THE *Wicked* KINGDOM

Lilian Morgaine

For everyone who wishes to escape reality

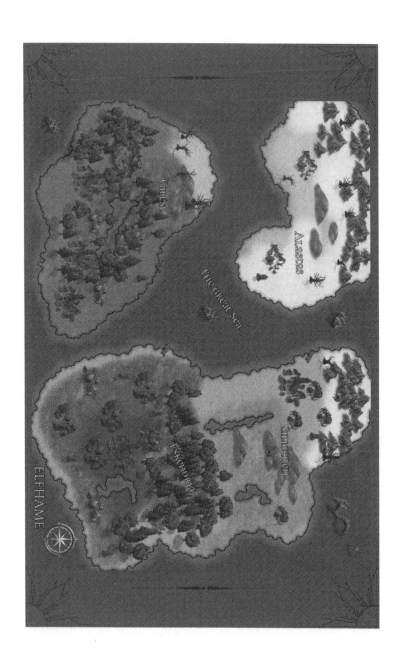

CHAPTER ONE

The forest is a labyrinth of ice and snow.

I am sitting on the branch of a tree, staring into the edge of the thicket for an hour, but it appears futile. The dusty wind has covered my tracks with drifts of snow but also hid possible tracks of prey. Today is an unusual day. This is the furthest from home I've ever been. I am afraid this would become more and more common as the harsh winter is becoming even harsher and food is running out.

The winters were hard; the animals sheltered themselves deeper in the forest, where it was not safe to follow. I only got the stragglers, which I'd hunted, one after another, hoping to survive until spring. A dying hope.

I remove a snowflake from my eyelashes with my stiff frozen fingers. In this region of the forest, the trees still have bark: a good sign, as it indicates there are still wild animals in the woods. When the trunks were eaten bald, it meant that my prey would have moved to the north through the territory of the wolves, maybe even to the forbidden city – where no one in their right mind would go unless they were seeking death.

This thought alone sends a shiver down my spine. I push the thought aside and fully concentrate on my surroundings again. After all, I have a task to finish – finding food.

Finding food so that I could survive the next week, the next day, hell, the next hour – that's all I could do. I would need luck to be on my side to find something in this snowstorm, despite my advantageous position in the tree crown. You could barely see five meters in the distance.

I drop my bow and slowly climbed down the tree. As I did I suppressed a groan. Because of the cold, every bone of my body hurt. The ice-encrusted snow crunched under my worn-out boots. My teeth are chattering. My vision is blurry. The snow under my boots make an inconveniently loud noise – it seems like I would go home empty-handed.

I only have a few hours of daylight left. If I don't go back soon I would have to walk home in complete darkness. The warning of the hunters still echoed through my head: "Huge wolves stalk these woods. Apparently, they're a great pack." I am also wary of rumours that eerie beings had been seen wandering around these woods: massive, terrifying, vicious creatures.

People said they were coming from the forbidden city but no one ever dared to look. People believed there were creatures living behind the city walls, desperate to hunt and kill. When my father used to take me on hunts, he forbade me to go even close to the border of our village. The forbidden city is filled with mystery and legends, ones that haunt children's dreams.

Townspeople implored ancient gods to protect their families and homes from whatever lay within the walls of the forbidden city.

7

Stories were told from villages closer to the city which were razed to the ground and the residents exterminated to the last. The reports of the incidents were dismissed as horror tales by the village elders.

I'd taken a huge risk by going this deep into the woods, but yesterday I'd eaten the last piece of bread and the day before the last bit of cured meat.

Yet, I would rather sleep another night with a growling stomach than satisfy a wolf's – or whatever else lays in the dark of the woods – hunger.

Not that I have a choice. This wintertime, I am gaunt like a tendon – you could count my ribs. On some days I have to force myself to continue this never ending fight against starvation. While I am as skilful and as silent as possible, sneaking between the trees, I am holding my empty and painful stomach.

At least there is no one left at home who I could have disappointed. My parents died when I was small. Since then I have lived in several places. No one really took notice or care of a small, thin child running around the streets. We all were hungry and no one could be bothered to feed an extra mouth. I became my only friend and learned to survive. I have glimpses of my parents in my memory. My dad used to be a woodworker and would take me on his daily hunting trips to catch something delicious. He was strict but he loved me, showed me how to use a bow and arrow. My mom worked in the local bakery. Everything my dad and I lugged in from the forest she turned into a delicious meal.

I remember it clearly the day they left me, it was a cold December night and I was getting wood for the fireplace. Once I returned, they were gone. No letter, nothing. I waited for them for hours, days, weeks. I was on the edge of dying until I got up off my ass and stole. I believed my parents were eaten by wild animals or maybe killed by one of the creatures that no one ever has seen. I've never found out the truth about their deaths, but I carried on, I had to survive somehow. I improved my hunting skills and went into the forest day by day. I tried to remember what dad had done to hunt rabbits and how mom prepared them for dinner with only a few ingredients. And here I am now, crouched in the thicket of snow-laden blackberry bushes. The dream.

I have a good view of a glade and a small brook which crossed the place through the thorn branches. Small holes in the ice indicate that it is still used as a water source. Hopefully, I'll have more success here. Hopefully.

Sighing, I push my bow upwards in the snow and lean my forehead against the rough curved wood. I wouldn't survive a week without food. There were already too many families who were begging for money instead of hoping for the grace of the wealthy townspeople. I felt with my own body how far their charity went.

I make myself more comfortable and start to breathe slower. I listen hard over the crying of the wind at the sounds of the forest. It's snowing and snowing – never-ending. The snowflakes are dancing and whirling like sparkling spray and the white covers the brown-greyish world with a freshly clean cover. And despite my hunger, despite my numb limbs my troubled, dull thoughts become calm at the sight of the snow-covered forest.

When I was younger, I admired how the beautiful, fresh green grass differed from the dark ploughed dirt or how graceful a smaragd brooch looked in a fold of emerald-green silk.

When I was a child, my thoughts and dreams were filled with colour, light and shapes. And sometimes I wondered how it would have been if we, for once, had enough food or had enough money to live a life like the wealthy side of our town.

But this was a dream, which didn't come true. I only have a few moments, like this one, where I admire the shining of the winter lights on the snow. I cannot remember when I took some time off to admire something beautiful or interesting. Stealthy hours with Finley in the barn won't count. These hours were driven by hunger, by emptiness: sometimes awful, but never lovely.

The howling wind weakens to a slight whisper. The snow is falling slowly, in thick and huge chunks which settle in the deep corridors and high treetops. How beguiling, this icy, soft beauty of the snow. The thought of going back to my village, to the streets covered in frozen mud, in the overheating narrowness of the hut I am living in, is repugnant to me.

There is a rustle in the bushes beyond the clearing. I instantly put the arrow on the string and I peek through the thorns holding my breath.

Less than thirty steps away is a small hind, not fully emaciate, but hungry enough to nibble on the bark of trees on a clearing.

A hind like this could nourish me for a week or even more.

My mouth is watering. As quiet as the wind, am I fixating on my prey. It is innocent and doesn't see its death coming. Carefree, it continues eating the bark of the tree and chews slowly. I can dry half of the flesh and the rest would be eaten immediately. I would sell the skin or maybe craft some clothes out of it. I need new boots. My fingers are shaking. So many nutrients, such a blessing. I take a deep breath and aimed again at my prey.

There, I saw, in the corner of my eye.

From the bushes opposite to me, two black eyes are looking into the clearing. The forest goes quiet. The wind dies. Even the snow dries up. Us mortals have turned their back to the old gods. If I could've recalled their names, I would have prayed – to all at once. Because there in the thicket lurked a creature I have never seen in my life. It was tall. My mouth goes dry. Is it the creature that the hunters had talked about. It looks human but it defiantly wasn't. They look off in the white landscape. If I wouldn't know better I'd say he is human. The way he holds tight to the bow in his hand. The long elegant fingers. His eyes are scanning the surrounding, yet, he hasn't encountered me. I slow down my breath, trying to stay calm. Has he come from the Forbidden City? I had always thought that these creatures were from fairytales but by its pointy ears I knew that I have seen an Elf in the thicket.

I should go away, save myself as fast as possible, I thought.

But maybe … maybe I would do the world a favour – my village, myself – if I kill it while I have the chance. As long as I am still unnoticed. To shoot an arrow into his head would be nothing. Legends say that once Elves ruled the world we now live in. But time passed and the Elves had abandoned us, the once so powerful creatures didn't feel like the mortals revered them as they should have done. It was understandable that we did not really enjoy their company. Who wants to have dinner with creatures so powerful they could crush your world in seconds? When I was smaller, my mother told me several fairytales of good Elves and bad ones. Of a land where no one has to hunger. Where magic rules the world. I believed her but once I'd grown up I realised that there is no such land. Yet, I look at him and can't believe my eyes. It shouldn't exist but it does. A thought crosses my mind. Will my arrows kill such a powerful creature or will it get annoyed and decide to kill me and everyone who is important to me? Is it worth the risk?

I pull an arrow out with a nimble, well-considered movement. I have to prevent this creature from seeing me. The arrow was long and heavy, perfect to hurt animals, but such powerful creatures? I am unsure. If I kill the Elf, the hind will flee. However, if I kill the hind, the creature will know he isn't alone and then I would become the prey. However, the Elf doesn't look as if he's eating raw flesh. He looks stunning. He is by far the handsomest man I've ever seen in my life. It feels odd. So many questions are wandering through my head. What is he doing here? Is he alone? What does he want?

My chest tightens, I can barely breathe steady. I don't know anything about the behaviour of these Elves, are they lone wolves or moving in groups? Maybe I am already surrounded by the other members of the pride. I hold my bow tighter and strain the tendon. I would consider myself talented with bow and arrow but I have never killed something this dangerous. I always thought I was lucky … until now. Now I have no clue where to shoot or how fast this thing will react.

I couldn't afford to miss it. I only had this one arrow, one try, which would determine if I lived the next minute or not. The Elf creeps closer and a branch snaps under his foot. Holy shit. What am I doing here? The hind freezes. It looks around and prick up its ears.

But the creature has the wind in front of the nose meaning the hind couldn't smell it nor hear it. The hind was still looking in the wrong direction. My gaze wandered between the animal and the Elf. He is alone, this was clear. If I fail, not only my life would be taken, but the hundreds of innocent people in my village would be sentenced to die. In the past years in which I have studied and become familiar with the forest, I have been in constant danger. I have taken risks and most of the time I have estimated my chances correctly. Emphasis on *most of the time*.

I tighten my bow, ready to do something reckless, but suddenly I'm looking into the obsidian eyes of the Elf. I grab my bow tighter and let the arrow go. I gasp. The black-haired Elf tilts his head across the clearing, not even bothering to move away. He grabs my arrow as if it was a balloon floating gently in the air. Oh saints! This is my end. I lower my bow without breaking eye contact with him. He clamps my arrow in his bow and aims at the hind on the clearing. I hold my breath, not knowing what to do or think. He shoots the arrow straight in the throat of the hind which cries out and falls to the ground. Its blood splashes in the snow. Wine red on snow white. Its brown eyes torn open, the hair on its neck bristled. I am going to die. Snow is falling beside me, it still hasn't stopped. I wanted to grab another arrow from my back just to notice I have used my last one. I stand there in shock looking down on the wine-red liquid dripping on the white ground. I didn't do this. I didn't kill the hind. My head turns around, facing the Elf. The snowflakes hinder my sight but the creature is lowering its bow. I am confused. Intensely dark eyes stare at me as if the ashes are captured inside them. His skin is as pale as the snow itself but his face is covered with a healthy rose tone. He doesn't look like he is starving or hungry. He looks too perfect to be true, too unreal, like something that has escaped from a fairytale. An Elf has helped me. The being moves his bow and I shriek, my eyes wide open. Fairytales are never taken as a safe source of accurate information, and what people tell about Elves differs, but one thing is for sure – they are dangerous. A veil of truth and trickery. Never make a deal with one of them or you will be doomed the rest of your days.

I stumble in a tangle of some branches, not letting the Elf out of my sight. I am astonished when I see the Elf simply hanging the bow over his shoulder. He is dressed completely dark, not the best wardrobe for hiding in the winter forest but who am I to judge? Without doing anything else, he turns around and leaves me on the clearing. He didn't kill me. My eyes follow him walking through the thicket for as long as possible. He walks like a man, nothing in him reminds me of animal behaviour.

I pull my bow closer to me as if it could protect me. The forest starts to live again – as much as it will in the winter. I slowly approach the dead hind, examining fur, hooves and teeth. I could make good money with this one, but I can never carry all of it home alone. I waste precious minutes – minutes where potential predators could smell the blood and try to get something out of it – skinning the creature and cleaning the arrow shot by the mysterious Elf. Well, at least my fingers are getting warmer. I put the flesh of the animal on my shoulders. I am quite a few kilometres away from home. This will be a long walk. I look back at the cadaver, its brown eyes still shining, looking up in the snowing sky.

For a brief second, I wish I could feel some sympathy for the being but I don't. That's life. We all want to live but only a few will survive.

CHAPTER TWO

My hut is dark and rundown. I don't have the luxury of a warm fire or even heating like the wealthy side of my town has. I often thought about leaving this place, too many memories are embroidered into these wooden walls which were all placed by my father himself. Even though we did not have much, we were happy. Sometimes I can still hear my mother's laugh echoing through the rooms. From time to time I crave a certain feeling, the feeling of security and being loved. The feeling when I would be hugged tightly by my mother when I felt sick, the feeling of listening to my father's adventurous stories. But that was then, and now I am here. The electricity isn't working anymore because I can't pay the bills. With what would I pay? I don't have a job. None of the money which is in a pouch of my pants is made honourably. Over the years, I became a good thief. Crowds are my favourite spot. People barely notice you and the rich don't even think of getting robbed. They probably don't realise they lost something, or they just don't care.

The town is divided into two areas, rich and poor. You can say my town is actually two towns with two majors and two political opinions. I normally sell my meat on the black market, I get good money for my hunt there, sometimes. I survive.

My go-to seller is the old Mrs Ivy. She has lived for far too long already but still manages to run her small illegal business. Even though she would never admit it, when the winters were hard and my parents just went missing, she helped me. I believe she felt sorry for me. Without her, I would have died long ago in the cold nights of the winter alone in my freezing house.

Since I grew older and started to hunt again, she always insisted on paying for her portion. I felt bad, I wanted to tell her how thankful I was for what she had done for me but she never let me argue with her. And over the years, I accepted it. It's not that I don't like getting money.

I lift the hint cadaver onto the small wooden table in the kitchen and place the carefully separated skin next to it. I can't wait to finally eat something warm. The feeling of a full stomach, the satisfaction! I gather wood from outside to light the small fireplace I self-crafted in the living room. I collect some herbs which I had stored in small boxes in the kitchen. My mother was skilled with choosing the right herbs for the right dishes. I am, well, ... trying.

While eating my portion of meat I can't stop thinking about the stranger I met in the woods. Not a stranger – an Elf. I know my sight wasn't excellent but I am sure this was an Elf. One of these creatures thought long-lost dead or extinct. People tell fairytales of their existence, acting as if they never really lived. And here I am, a person who actually saw one. Stories tell that the Elves were warriors, born to kill. With their pale skin and their sharp eyes, almost animal like. Their one true instinct is to kill.

He didn't look scary, with no sharp teeth or long claws. His skin was pale but he didn't look like a corpse. And the fact that he spared my life and left me the hind, without wanting anything from me in return ... Maybe he will come back, try to find me. He might bring an army to destroy my village and everyone living in it ...

Aedlin, stop. Why would that happen? I really should stop overthinking. Maybe I saw something wrong. Maybe it was an unknown hunter who felt pity for me.

I continue chewing on my food, which suddenly tasted dull, yet, the warmth is filling my body, starting in my stomach and going down to my toes. Tomorrow morning I will head to the market to sell the skin of the hind and finally buy new boots.

By looking at the burned down candle in front of me I realise how late it has gotten. Tomorrow will be a new day.

During my sleep, I was haunted by a pair of inhuman dark eyes.

-

The sun shines brightly into my dilapidated bedroom. I sleep on an old rusty bed which is actually way too small for me. I'd gathered several furs over the years which helped me stay warm at night. Still, I feel stiff while standing up. My body is cold and my toes feel frozen. This winter is unusually cold compared to the others. I look outside on my porch and gaze into the snowy landscape. It is so early that the snow remains untouched. It looks like little fairies sprayed glitter over the fields overnight. It is a deadly beauty.

I get ready and prepared my goods for the market. The sun is rising over the horizon and I can hear how the birds start to live. The snow crunches under my boots. The world is icy and soon my nose turns red from the cold. I hold my grip tighter around the backpack in which the hint skin is stored. On my way to the main plaza, I see how the town began to live. People run to their work. Mothers with their children go for a daily walk to get some bread from the local bakery. Of course, this early in the day you only see the less fortunate side of the town. The wealthy people like to sleep late into the day because they don't have to worry about getting their food before others take it. I dislike the power game among us. We should work together but one works to feed the other.

People lie. Most of the time to get themselves in a better position. I lied. Everyday. To survive. I am not proud of it. I remember my mother telling me that telling the truth is always the right thing and if you do enough right things you will be rewarded. Well apparently, you won't. To live through the day and see the sunrise again I had to become a different person with different ambitions and opinions. I'd say it's my talent to be someone else but me. Sometimes I don't remember who I really am anymore. Am I the hunter who loves to sit in trees and shoot the final killing arrow? Or do I like to trade on the market for the best price? What about stealing from the rich to feel something similar to the emotion of achieving? I really don't know.

I continue my way through the alleys of my town, facing people sleeping on the street; sometimes they have black limbs or motionless bodies. I know death, I kill for survival. But seeing human bodies sprawled out on the dirty stone of the streets ... This is something else. No one cares about them; they won't be taken away, they will lay there until their body gets eaten by animals or they decay. I try to breathe through my mouth and not look at the people who once had a life, even if it wasn't a good one they lived. Sometimes I wonder if they are looking forward to the thought of dying: no more suffering or hunger. It makes me furious how our system make people want to die. Life is so much more than fulfilling a purpose. It is a time that belongs to you, it's your individual show, you are the director and actor. Even though I sometimes feel like I'm being dragged down to the ocean floor, suffocating from all the stress and tears. But then another day starts and I can try again, try to live a better life; a life I want to live where no one tells me what I can and can't do. Of course, it's rather hard facing the truth that I barely survive a cold night. But I let myself dream. It's the only escape I have from my day. Books help me. Books create a world where I can escape to. Where I can escape my reality. But fleeing from the truth isn't filling my stomach.

-

The market is already packed with merchants from all the nearby cities. I sneak through the people trying to find Mrs Ivy. Her stand has always been at the same place, on the edge of all the chaos. From far away I can already see her curled snow-white hair. She isn't the kind of person you would invite to afternoon tea. She rather looks intimidating, some might even say scary. Her cavernous skin emphasizes her long working days. No one really knows for how long the woman has lived already, people say she might be a witch. This is ridiculous: she might be very old and looks scary, but her heart is pure, and she isn't brewing potions in her basements ... as far as I know.

"Ah hello, my little evil!" Her voice is remarkable. Mrs Ivy sounds like she's been smoking three boxes of cigarettes every day for her entire lifetime.

"Mrs Ivy." I nod towards her.

"What did you bring me today, girl?" I follow her gaze to the sack on my shoulder.

"Something you haven't had in a long time." I smirk. Mrs Ivy takes whatever she can get without asking too many questions. Her old hands go to grab the fabric greedily but I push them away. "How's the market? Any weird occupants?" I ask, hoping she would know something about the stranger in the woods. Maybe other people have seen it on their hunts as well. Maybe I won't go insane.

"Girl, don't speak in riddles to me! If you wanna know something then ask, it's simple." She straightens her back and puts her left hand on her hip. I roll my eyes.

"Have you heard of a man who creeps around in the woods?" I whisper so no one else in the market could hear me. I don't want people to think I am crazy.

"A man in woods? That's the start of a bad story. Child, the woods are dangerous. Little girls like you shouldn't go alone, but then again, you never listened me! Why start now? To answer your question, no, I've not heard of man being seen in the woods." Her eyes drop to the sack on her old rusty table. I unfold the fabric around the hind skin.

"By all saints, where did you go to get this?" she asks stunned, all while examining the texture of its fur and veins. "Aedlin, I thought we talked about stopping going deep in the woods," she adds, not waiting for a reply. She immediately turns around and grabs a sack of coins. "Here, my girl, this is yours!"

I open the old brown purse to reveal six gold coins. Six! That's more than I've made in the last months! I stare at Mrs Ivy in shock. She's too busy looking at the skin. She hushes me away. I won't question her decision if she thinks it's worth it. I won't complain.

I can hear her whispering under her breath, "I haven't seen this in months." I bet I got a good catch for her today. I smirk while walking through the market, securing my coins in the leather purse inside my coat.

-

The market has gotten even more crowded over the past few minutes, with more and more traders trying to get rare goods at remarkable prices. I try to squeeze through the crowd, noticing that some people from the other district are lingering around. I ask myself what they are possibly doing in such a place which is filled with filth and poorness. My eyes scan the surroundings. Every person might be a new target for my long and quick fingers. I spot astonishing purses and expensive looking jewellery. I catch sight of a nice bracelet hanging around a middle-aged woman's wrist. Bracelets are a joke to me. To steal them is as easy as making a baby smile. I speed up so I can catch up to the woman. She seems to be alone. I have to be aware of my surroundings. I bump into her, catching her with both arms when I see that she stumbles, as if she's going to fall. She cries out.

"Be careful where you walk, rat!" Her hatred-filled eyes are focused on mine. I've gotten used to this expression over the years.

"I am sorry, Ma'am." I bow my head to hide my smile from her. When I was smaller, people showed empathy for me, but never more than just a pitiful smile; however, as I grew older, they increasingly saw me as an unpleasant person.

"And take your filthy hands off my exquisite garment!" the woman adds. She shakes my hands off, not noticing how I'd already slipped her very exquisite bracelet from her very own wrist. I stop in the middle of the crowd and watched the woman leave, not knowing that me, a filthy rat, just stole her precious jewellery. I know stealing is not good – never do that! But it's fun. The rich never expect me to be so skilled. To them, we are uneducated and don't know what manners are. Tricking one of them has always filled me with excitement. This thought makes me smile because it reminds me that we are somehow all the same. The rich and the poor, both human. When I was younger I thought that the rich were better in everything.

I wasn't allowed to go to school to have a good education because of my impoverished family. However, I learned reading and writing from my mother and father who were eager to teach. I never had to sit a test, however, I learned from experiences. And this is what differentiates me from the rich children. I know how to live, they only read how to. Yet, it has always been the rich people who have achieved something astonishing, and now knowing the fact that I am so highly skilled in something that no rich one I know is – it fills my heart with joy.

I store the bracelet in the pocket of my coat. Later on I will sell it to some trader from across the world. Yet, I am moving towards the forge, where a guy who owes me something for not getting killed works. Yes, you heard right, I saved someone. Feels so good to have someone in my debt. His name is Finely. We got to know each other years ago on the street. His father died in a mine accident years ago and now it's only him, his mother, and his – hold up – five additional brothers. In times like these, having to feed so many mouths isn't easy. Finley started working when he was fourteen. By that time I was already all on my own and from time to time we met and became somewhat friends. He went hunting with me, I tried to show him but he's not very skilled in walking quietly which chases away the prey. We gave up pretty quick. Now we have an exchange system going on. I give him food sometimes while he gives me new bows and arrows. A win-win situation. As time passed between us, we also started to help each other to fill the empty voids in our hearts. It was never serious, only some games. It made me feel wanted, like someone was taking care of me. Taking care of myself the whole time gets tiring, and not having somebody to vent to is frustrating.

While walking towards the old forge, I eat a piece of the bread I just bought. Yes, I bought it with my own money, ha! It is still warm. I am overwhelmed by all the different sensations!

I don't even bother to knock at the door; I just storm inside, interrupting Finley's work.

"Old saints!", He jumps, "Aedlin, how often have I told you not to burst in here like that. I'm working with hot metal and I could get hurt!" he said while putting down his equipment.

"Not enough I guess, since I'm still doing it!" I smirk while walking around in the room. It's hot here. I could take off my coat in here even though it's winter. Weapons are everywhere, on the floor or hanging on the walls. I don't even know how to use the majority of them.

"Bread?" I ask while lifting myself up on the desk, which seems to have the least materials on it, offering the other half of the loaf.

"No, I'm fine," he says, bad-tempered. "What if I wasn't alone here? What if the master was here? You know that you are not allowed here."

He steps closer out of the glimmering heat of the melted metal. He is definitely a head taller than me. I made fun of him when we were smaller because I was taller than him, well, guess who now makes fun of me. His dark brown hair is falling into his face. This look makes him seem somewhat mysterious. I can see how the other girls from the town look at him. Am I jealous? No. They can stare as long as they want to, they probably won't get much back than a kind smile. Finley and I have been friends for a long time, and for a long time we only had each other and yes, our actions lead to something. And yes, he looks even better with no clothes on, if you were wondering. But it's been years. I felt lonely, so did he. There weren't real emotions involved, it was just the need to have someone familiar by my side. But it's over, we don't have time for romance or anything like that now. Who knows if we will survive the next day?

"Well, I got lucky I guess. You know, sixth sense – I could smell you were alone." I smile when I saw that one corner of his mouth went up.

"What do you want, Aedlin?" He puts his hand on the support beam. I jump down from the counter and focus on the bread loaf in my hand.

"Have you heard any news from people wandering in the forest?"

He looks at me with a frown.

"Besides you I don't know anyone who is hunting in these woods, why?"

I swallow. Finley has always been the logical one. He takes facts for granted, whereas I live in my dreams from time to time.

"I saw someone there. Someone I thought didn't exist."

Finely takes my chin in his hand and pulls it softly up to him so I have to face his autumn-coloured eyes. "Aedlin, don't speak in riddles." I swallow but don't break eye contact.

"I saw an Elf."

He drops my chin as if he'd just been burned by my skin. "Don't be ridiculous. Elves don't exist anymore."

"Oh really, Sherlock! I didn't notice."

He rolls his eyes and focuses them back on me.

"I am certain I saw an Elf!" I insist.

"Have you been reading too many of these Fantasy books?" He smiles and messes up my hair.

"Finley! I am not joking." I trie to strengthen my voice, while dodging his hand and I can see that Finley finally understood the situation.

"If I believe what you say, why are you standing in front of me, unharmed?" He raises one of his dark eyebrows and crosses his arms in front of his chest. He has a good point. Why would a creature who has terrorised my country for centuries let me live?

"He didn't see me," I try.

"An Elf with extraordinary sight didn't see you?" He huffs. "You probably just encountered another brave hunter."

"Okay, to be honest, the Elf saw me," I confess. "He looked me in the eyes, stared straight into my soul. He had obsidian irises and was dressed in all black. His black hair was pulled backwards revealing his pointy ears!"

"So you want to tell me that you had an encounter with an Elf in the woods who was hunting there as well … here in the human world?" Hearing him saying it like that does make it sound stupid.

"Well … yes."

"Aedlin, you know that this sounds crazy."

"I swear to the saints, that's what happened." I grab my bow and arrows which are laying on the counter.

"If it was someone else telling me this, I would say they were crazy, but …" Finley takes a deep breath in. "I believe you."

My jaw drops. What? I didn't expect that.

"Don't look so surprised, I'm your best friend, of course I believe you. Take me to the spot where you saw him, maybe we can find some clues." He looks eager, but as mentioned earlier, with his height and loud walking, we would be the perfect dinner for possible predators.

"It's still early," Finley continues, "I'll tell my master that I don't feel well and we can go there now. If Elves are actually alive, our village has to know – we need to be ready for possible attacks."

I sigh. I can see that we are thinking about it differently. For me, the Elf is a source of information and possible new knowledge; for him, the Elf is a danger that needs to be taken care of. Perhaps I should've felt frightened of future attacks, but I don't. I only feel a strong sense that the male Elf wouldn't hurt me.

-

On my way back I cross the market and bought new boots. The astonishing feeling when I threw my old ones away was amazing. Now equipped with new warm boots, my winter coat and my bow, I am waiting on the porch of my small hut. We agreed to meet at mine as it's near to the forest entry. Also, most of the neighbours I used to have are dead, which gives us the security that no one will see us, or if they do, they're too old to actually do something against it. It's not forbidden to go in the woods to hunt, but it's better to not be seen. The rich rather want us to buy from their shops and markets, however, they are overpriced as hell, and I prefer to go hunting myself.

The sun is still high, giving us enough time to get to the place where I had the confrontation and back home. Once Finley has arrived, I tried to remember the exact path I'd gone on, but it's hard due to the amount of snow. My tracks are gone and every tree is an exact copy of the next one.

The wind whistles around our ears so I try to hide my face deeper in the collar of my coat. Looking at Finley, I see that I maybe should have brought a scarf and beanie. I can feel how my ears are freezing. Even my long thick hair won't help much. However, after endless hours of sitting in the thicket waiting for potential prey, my body got used to the cold. I grab my bow tighter and made sure I have the dagger from my father on my waist. I would say I am far more skilled in wielding weapons than Finley is. However, he has the advantage of height and strength. He can easily carry me until we arrive at our location. I guess his go-to defence is combat. Which is why he also brought a dagger with him. Let's hope he doesn't need it.

The forest is deadly quiet. No animals are to be seen – it's as if a plague has killed them all at once. Even the trees look dead. This winter is unnatural. It's killing all life.

I get the feeling that the deeper we go, the colder it gets. I can barely feel my fingers anymore. Finley has gone quiet behind me. There is nothing we can talk about. We appreciate each other's quietness. I forgot how long the walk was. The sun is moving to the horizon now.

"We'll be there soon," I tell Finley, hoping I'd be right. He just nods silently. His mouth is pressed tightly, his jaw tense. I grab my bow as tight as possible, ready for any possible encounter. We cross a stone outcrop, and when standing on top of them I am able to see the clearing.

"There! I told you I know where to go!"

"Sure. You were as lost as I was!" he jokes. We climb down and move to the opening. And there I see it, the remains of the hind. It's not much, looks like other predators smelled the blood, but the bones are here. Proof that I am not crazy. I pick up a bone. "Here catch!" I throw it towards Finley who turns to avoid the bone.

"Hey!" For the first time in days I laugh because this was just too hilarious.

"Stop laughing at me and throwing disgusting bones at me!" he says with a smile. He picks them up and examines them.

"The Elf was there." I point to a opposite us. "I saw him leaving through the thicket this way," I continue and move to the place I just mentioned. I try to examine the icy floor but nothing is left from the Elf, no traces, nothing. It seems as if he had never been here.

"Hypothetically," Finley says from behind me, "If the Elf really was here, then where did he come from?" I roll my eyes. He still doesn't believe me. I turn around on my heels and try to find some strange stone structures or buildings in the surroundings that could indicate the way he went.

"I have investigated this forest for years and never came upon a structure …" I stop. "Of course! How could I be so blind?!" I turn around, facing Finley, who has no idea.

"The Forbidden City! It should be close to this clearing. What if the city isn't occupied by monsters but is instead the gate through the worlds?" I say enthusiastically.

"No!" Finley says firmly. "We are not going there. It is forbidden." I roll my eyes. Since when had he become so strict?

"But what if something happened? What do we know from this place? Nothing. Either the old people refuse to tell us or no one actually knows. People avoided this place for centuries and why? What if more are coming? What if they invade the town and hurt your mother or Peter? Jackson? Phillip?! And you know that you could have done something but didn't because you chickened out." I realise I'd gotten louder so I cough trying to calm my temper.

"Don't involve my family, Aedlin," he says quietly.

"Then help me find the source."

Finley walks around the clearing, wasting useful minutes of sunlight. Finally, I see him nodding. "But Aedlin, you will listen to me. When I detect danger, you will do what I say – no playing lone wolf. We are a team. Better being on the safe side than being killed by an immortal creature."

"Agreed."

CHAPTER THREE

I lead the way even though I am not quite sure where to go. I've never been to the Forbidden City but I've examined maps with my father. And I know the whole forest inside out. I know we have to pass a small river and some distinct tree collections.

The sun has set and the dusk has settled over the forest. However, we could clearly see where the Forbidden City starts once we reached it.

The city is surrounded by a huge wall which is covered in moss and grass, making it look abandoned or even haunted. These walls used to help protect the villagers from possible fiends, now they protect us from whatever lies behind.

We are standing in front of a gate.

"You stay outside, checking to see if anything wants to come back home with us, and I'll sneak in and check the inside out."

"No, I won't let you go in there alone!"

"Finley, let's be real, I am small and fast. I will be just fine."

He doesn't seem to be convinced.

"I promise you, I will be careful and come back at any sight of possible danger."

"All right, I'll trust you, but if I have to save your ass from whatever lies in there I will beat you up." I smile.

"First you have to catch me, then you are allowed to beat me up."

Finley grins but then looks serious. "Be careful, Aedlin."

"Always."

And with that said, I turn around and enter the Forbidden City, the one where the elders say not to go unless you want to die. I wouldn't say I want to die but I don't want to live a boring life either. I look back at Finley standing in front of the gate, patrolling the entrance. I carefully walk over the half-stone half-gravel path. It looks like an old village where no one lives anymore. At first sight, I don't see anything paranormal. The huts are rundown. Windows are barricaded with wooden pallets. Some roofs are sunken in. I examine the ground as best as possible with the steady fading light. No prints to be seen, as if I am the first one walking these paths after a long time. But then I realise something. The snow is also missing. Before entering, the ground is covered in snow but here barely any snow is laying around. It feels warmer, too.

I try to come up with an explanation, but nothing makes sense. I move further into the town. There we have abandoned shops, an old church, a school and a market area. Everything that would have been normal in a city.

"Hello."

Hm? I turn around.

"Finley? Are you here?"

Nothing. Strange, probably just the wind. I grab my bow tighter and move through the ruins of the town. Is it just me or does the wind get stronger as I move forward? I pass abandoned alleys with nothing more than leftovers of a civilisation. The whole time, one thought stuck with me. Why is it that people say this city is cursed? Am I gonna die tomorrow? Or will everything I touch be poisoned? I don't know.

I curse under my breath. Finley was right, nothing exciting is waiting here for me. I stop in front of a church which towers over the houses of the city. It's a small church but considering the size of everything else in this village, it looks imperial. I can't not look at the detailed walls with its colourful windows. Every single house I have passed looks old and rotten but this church looks as if people still maintain it. The wind messes up my hair and I try to straighten my long red curls but it won't listen to me.

"Come on in."

I stare at the gate of the church. I swear to the saints, this voice came from the inside of the building. I was never a fan of horror stories but I am certain that this could be the beginning of a new one which children would be terrified by.

I shouldn't go. I should turn around and go to Finley to tell him he was right and this all has been useless. On the other hand I could go in there and discover a bit more. What might be in there? Who am I, a little girl who is afraid of a voice calling for her? Okay, saying it like that sounds slightly wrong. I swear I am not insane. I am just seeking some adventures, that's all.

I look around, making sure there really is no one who is playing with me.

I put my hand on the old rusty door knob and push it open. The door opens with a squeaking sound. Nice. It is completely dark outside, as I assume would be, but in the church there are candles lit on the walls and altar.

"Hello?" I say quietly.

"Good evening, Aedlin!"

Okay, now it gets spooky.

"I am so happy to finally meet you!"

His voice gives me goosebumps. Or its voice. I can't really tell if it is human. It sounds smoky and rough. I surround the altar from which I believe the voice comes, but it echoes through the whole church.

"Who are you?"

"I have had many names over the centuries ..."

I choke. Did it say centuries, like not decades, but centuries?!

"Some call me Hope, the saviour, others, the evil, the devil, the talking shadows. You can decide, love."

"How come that you know my name?" The grip around my bow tightens even though I have no idea where to shoot. I hear the voice but can't see the body. I fully surrounded the altar and haven't seen anything obscure.

"Your name is known from where I come, they praise you like a goddess. The goddess of light. The cure to all misery. The Queen who will put me under the earth." I feel a cold breath on my cheek.

"I want to warn you, little girl. You are not my enemy and I am not yours ... yet. But if you try to challenge me, I will not be sad to put an end to your life. However, it would be a misery to end such a potential life."

I try to make out where the voice is located. Suddenly, the hall goes dark; all the candles blow out, besides one which is carried by shadowed hands. Its light brightens the face of the voice. Their facial features are hard to make out. They consists of shadows moving around their head.

"*Aedlin, if you can help me I will make sure that the Elves won't come back to haunt your village. If you agree to assist me in just a small task, I give you my word that nothing will harm your people or the young handsome boy outside of the gate.*" As if nothing has happened, the candles light again and the shadows vanish; gone were they and I am left alone with endless questions.

I waited for a couple minutes in the aisle of the church, looking around. Then I examine every inch of this goddamn building. No tracks left from the intruder. As if this had never happened. What it said was nonsense. Like hell, this thing probably has a massive ego to be calling himself the evil or the devil. Saints. And wouldn't I know if I am ... what did it call me again, a goddess?! This place gives me chills.

As I walk out of the church and towards the gate where Finley waited, I have the constant feeling that eyes are following me.

-

On the way home, we don't talk. I don't know why I haven't mentioned my strange acquaintance to Finley. Maybe I don't want him to think I'm weirder than he already believes. I just don't want to see his face while he says, *I told you.* I hate it when he says that. We are trudging through the snow. The moon has appeared in the sky. It is shining through a lattice of leaves. Tall, shadowed pines are stretching up like arrows into the sky. I can hear the flutter of wings which are unseen and in the far distance the howling of wolves. We should move faster. The air is freezing cold but I smell pine needles and fresh air. This night could be considered beautiful if I don't have to worry that my nose would fall off due to the cold. My teeth start to shiver and I can see that Finley is fighting it as well. I know where we are and I know it's not far until we reach the town but each step is getting harder and harder. As we create distance between us and the Forbidden City I can't shake the feeling of being watched. I still feel the voice of that thing on my neck. It's a cold, rusty voice. The thing it said to me, about who I am in his world. Does that mean this world is not the only one? Does it mean that the fairytales are real? Is it possible that we live side by side with another civilisation but we don't know about it? I try not to get my hopes up that this man really was an Elf, that this country isn't the only one.

I was so lost in my thought that I didn't hear what Finley said to me.

"Hm?"

He rolls his eyes.

"A penny for your thoughts. We're home."

Only now I realise that we have left the woods and entered the main path to our town. I can spear my hut in the distance.

"Thank you for coming with me."

"No worries, Aedlin, but tell me, did you really see nothing back there? You were awfully quiet on the way back. You alright?" By the way his dark hazel eyes wander around my face to see if I am hurt, my heart makes a little bump. Why couldn't I accept him? I may have lied earlier when I said "we" decided it was better if we were friends. The truth is ,I decided that. I told him that I don't want this to be more than a friendship. But I catch myself wondering why I did that. Finley is caring, loving, funny, adventurous. All the things I like. Why won't I let him in my life? Be a real part of it? I don't know.

I don't answer him. I only go on my tip toes and give him a kiss on his cheek which is rough from his beard.

"Good night, Finley."

I pass him and go straight to my hut. I know that he is looking at me because I don't hear him going away. I suppress the urge to turn around and ask him to come home with me. Not because I want physical attention, just because I can't stand being alone anymore.

I fall into a restless sleep and am haunted by my nightmares. All include a rusty old building and a voice I already detest. However, I have never been really alone. The dark eyes were following me everywhere. And despite the troubled emotions I felt when seeing the shadows, the obsidian eyes feel like home.

Chapter Four

The next morning started as the past had. The snow looks welcoming, like it's not trying to freeze you to death. Even though the hut was cold since I forgot to gather firewood for the chimney yesterday evening, I woke up soaked in sweat. The night wasn't pleasant. Waking up from one nightmare just took me into the next one. But all of them were utterly similar. First, I saw darkness, but it quickly turned into chaos. I heard uncountable screams. Painful ones. I saw fire. People getting burned. I have never been long enough in one to fully understand its meaning. Yet, they were disturbing. I saw creatures faces I have never seen before. Every night I hope I will fall asleep and won't see them, however, I get disappointed way too often.

I put on my warmest clothes and get ready to go to the local library. I have to find out more about the stories told of the Forbidden City. The library is my second home, even though the one in our district isn't filled with epic fantasy or romance novels like the one in the Golden district is.

I was about to leave my hut when someone knocked on the door. I stopped my movement in confusion. I don't get visitors. The ones that used to come here when I was smaller and my parents were still alive have passed away ages ago.

"Who is it?" I ask carefully with my hand to the dagger on the kitchen table.

"Put your hand away from your dagger, Aedlin, I have something you want." Upon hearing Finley's voice, I have to suppress a small grin. He knows me too well.

"Come on in," I say.

Finley opens the rusty wooden door and the air is immediately filled with the smell of freshly baked bread. My eyes shoot to the little box he is holding in his hand.

"I was worried about you, and it was quite cold last night. I wondered if you'd eaten," he says and I can hear the worry in his voice. To be honest, I haven't eaten yet. Or yesterday evening.

He hands me half of the bread and leans on the table. Only then does he notice my clothing.

"What are you up to? Do you want me to come with you?" His voice is soft and brought a strange feeling to my stomach. As much as I wanted him to help me in the library I cannot allow that. He has a job which he needs to do, and I cannot tell him what I am looking for in the library.

"Oh I ..." I take a bite from my bread to give me some time to think. "It's nothing. I just wanted to stroll through the city."

He narrows his eyes. "If you don't wanna tell me what you're up to, it's fine, but come on, did you really think I'd believe that you'd go for a walk?" He grins and leans forward. Our faces are only inches away and I can see the small freckles around his nose and cheeks. His eyes are like honey, you want to sink into them. What has happened to me? When did I start feeling like this towards him? Or were the feelings always there, and I just suppressed them?

"If you need help with whatever mischief you're dealing with, just call for me. I will be there." He doesn't move back. We silently stare at each other. His eyes flicker to my mouth and I swallow. I take a deep breath and I finally find my voice again.

"What are you doing, freak, wanna lure me in? Or do I have something gross on my face?"

He steps a bit away from me.

"Maybe I want to lure you in, but maybe I've already done so. Or you have a huge pimple on your nose. We will never know." He smiles.

"Shut up, Finley!" I laugh.

-

On the way to the local library, I take the path through the market. I stop by Mrs Ivy but she has better things to do than greet me. She is busy negotiating with customers. I have to smile. The old lady seems to be fragile but she has fire in her heart.

When I arrive at the old library, I feel unsure about my decision. What if I find something so immense that it will change my way of thinking? But hasn't my thinking already changed?

I open the old door and I get overwhelmed by the smell. The scent of old papers and books floats into my nose.

An elderly lady is sitting at the front desk and crocheting a scarf. She wouldn't even notice if something was stolen, and anyway what would she do? Throw a needle at me? The library isn't impressive. I've sneaked into the Library in the Golden District and it was an astonishing architecture masterpiece, but this old shabby hut is barely standing. It's constructed from wood and you can see that a huge chunk of time has passed since it was renovated. I think more spiders are here than books. Disgusting.

"Excuse me..." I look at the name tag of the woman on the front desk. "... Mrs Greystone. I am looking for papers about the forbidden city."

She doesn't even bother to look up. She mumbles under her breath and the only word I make out is "underground". I thank her and leave her be. Kind lady.

I move towards the stairs that lead to the level under the main floor. The steps squeak under my foot. Nice. The light is dim and the smell is questionable. I thought that upstairs was a mess but looking around this floor I can clearly see that something died here and I really don't want to know what.

I move through the corridors. The shelfs are sorted after names. I just hope that the papers I need are under "forbidden city" since that's what we all call it.

I go over every single book on the shelf. I almost give up and want to turn around, accusing myself of being stupid. But close to the edge of the shelf I found a book so covered in dust that I have to cough when my hand moves over it. *Swinford: The Forbidden City.*

Swinford – that's its real name. I open up the book and dust floats towards me.

"When was the last time someone opened up to you?" I check the publication date. I'm staggered. This book which I am holding right now was written over two centuries ago. I am holding history. I look around the room.

I am alone.

I take a seat on the not so clean floor but I don't care right now.

I open up the first page.

Collection of events in Swinford.

Day one: After Elves have attacked the humans. After centuries of a peaceful alliance, the High King Maxon has declared war amongst the folks if we don't obey.

Day two: We got caught by surprise. We thought that the folk would stay peaceful until after the heir got crowned, but everything turned upside down.

Day five: More humans were found dead. Cause of death: murder. No animal kills with a sword to the heart.

Day fourteen: We prepare for war. We have found a weapon to kill the devil creatures. The major is launching the invasion. Some say he is crazy, others see him as a saviour.

Day thirty-seven: The war began. Humans didn't obey the High King. The Elves attacked us ruthlessly. They have forgotten our decades of trading. We can't tell why. We lost a great deal of soldiers today. Even though we have the weapons, we don't have the skills. We are only humans.

Day fifty-eight: The two parties are still fighting. Too many people are dead, be it human or Elves. We should stop but orders say otherwise. I can see how the human army gets smaller and smaller each day. I don't know what to do. I lost two of my best friends. I am

43

not sure if this war is worth the suffering. The Major says otherwise. He shouts, 'Keep formation!' That's all I can remember. I don't know when I have last slept. It's been too long.

Day eighty-nine: We lost the city. Or we won the city. I can't really tell. The dawn is settling but the Elves are gone. The city is empty. No soul left. People tried to enter the city to celebrate their victory. But the city gates didn't let any pawn in. As if there is an invisible wall we cannot overcome.

Day one hundred and twelve: The wall is still standing. People cannot enter the Swinford. The mayor decided to tell the ordinary townspeople that they are not allowed to go to its grounds because it is considered to be cursed. And everyone who is willingly stepping into the gate will die. I don't believe him.

That's why it is called "The Forbidden City". It all starts to make sense. I see that this diary entry was just a glimpse of what this book contains. I believe people from all decades have written their experience down. While the time has changed, one thing has stayed the same:

"People cannot enter the gate."
"An invisible wall preventing us from invading."
"Even with force we couldn't break down the wall."

I entered. I went through the gate. I searched the town. Was Finley able to pass? I recalled him not trying yesterday. He was positioned before the gate. A shiver went down my spine. If something had happened he wouldn't have been able to help me. I was on my own, again.

44

The records said that the Elves disappeared and never came back. As if they vanished into nothing. What if the Forbidden City is just the beginning? What if it's a gate? I remember the voice saying something similar: *"His world."* It didn't say *this* world. It said *his*. This would mean that we weren't talking about the same world. Is it possible? But I've searched the whole city and there was nothing. No secret gate or entry. Everything looked normal, abandoned. I needed to have more information about the other side.

Why was there war after a long period of peace between the human and the Elves? What changed?

I flick through the pages trying to find anything useful. I read hateful notes addressed to the Elves. Humans really despised these creatures. Towards the end, their emotions became neutral. They started to question the purpose and existence of the Elves. I keep rethinking my visit to the city. Yes, it felt weird. The air felt different. Heavier. And considering the conversation I had in the church …

What if the Elves were planning to come back? What if we are all in danger? But why me? I have no say in this world. They should have chosen another person, a Golden person.

I close the book, and a small paper fell out of it. I examine the paper. It looks not as old as the book itself. It is soft and white, not rough and yellow. I unfold the note.

To Aedlin Orbwood,

To the person who does not know her heritage yet and seeks answers that cannot be given by her people. Do not hide like a coward in your puny hut surrounded by the spirits of your dead family.

It is time to become serious about who you are and your future. It is time to stop pretending.

Enough time has passed already.

I stare numbly at the antagonistic note. I look around trying to spot the person who might has put it in here. Is Finley pulling some sick prank on me? This is impossible, but how would he know I was here? The note doesn't seem like something he'd write. Hardly anyone knows my full name. Only close friends know that I am Aedlin but I protect my last name like a treasure. If people know your name, they have power over you. And I don't want anyone to have this kind of say over my existence.

I get up from the floor and stretch my cramp muscles. I put the book back into the shelf and store the paper note in the pocket of my trousers.

I didn't slouch through the market but immediately went home. I wasn't hungry but I force myself to eat the rest of the hind I hunted two days ago. The note stayed in my head the whole time. I had to get it back out and read the mysterious lines over and over again. Who is this? Could it be the shadowed figure in the church? I flick the note away.

Two days later, I am sitting alone in my room in the dim candlelight, I inspect the note over again. Every word confused me.

It's time to become serious about who you are and your future.

46

Before I can stop myself, I reach for a paper and some leftover ink. I began writing:

To the person stalking my walking hours. I don't know who you are, but somehow you know my name. I am not about to exchange secret notes with a stranger who won't even sign their own name. I am well aware of my situation and future. I believe I can say that best considering the fact that I am me and you are no one I know.

I drop my face in my palms. This isn't who I am. I know nothing about my future. I don't know if I'll live to see the next week, or what I will eat after my rations are over. I mutter a curse under my breath. I crumble the note and throw it into my closet. Trying to ignore it.

That night, my exhaustion is not eased by those same recurring dreams.

Every night, I get chased by shadows and asked hazy figures of names, only to have their words vanish into the wind.

The next morning I shrug on my daily clothes, not even trying to run through my hair. Grabbing my reply off the closet, I resolve to give this person a piece of my mind. I hardly care if I offended some stranger. The note went into *Swinford: The Forbidden City* and I expect it to be the end.

I was wrong.

The person exceeded my expectations with their stubbornness.

Orbwood,

I am not stalking you. I observe. Wanting to see if you are worth my time. I am yet a stranger to you and believe me, I have little better to do than keeping an eye on your wellbeing . I am your guardian angel. However, if your last note and desperate attempts at defending your dignity is what you believe, then you are not worth a whit of the ink on this page.

But let me tell you this – I may have answers to your questions.

That should have been the time when I stop writing back. What am I doing here actually? I should focus on the essentials of life. That should have been the moment when I throw my hands in the air and never thought of this ever again. But I cannot let it be. There is someone out there so versed in words and suspicious, but they're offering help.

I take the note and leave the library. I am lost in thoughts, not noticing that Finley has approached me.

"What's that?" he asks. I let the paper drop in my pocket, trying to cover how shocked I am by his sudden appearance.

"Nothing." I shake it off. "Hey, what are you up to? Maybe we can go hunt?" I suggest.

"You want me to join your hunt? Me who is, quoting you, 'unable to walk'." He grins.

To be honest right then I welcome everything that could lead my thoughts to another point. "Yes, maybe you could improve your steps. You know if you don't try you will never know," I say half-hearted.

I am surprised that he agreed to my idea.

On our way I can feel the note heavy in my pocket. As if it is something I should feel guilty of. Finley is talking about his day and the birthday of one of his brothers. However, I catch myself wandering off with my thoughts to the phantom in the dark.

I search the forest for possible inducers and just hear and agree with his stories.

"Aedlin?" he asks.

"Yes?" I mumble under my breath.

"What do you say?"

"Hm?" I turn around to face him.

"You didn't listen, did you?" He stops walking.

"I am so sorry, Finley. I am not myself. I … I am really sorry," I admit.

"You've not been yourself lately. Did the note have something to do with your strange behaviour?" he enquires.

"What note?" I stupidly ask.

"Don't try lying to me."

"No, no all fine, I just need some time."

"Some time apart from me?" Finley asked quietly. Only now I look up and see his face. He looks tired and exhausted. It's been a couple of rough days lately.

"I just need to get something done. After that I will be the old me again," I say. Finley smiles sadly. I hate to see him like that. He is always so full of energy but he looks tired. And I believe that, to some extent, it is my fault.

"I can't wait for it." He grins and I cannot stop myself from smiling as well.

-

In my hut, with a filled stomach, I take a candle to my room. Grab a pen and started to write.

To the stranger, whose name I still don't recall.

Maybe we should stop being cowards and maybe I should demand answers to my questions. Yet, who am I to trust a stranger? I read about the local history of the war between humans and Elves. The war in which the Elves unleashed a magic not only capable of warping men's minds and bodies into abominations, but it is also written that the magic was set free and people were murdered by it. Why do people fear the Elves? Who's fault was it? And what is my position in all of this?

Aedlin Orbwood

Days have passed and during the sun hours, I've almost forgotten about the secret notes I was passing with a stranger.

However, the nightmares I had every night reminded me of it. I refused to admit that I went every day at the same time to the library and check if the stranger had replied to my questions. I almost lost hope until one afternoon when a note fell out of the book.

Orbwood.

You were reading about the War of the Forbidden City. I hope you are open to receiving a great deal of information that seems to be impossible for your small human brain to accommodate. Maybe in this point you are right: there are good men among the wicked in this world, donning the fleece of the innocent. He who set free the magic and chased after the mortals, and warped their bodies, minds and hearts, is wicked indeed. But the actions of this man should have condemned only him and not all those who wield magic. Mortals fear us—

"Mortals fear us" – there is only one creature who says mortals. Elves. My stranger is an Elf. I am exchanging notes with a powerful being.

—due to our power. We have something that they don't have. And your breed is so small minded that they cannot comprehend this knowledge. ELVES are the creatures of knowledge whereas humans have a tendency to physical affirmatives. Never thinking, always killing. I am not saying it has been all their fault, but if they just listened it would have been different. However, Elves are not an easy companion.

Your position is the cure. Your existence has been foretold for centuries. If you believe your history is complex and difficult to follow, then your small human brain will explode when reading about my history.

Are you going to be the cure who could have saved lives but chose instead to be a nobody? Or will you follow where your heart leads you?

When will you stop being afraid and learn more about who you are?

I stare at the note. I don't know what was more agitating: this person's tone or the fact that they were right.

I have to know more about their history.

I have to get into the library. The Golden one. The one occupied by the rich. And I will need help. I take the note with me, unsure if I will ever reply and go to Finley's house. Today is Sunday, he won't be working. He is the only person who can help me.

I knock at the door and a woman in her mid-fifties opens it.

"Oh, Aedlin, what a surprise! Finley didn't tell me you'd be coming, hun." This woman had gone through so much suffering and she could still smiles at me as if I am the light at the end of the tunnel.

"Oh no, Mrs Hummingbird, he doesn't know I'm here. It was more of a surprise visit."

"Oh, my dear, please call me Elise. We talked about this." I smile at her. "Finley! Aedlin is here, can you please come into the kitchen?!" she cries out.

Their house looks nice. Over the years, they did it up a little, since all of her children are working. Having five incomes is better than having none. The hut was not splendid but it is cosy and warm and a scent of hazelnut is in the air. I fidget with my hands, not knowing where to put them. Elise has always been kind to me but I have problems opening up to her. I don't know what we should talk about. I can't sew or crochet. I hunt and kill. And looking at the fragile woman in front of me, she couldn't handle her emotions when I told her I have to kill innocent rabbits for dinner.

An awkward silence has established between us but luckily Finley appears in the door frame. I sigh.

"Thank you, Elise, for the hospitality. I have to kidnap your son real quick!" I walk over to Finley and grabb his hand. I can feel his unsureness because his movement is uneasy. I rush out of the house and cannot hear Elise's answer.

"Aedlin, what's going on?" he asks, demanding. We stop and I realise I am still holding his hand. I quickly let go of it.

"I need your help, Finley." I fidget. "I have to get into the library."

He looks confused. Sometimes I think his brain is the size of a walnut. I add, "The one across town. The Golden One." He widens his eyes in realisation.

"Aedlin, we are not allowed to go there! What do you need from there? What's going on?"

I sigh and turn around, not knowing what to tell him. "I need books. Books that are not available in our small library."

"Books about what?" he demands to know, still not moving.

"Books about history. Finley, please just trust me and help me. There is nothing you really have to do. I just really have to get some books!" I moved towards him. "Please!" I beg. He sighs.

"Alright, Aedlin, let's do this!"

-

I have to admit this isn't the first time we've sneaked into buildings in which we are not allowed in. We actually had special garments for such occasions. For the first time in days I've brushed my hair. I try to braid it into a high bun and stepped into a dress I stole months ago from a store. The fabric is soft, nothing like my rough hunting clothes. The dress has a cream colour and is overall quite unspectacular for Golden people, but for me this dress is the cherry on top of the cake.

When I finally check myself in the mirror I see that some wild red curls got loose from the bun and hung beside my face. I hate to admit it but I like myself. I look good but this is not me. This is someone who tries to fit into a world that is not hers. My gaze focus on the note laying on the kitchen table. It is an invitation but also a challenge. I a going to find out more about this secret world.

I wrap myself into my warm coat. It will look odd to people who would take notice of me but I a good at going undiscovered.

I meet Finley at the border of the Golden district. He looks stunning. Finley is wearing a grey Sacco and has brushed his brown hair back. I try to ignore that my heart is beating faster.

The Golden district is normally heavily guarded. The Golden people thought very poorly of us. They were afraid of possible dangers.

"Hello, hello! Who is that and where is my friend?" Finley says and I immediately have to smile.

"Stranger, who allowed you to talk to me?" I say in a high-pitched, mocking voice. He has to smile.

"Of course, my lady. I beg for forgiveness." He takes my hand and pressed a kiss on my knuckles.

"Apology accepted." I laugh. "Okay, let's keep going." Finley offers his arm and I hold onto it. It am always better to walk in pairs in the Golden districts. People here are usually in company on their afternoon walks.

I try to ignore his appearance. This isn't part of the plan. I have to focus on what I need and not on my teenage love. I take a deep breath and we step through the gate into the Golden District.

As I thought, the guards weren't looking twice. The Golden district is so different in every aspect.

The pathway is lined with hazel trees and Ostryas teeming with purple irises and red poppies. Even though the winter is raging, a light breeze carried the scent of spring and the honeyed air was mild.

In my district, the flowers had slender stamps and their leaves were crisp, brown and curling like a finger of a corpse. These flowers represented death. But here everything is filled with life. The houses are painted in a light colour. People are walking around the well-designed marked area. I can see frozen fountains and bakers selling their biscuits. How unfair life can be. I hold on tighter to Finley, not trusting myself to not run off and steal some of the divine baked goods. That wasn't the mission.

In my district, we can't really distinguish between the city hall, library or ordinary houses; here, on the other hand, each house is individual with its own unique bright colours and sculptures.

I know exactly where the library is. I have snuck into this building countless times. However, I always knew about the dangers of such risky adventures. If you get caught, fatal consequences await you. I am unsure why the Golden make such a big deal out of us going into their district. However, I believe it has something to do with the fact that we are considered filthy. Lots of my people carry diseases, diseases that might kill somebody. Nevertheless, I am quite sure that the Golden do not have to worry about their healthcare system. They have plenty of medicine and doctors, whereas we are doomed to die on the street. It always makes me angry to face this inequality in the town. How can it be fair to have a certain living standard based on your bloodline? Though, I have no power to make changes in the near future. Which is why I accept the risk of being killed. If it brings me joy, hell, why not?

Finley and I haven't talked the whole way to the library. I was afraid that our way of speaking would reveal that we weren't from here. However, this is rather unlikely. The Golden ones are living in their rich bubble. Still, we do not want to take unnecessary risks. As expected, the door to the Golden Library is guarded. Normally you need an entry pass, which we do not have but we have thought about this.

"Card," says the one guard to my left. Even though they have everything in excess, the guard looks as if this was the worst working place he could ever be in. Ungrateful bastards. I rummage in my purse 'looking for my card'.

"This is ridiculous! I've forgotten it at the mansion," I say trying to sound like a Golden One.

"No card no pass, this are the rules, sorry, Ma'am," the guard on the right says. As if I don't know the rules.

"Sweetheart!" I say, furious. In this part of the town, Finely and I are madly in love. We have to play a role. "They won't let me in! But I must go!" My voice is on the edge of a shriek.

"Honey, I am certain you wish to enter, however, your cute little brain has forgotten your card," Finley says with a soft voice which tickles the top of my head.

"But going back home and coming here *again* will be *such* a hassle!" I try to sound theatrical.

"I know, I know. But there is no other way." He pretends to calm me, patting my arm. But now comes the moment, the finale of my performance. I take a deep breath and start to cry. Crying like a five-year-old not getting the toy it wanted.

"By all saints," says the guard on the left and rolled his eyes. "If it is that important then we can make an exception, but please be quick." He sighs and opens the door.

I wipe away my tears and smile. I take Finley's hand and pull him into the huge entry hall.

Each time I am fascinated by its beauty. The room is filled with white marble and golden details. Everywhere you look you could find bookshelves or small seating areas. Servants were running around offering tea or coffee to the visitors. It is as if you're in a palace. Not comparable to our dusty little library, this one is comparable to a dome.

"I am amazed by how this always works, honey," Finley whispers in my ear and goosebumps spread around my neck. "Your tears were magnificent." I have to smile.

"Thank you very much, my sweetheart."

I walk steadily through the shelves trying to find answers to my questions. It is overwhelming, the collection of books. I can have taken all of them, but no. I need the essentials. I am unsure how long I was looking through the shelves but at some point Finley came up to me.

"I don't want to pressure you but I think it would be better if we leave soon."

I nod and tried scanning the books one last time.

After a few more minutes I have decided to take five books with me – all about the Elven Realm and its creatures. I walk up to Finley who is seated in one of the armchairs, drinking tea.

"Really?" I raise my eyebrow.

"Hey, if you can enjoy this, why can't I?" He smirks. I have to laugh.

We leave the library as nothing had happened. The guards don't even look at us twice.

We walk past the bakeries and I am this close to buying some but then remember that this district has different currency. Another regulation to distinguish between us. If I try to buy something now with our currency, we would be blown up.

We walk up to the gate we first came through which is still guarded by two men.

"Pass please," one of them asks. I look at Finley. We never got asked for a pass at the gates.

"Pass?" I ask.

"Yes, Ma'am, your identity card," says the guard in a monotone voice. I pretend to look in my purse for my card.

"Oh, I believe I've forgotten it at home. I am so clumsy."

"With no identification card I am afraid I have to arrest you for pretending to be people you are not." Oh no. This is not good at all.

"Officers, please. I feel hurt being associated with the filthy part of the town!"

"I am sorry, but we have to follow the rules." The man steps closer to me but I dodge his hands and kicked him in the guts.

"Hey!" he screams.

"I didn't want to do this, this is your fault for wanting to see my identification card!" I mock them. While Finley was busy taking out the other guard I continue to dodge the attacks of the man. Holding books and fighting requires a lot of skills. And then I have a thought. Why not use the books to fight? I know my heart will hurt but I don't want to be put in jail. I reach back and slam the book in the officer's face. He crumples to his knees and falls face forward.

"Finley?" I turn around to see him knocking out the other guard. Our eyes meet and I had to laugh. This situation was too absurd.

I look around, hoping no one noticed this small hassle. When I make sure no eyes were on us, we quickly vanish into the grey and dirty part of the town.

"Great punch, sweetheart," I joke.

"You weren't that bad either, honey."

I stop on my heels.

"Not that bad? Who are you kidding?" I smirk. Finley stepped closer to me.

"You're saying that you were the better one in this fight?"

59

"I am certain, I had to fight with books!" I go on my tip toes to seem taller which was ridiculous. Finley is at least one head taller than me.

"Okay this one belongs to you, honey. But next time it is my turn." He grins.

"Deal!"

Finley narrows his eyes.

"What?" I ask.

"You're bleeding."

I frown and touch my cheek. Checking my hand, I see some blood on it, however, it doesn't seem like a lot. I will easily survive that. I have to take a deep breath but instead of it calming me down, I take in his scent and my stomach did a one hundred and eighty.

"So did you," I whisper. I can feel his breath on my cheek. His eyes are focused on my lips. Since when does he come so close? Do I want him to be this close? He looks me in the eyes as if in them are the answers to his questions. Does he close the gap between us? Suddenly, his lips are on mine. I am confused. This happened often in the past and I was sure it was always quite meaningless, however, this kiss had meaning. I am not sure what the purpose was but I find my muscles strengthening again and burrowed my hands in his hair. His lips are soft but the kiss was everything but gentle. I could feel desire, pleasure, lust. However, one thing is missing – the butterflies in my stomach. This kiss is nice but it rather had the wrong effect. I am the one pulling away from him. His eyes darkened but cleared as quickly.

"Thank you for joining me today." I take a deep breath. "See you soon." I turn around and walked to my hut, not wanting to think about the kiss and what it has changed between us.

CHAPTER FIVE

I let myself fall exhausted into bed. I took five books which are now laying in front of me. In the next hours I read through each and every book, not realising how the night turned into the day. In the morning, I rubbed my eyes, trying to bring back life into my body.

The books told a story from centuries ago, beginning with the launch of the Crystal War between two hostiles fronts. Humans and Elves still lived in peace. However, the conflict mentioned in the book which was stored in the archive was not mentioned in the history books. It made me believe that this was just a small part of the bigger picture. The Elf Empire and the Human Empire were once part of one single, powerful country. Until the Crystal War. This was when the human and the Elves contract broke. However, this wasn't the last war the Elves were involved in. Thirty years ago, which isn't that long considering that Elves are nearly immortal, the Elves fought against the Shadow Legion. The details were quite shady and sources said different things. But what I could tell is that the Shadow Legion were once a serious threat for the Elves. Due to the breach in regulations, the Elves were on their own with no help from the mortal side. If humans consider the Elves a powerful being, how mighty is the new threat?

The Shadow Legion is an army created by the Dark One. His army is filled with creatures half dead which all follow his lead. Is it like a virus? Do Elves get infected by the Dark One and then they mutate into such beings? Can humans be affected?

My quill pauses for a moment, hovering over my blank page. Is their magic really dangerous? Or just different from what people consider normal?

I continue reading another book, *Affinities*.

I forget to sleep or to eat. The only task I can do is to acquire his mysterious knowledge captured in these old books.

Affinities are the magic associated with one particular element. I figured out that not all Elves can have affinities. However, most of them do wield an elemental power.

The note of the stranger lingers in my head and I grab a piece of paper and ink to write my thoughts down.

Stranger,

I've moved away from the introduction in your history. I believe I am familiar with the basics. I want to learn more about what Elves do, what magic is. I found a book that talks about magical affinities. As I understand it, in their early states of existence, Elves and humans believed that magic had its origin in the element itself. As far as I know, there are water, fire, wind and earth affinities.

Aedlin Orbwood

As much as I don't want to, I find the words of the stranger's note embedded in my head. At every opportunity over the next weeks, I try to find excuses for Finley who kept asking what was the matter with me. I withdrew myself to sneak into my house and read the books. I walked around the market listening to the daily chit chat, hoping for any sights of the stranger who had been wandering around in the woods. As the notes from my stranger became more frequent, so did my appreciation grow for them. I had finally found someone I could share my thoughts with and they give answers to all my questions. The stranger's knowledge seems to be endless.

Orbwood,

What is magic, you ask? I am afraid you will not find that answer in these books you seek, it is rather a question more suited to be seen with your own eyes. I am willing to give you answers to your questions, yet, they are limited. Tell me, how far have you studied my history?

The Stranger in the Dark

Something about their words seep deep into my mind. Pride swells in my chest when I find something that may be considered acceptable by the stranger. It is undeniable – I have a weird stranger to impress.

Stranger,

Currently books are the only thing I have for absorbing knowledge. My world is not filled with magic, my world is mortal. For me this knowledge exceeds my imagination of reality. Things that never ought to be possible are, the possibility of curing death. As the books state, there are several Elves who have the possibility to cure death. Giving them the ability to locate illness in the body. Might that be considered dark Magic? My people have killed hundreds of innocent people because they thought they are witches for curing a cold. Where these people Elves?

Aedlin Orbwood

My days became repetitive without realisation. Reading, a note from the stranger, eating, sleeping. I found a rhythm to maximise the time of reading a day. The more I read, the more I realised that I have lived only half a life. How can people not wonder or know about this other place? About magic! About wars fought by immortal creatures. I have always been eager to learn more, even though I have never had a school education. Although my parents were quite educated and they didn't hesitate in teaching me about the world, this new world is a challenge for me and my mind.

Orbwood.

I see that you are eager to learn. Very well, now that you show interest in the situation. I will indulge you. These people you are talking about were no Elves, they were considered sorcerers. A kind that looks like human, yet, possesses inhuman abilities to wield Dark Magic. They were all killed in the Salem processes, claimed to be witches, to be evil.

The Stranger in the Dark

I find myself wondering what Affinities are out there. I follow the flame dancing on top of the candle and I keep wondering how it would be like to wield the power to manipulate and manifest light. I stare at the flame with the stupid attempt to manipulate, control it. I don't have to mention that it obviously didn't work. I make the nights to days trying to escape my nightmares which still plague me. Now with my knowledge, I try to connect my dreams with the acquired knowledge but it is hard. Sometimes I see beautiful landscapes covered with not from this world flowers, but sometimes I relive my encounter with the shadow being.

Dear Stranger,

I think this knowledge should be shared with mortals in a way that is easy to understand – like you have done with me.

I am not special. I am an orphan killing to survive. I have never been someone who is special. Why have you reached out to me?

65

I would like to understand what you see in me, why you bother sharing all this knowledge with me. Couldn't I be a possible threat to your world?

Sincerely,

Aedlin

While we continued to exchange notes, I felt the urge to re-examine the forbidden city. For the last couple of weeks, I felt a sensation drawn towards it. I clearly saw the city walls in my dreams. Something important was going on with this small village – I just haven't figured out what.

I had limited encounters with Finley. Since the kiss, I try to block him completely. I don't think he would understand the notes and knowledge I'd gathered. No one other than the secret messenger shares my enthusiasm for magic and the Elves. In my town it's feared and if I try to lead the conversation into this direction I get blocked. As a result, in an odd way, the stranger is becoming easier to confide in and speak openly to than my close friend, Finley. I find it more and more easier to reveal things about myself to them.

Aedlin,

I see you as an opportunity to save what you do not know yet. Consider me a consult for my kingdom. Someone who estimates and judges. People rely on my capability in assessing the situation correctly. I see something special in you, you have not yet encountered.

Do you have others in your town you can openly talk about your opinions with? Or am I the only one?

The Stranger in the Dark

I am not quite sure how to respond, so I spend the night tossing and turning in my bed. If I confess that I had begun to see the stranger as a friend, what would that mean? I start to rethink what I've read about the forbidden city that no human can enter, and about what the Dark One told me in the church. That I am supposed to be the saviour of the Realm.

The Dark One made clear that I could be his key to success but that would mean me joining the bad side. I cover my face with my palms. What am I doing here? I remember that only weeks ago my only concern was to hunt enough food to survive and look at me now. I am reading through the night and hoping to receive a new note from the stranger. How are they doing it? How can they receive the note and return a new one without being seen by townspeople? How come if I ask the old lady in the entrance of the library if someone went down to the ground floor, she always says no. Are they one of the Shadow Legion, moving in the dark?

Dear Stranger,

Perhaps I do consider you as someone to be trusted. The last human I spoke to about magic cursed at me and cried out that I should leave immediately, that I am a witch.

Your worst offences are your assumption of my capability and the fact that you have not told me your name yet. Who exactly are you?

Sincerely,

Aedlin

Days passed and life kept going. I finished the books about magic and tried to gather more in the local library but nothing was to be found. I desperately waited for an answer from the stranger but nothing happened. No reply. So after some days of reconsidering what I said, I gave up on waiting for their reply. I started to go hunting again, having the need to go out. I could no longer sit in my room knowing this whole world exists somewhere out there. I met up with Finley and we talked. I told him everything. I told him about the notes, about the books and about my theories. Everything. I couldn't hide it anymore. Having lost the stranger, I had the urge to talk to someone close. I found it weird that I rather would have talked to a complete stranger than to the guy I've known my whole life.

"So you're telling me that you have exchanged notes with, what you believe to be, an Elf, talking about magic and even more confusingly, they taught you their history?" Finley gags, perplexed. "You know that this sounds a bit sketchy." I cover my face with my palms. "I know. I know how it sounds but believe me, it's true. There is a world out there we weren't allowed to discover."

"But don't you think they had a reason to 'hide' it from us? Elves are dangerous!"

"That's what they keep telling us but I've exchanged words with one of them and they are highly intelligent creatures. Something about this whole situation has to do with me because they kept writing back. My dreams! The forbidden city! It has to make sense." I look up and meet Finley's hazel brown eyes. I can tell that he thinks I am going crazy. "You don't believe me," I said say thoughts out loud.

"Aedlin ..." he starts but didn't get any further.

"I see, Finley, I swear to you that I am totally in control of my mind. I know what I've read and I know what I felt in the city. But ... if you don't believe me, then I guess this is not going to work. I don't need someone around me who thinks I am a stupid little girl. I am educated and I am smart and I *will* figure it out – with or without you!" I stand up.

"So the books were for your magical bullshit?" he says, grinding his teeth.

"Magical bullshit?" I spot it. "This is not bullshit. These are indicators for life, a life we were unable to learn about. New civilisation, languages, cultures and even more. Isn't it exciting?" I try for the last time.

"It is dangerous, Aedlin," he says. "Why do you want to be involved in something people have fought for it to be forgotten?" he asks.

"Maybe because I am open to new adventures, I am sick of this life here." I gesture to the surroundings. He sighs.

"Aedlin, I worry about you! You have no idea what you did, blocking me off the past weeks." Finley steps closer to me, but all the feelings I thought I have towards him are gone. I push him away with my hand.

"No, Finley," I mumble under my breath.

"No?" He steps back. "Why are you playing with me? I showed you clearly what I feel for you and I thought you felt the same … but something has changed." He huffs. "Has it something to do with these notes? Is he your secret lover? An Elf?!" His voice grows louder.

"Finley, stop talking nonsense! I don't know who they are and they are definitely *not* my secret lover. Neither are you." I take a deep breath. "Yes we kissed, yes I thought I wanted it but I realised I don't like you that way. We are too different."

"Indeed, we are different. You are living in the past, seeking danger and risks. I have a family, a family I have to protect! I can't … I can't keep worrying about you as well." His voice grows quiet.

I know what this is, it's a goodbye. All the years we were together, he was my best friend. A friend who made me enjoy life. But we grew up to be adults, to be responsible for our own lives. We cannot keep playing a game, we have to face reality and his and mine are different.

"No one asked you to worry," I say and leave. I leave him standing there and he doesn't try to come after me. He doesn't stop me.

He lets me go.

Chapter Six

I walk home, not caring if people look at me or what they will think of me storming through the streets. I go straight home, pack a backpack with food, water and books, grab my bow and go straight into the forest. How could I believe that Finley would help me? After all we've done together, he lets me go. Just like that, years of friendship are thrown away. I didn't notice that tears made their way down my cheeks. I was foolish. First, my strange pen pal abounded me and now Finley. Maybe it is better this way. I am fine with risking my own life, I don't want innocent people to be involved.

I stop and take some deep breaths of the fresh cold air. Who am I to cry about some people leaving me? I am used to being alone. Have I become this attached to him? Well, I work perfectly on my own, so I'd be fine. It has to come this way. Finley has a family a mother and brothers. He was right, I am an extra worry. he had to let me go, to protect himself and his loved ones. I walk determinedly towards the Forbidden City with only one goal in mind – discovering what the myth is about. It is as if nothing else existed anymore besides a feeling of being pulled towards the city, getting dragged to these old stones.

I have been so focused on my thoughts that I haven't taken notice of the winter wonderland around me. During the day the forest doesn't look as intimidating as it does in the night time. The birds are singing but I can still see how death wanders through the trees waiting for its next prey. I snuck over overhanging limbs across the path, and followed the barely visible path to the Forbidden City.

Over the decades, bushes have grown over the track making it nearly impossible to discover the city walls, as if this was the aim of the people who once lived in the town.

The sunshine brightens all the surroundings, making the snow shimmer. The pine boughs are weighed down with snow.

The closer I get to the city, the darker and colder it got. I can feel a biting wind on my face and I try to cover myself with my coat. My side became progressively worse due to the flurry of snowflakes. I can feel how the flakes built up quickly in my hair. I am on the edge of turning around, when I see the city wall of the Forbidden City in the distance.

I go closer to the iron gate where the doors were shut. I don't remember closing it the last time. I push it open and a loud creaking sound appears. My mouth is sour and dry, not knowing what to expect. The gate swings open. I should not enter, this is a suicidal mission, yet, I have to find shelter soon due to the blizzard getting stronger and I am not prepared to go all the way back home in this weather.

I take one step at a time through the gate. I expect some sort of drawback which would indicate that I am not welcomed in here as the many authors have written down, however, I feel nothing. I step through the gate as I would through an ordinary door.

I scan my surroundings, trying to find anything unusual, yet nothing seems to have changed; however, due to the heavy falling snowflakes it is nearly impossible to see. If someone or something is hiding in the bushes, I'd be dead before I noticed.

Looking at the shabby huts I realise that I would not seek a safe shelter chasing one of them. I am in need of a building strong enough to let me live through the night. I try to tie my hair into a messy knot, though the wind made it impossible. I hold my hair out of my face, trying my best to find a suitable place. The air is now freezing cold. I start to shiver, since my clothes are all soaking wet. I put my hands to my mouth and let out a breath, hoping it would warm the insides of my palms. Once the air is out I can see small clouds of iced oxygen in front of me. When I look at my blue finger tips an idea pops up in my head as if lightning struck. My eyes search as good as possible for the old church which was made of bricks and stones.

I grab my bow tighter and tried to proceed through the storm to the building.

The snow shifts and drifts and the surroundings are obscure. The wind is howling while the flakes pelted against my frozen cheeks. I feel a rising pain in my fingertips, which is a good sign, I have certainty they are still alive, yet, it is utterly uncomfortable.

Many churches I know have a tower at the west end of the nave. Some were even topped by spires. So is this one. If I focus my eyes on the top of the tower I am able to see the bell hanging. Once

73

this bell was the only indicator for many people's lives and now it hangs there, abandoned, useless.

The building is surrounded by Yew trees due to their longevity. My mother taught me once when I was smaller that such trees symbolised the saints burial grounds, owing to their great age. The meaning behind the trees has always been beautiful for me. Yew trees stood not only for death but also for resurrection. Their meaning often helped ancestors to mourn the death of a family member better, knowing that death wasn't the end. I sometimes like to think this way about my parents. That they are not completely gone from this world.

I drag my focus away from the trees and look at the church entrance. With my last ounce of strength I push the door open and slide into the warm hall. Safe from the freezing wind, I let out a breath that I didn't know I was holding. I rub my palms together trying to bring back life into them. A resin incense of benzoin, frankincense and myrrh flew into my nose. Once when I was smaller, me and my family used to go to church in the winter season. I never really understood why, I simply was too young. Yet, this smell brings back so many memories I thought were lost. It wasn't comparable with when I was last here. Let it be fear that dragged out the smell of the church once I encountered the Dark One.

Before I can rest, I have to examine the church and try to find possible threats.

There is a rail which acts to separate the sanctuary from the place where the congregation sits, known as the nave. In the nave there were often rows of pews where the congregation sat in rows on benches.

Around the church there are fourteen framed pictures, known as the Stations of the Saints, which show the foundation of my culture. However, the pictures differ from the one I used to see in my town's church. Seven of them were saints I was taught to pray to every night, yet the other seven I did not know. They all shared a remarkable feature – pointy ears. I step an inch away from the picture to see it in all its dimensions. This is clearly an Elf.

I walk towards the Altar, where usually the Holy Nietza, the book written by the saints themselves, is placed, if you believe the priests.

After I walk silently on the stones in the church, I discover nothing unusual. I exhale and return to my backpack which I have left on one of the benches. I sit down onto the dusty pillows and take a moment for myself. I stroke over the rough texture of them with my hands.

A sudden dizziness surprised me and I put my hand on my forehead.

It is spinning. I am freezing cold, even though the church protects me from the snow and wind, due to my wet clothes I struggle to increase my body temperature. I look around trying to find anything useful to warm me, like a blanket, but nothing was to be found. I snuggle into the uncomfortable bench and held my knees tight to my chest. I am focusing on my breathing, hoping the shivers would lessen.

My eyes became heavy and I try to stay awake – I have to be awake.

Nevertheless, the darkness feels like a welcoming friend and I cannot fight any longer against the desire to close my eyes.

I finally let the darkness take over my numb limbs and fall into a troubled sleep.

-

I hear the bell. Birds are chirping and the resin incense and myrrh was replaced by a floral scent.

I shoot up and open my eyes. Bad idea. My vision blurred and I have to support my upper body with my hands to prevent it from falling back. I am still in the church, good. I check my backpack for my bow and arrows. I take a huge sip of my water and bite into an apple so harshly that juice runs down from the corner of my mouth.

I listen closely to my environment. The blizzard has stopped. I can hear a light breeze making branches scratch on the church walls. I get up slowly and stretch out my frozen limbs. I am surprised by how warm it is in the church, it was nothing comparable to last night's coldness. My steps echoed off the walls as I walk towards the metal door. I gaze over my shoulder back to the hall which gave me shelter. This is quite an unusual experience.

I grab the doorknobs with both of my hands and open it with a groan. I look out and froze on the spot.

After so many months of cold weather and brown landscape, spring seems to be something magical. The once-dead trees look greener and the flowers are blooming in every possible colour. I see animals eating from the grass on the ground. This has to be the work of magic. The air feels lighter and if I listen close enough I can hear a faint sizzle. I turn around to see the church but where the church once stood is now a small hut. *No, no, no.* I look through its window, no one is there. I open the door hoping to find something that indicates this was the church but I was disappointed. Besides some brooms and wood, it is empty. I close the door and open it again, hoping I'd be back home. I walk over the threshold, nothing happened. Wherever I am this wasn't home.

This isn't the forest I grew up in. I know the forest. This is not it. I grab the bow and tightened the string.

The sun is shining as it did yesterday before the blizzard came, yet it is warmer. I feel sweat running down my spine. I can hear a source of water lapping.

After I secure the area, I drop the bow. Could it be? Is this the other world? That would be one explanation but it would also mean that this world was real. Reading stories about it is different than really experiencing the change. I fall on my knees and brush my hands through the fresh grass. I can identify berry bushes, brambles, ivies, ferns and so much more that my mind has trouble compensating for all of the new sensations. It's been too long since last spring. The air is filled with an earthy smell but with a sweet scent on the end. I lift my face, letting the light and shadow dance on my face. I hear humming bees and bumbles. I get up and walk toward the new forest. I inhale a minty smell and continue on, delighting in the sound of my feet sliding through the leaves while walking towards the forest. This is what I wanted. I cross the threshold and I am in a new region.

The trees lash and crash against each other like drumsticks in the hands of a giant. This forest is the definition of life. I explore further in the strange woods, always on guard. I turn around at the sound of cracking branches and freeze in shock and amazement.

I look into the eyes of a deer. More a stag, I'd say. It's antler is massive and seems to have fire tips. Its fur is shimmery brown, with some red and orange parts, making it look like it's burning. The most impressive feature of the stag, though, are his eyes. Its turquoise eyes, staring right into mine. Shall I run? Stay calm! Roll on the floor to show I'm submissive? I don't have much experience in dealing with deer that size. It huffs and turns around, disappearing in the forest as if I am as boring as the falling leaves. The light is dense as I proceed into the woods. Not much sun is coming through the tree crowns, yet it gives the place a magical atmosphere. Even though the sun is not reaching my skin, it feels warm and I have to take off my jacket and tie it around my waist.

On my way to I don't know where, I encountered several weird looking animals. Rabbits with two heads and birds in several colours, shapes and sounds. I saw a plant eating a mouse and took a big step around it. I was not planning on being eaten alive. This forest had more diversity than my whole town.

I found this place obscure but oddly fascinating. I stop every time I encountered a new animal and I tried to examine it as best as possible without getting hurt or killed. I am wandering around for hours, trying to dodge low hanging branches and logs on the ground.

Surprisingly, I notice that it soon got dark and I don't know which option was safer: try to find a spot to rest or keep moving until I found something useful. My shaking limbs decided for me. I look around to find a good tree on which I could climb and rest on its branches. I don't trust the animals here; if I sleep on the floor it would be my death sentence.

After a desperate search I found a semi-comfortable spot. I secure myself as well as possible on the tree branch using my backpack and coat. I allow myself to take a deep breath, close my eyes and appreciate the warm feeling on my skin. Even though the night says hello, the wind is still soft. My feet hurt and I drank my last sip of my water and bit into the other apple I took with me. I don't even have energy to read some pages in the books I brought. What would Finley say if I told him about this? Would he share the enthusiasm or would he start to run away? I know my answer.

With a grip around my bow, I fall into an uncomfortable but restful sleep.

CHAPTER SEVEN

I was woken up by the sound of voices mumbling around me.

I try to be as still as possible and focus my breathing on sounding normal, peaceful. I squint my eyes and see two men standing in front of me. Even though I only look for a short time, I see their ears. The pointy tips are unmistakable.

"Henry, the mortal is becoming conscious. Haven't I mentioned using more of the potion?! Useless!"

My eyes fly open at the chemical smell filling my nose. I see two faces clearly now, but I don't have much time to scan them. I try to flinch but strong hands are holding my body in place. I was hit in the face and soon the darkness is calling for me and I couldn't fight it off.

-

It feels as though someone has taken an axe to the back of my head, split it open, and allow my brain to leak. I open my eyes to the vibration I feel under my hands; the sun is dazzling and my vision blurry. I think I can see strangers' knees but as soon as I start to reach for them, my consciousness gets dragged back into the darkness.

I don't know how long this had been going on.

I hear people talking, hushing and whispering around me. Every time I think I am coming back to consciousness, I am left alone with my thoughts, again.

I come around once again and this time it feels differently. I slowly open my eyes. No chemical substance was pressed on my face. I feel a smooth texture under my hand palms and realise I am laying on a foreign bed. I shuffle the blanket to the side which is covering my body not without admiring the smoothie grain. I look at my legs and see that I am not wearing my clothes instead some attire I don't recall owing. I straighten my body and study the room I found myself in. It is beautiful. Not comparable with the pathetic hut I had at home.

Its walls are not shabby, but painted in a grey-creme damask. The furniture is assembled in a delicate greenwood and not a scanty umber timber as it was at home.

The chamber is spacious and the window walls on my left fill the room with light. Different kinds of flowers blossomed on the counter opposite of the bed.

I swing my feed to the corner of the bed and hover above the carpet. I get up and by the feeling of my bare feet on the soft floor, I have to suppress the urge to run my fingers through the texture. I look out of the window, try to open it but it was locked.

From the corner of my eyes I see something white and realise in shock that I am wearing a white nightgown.

I grow goose-bumps at the thought that foreign people have touched me and exchanged my clothes.

I scan the room with my eyes looking for my bow or any of my possessions. Nothing.

A soft knock on the door. I don't have time to hide before it opens.

A woman with black curls entered.

"Oh you are awake, how lovely." Her voice is soft and nothing like I would have expected an Elf to talk. I frown and move into the furthest corner away from her.

"Where am I?" I am surprised by how rough my voice sounded.

"How long have I been kept asleep?" I demand. The woman looks at me with a peaceful face which annoys me even more. She looks approximately the same age as I am, yet her flawless skin has an unnatural shimmer.

"I am not obliged to answer these questions, Aedlin." I widen my eyes by the sound of my name from her lips. She speaks my language. Though she has a slight accent when she talks. I blink a couple of times, trying to understand the situation.

"How do you know my name?!" I realise that my voice sounds a bit hysteric. I wanted all of this. I took the risk and wandered off into the mystical world, and this is what I would have to face. Yet, being kidnaped and knocked out wasn't included in my plan.

"I advise you to stay calm, your presence is requested," she says calmly, moving closer to me. I don;t try to move further back.

"To whom will you bring me?" I ask firmly.

"This I can answer." She smiles at me. "Your presence is requested by the High King himself." High King – I've heard this word before in one of my books.

"Come, let's dress you into something more appropriate than this gown." The woman offers me her help but I refuse. I am no fragile woman who wants others to help her. I look her in the face and open the door to my right, not knowing what was behind it. I shut it with a loud noise. I am in the bathroom. My gaze falls on my clothes finely placed on a small rose chair.

-

Just a few minutes later I was dressed in my filthy attire. This feels wrong. Yet, there was no time to waste. The woman drags me out of the room into a huge hall.

"Aedlin, I believe it is only fair for you to know my name as well. I am Salem." She chuckles. I cannot reply. I am just so consumed by the building I am in. This has to be a palace by its size – not that I have ever seen one in real life, but this is how I have always imagined them to look like in the novels I read. Salem comes to a halt in front of a huge white wooden door guarded by soldiers.

"From here on, you are on your own, but if you request me, I will come. I will be close, Aedlin." She says my name with such a calming voice that it is hard to dislike her. She squeezes my arm and leaves me alone. The two guards knock on the door and after a short "Yes" they open it.

I can feel how my knees are weak and I try to suppress the urge to fidget with my fingers. I don't know how to act around a High King, someone so prodigious. I still cannot fully comprehend it.

I enter the room that seems to be the throne room. There are three thrones located on a pedestal in front of me. In the middle, a man in his fifties is sitting on a throne. His hair and beard has turned grey, but nonetheless he looks stunning for his age.

His crown is made of an accumulation of golden branches. The picture before me looks majestic. The throne to his right is empty but the one to his left is occupied. I turn my gaze and met the eyes of the young man seated there. My breath stopped for a second. His eyes are ocean blue and he is focused on my being. His expression is numb but I can see his curiosity about my presence.

Despite his eye's hardness the man sitting there is incredibly handsome. Almost too perfect to be true. However, one thing stands out – the ears. The pointy tips coming out of the hair. So it is true. I was never delusional. I had seen an Elf that day. And now I am standing in front of the High King and probably his son.

I stop before the throne and tried to fall into curtsey. Bad idea if you've never practiced it before.

"You may rise, mortal," the High King orders in his voice deep. I straighten and focus on the High King. I am well aware of the guards close to me and feel naked with no weapons on my body.

I know how danger feels and this man, sitting on his throne with his golden crown, screams danger.

Silence.

I still haven't moved my eyes. I am not sure what I am trying to do but I know if I look away, I would be dead. If you turn your back on the predator, you will be its next meal.

His son is lifting himself off the seat, walking towards me. His shoes were clicking on the floor and echoing in the hall. I can feel the tension rising in the room.

"Aedlin, little fire, what a lovely name for such a pathetic looking creature." I hear the disgust in his words. I stare into the cold eyes of the High King's son who puts his hand on my chin, turning my face to both sides, examining every part of it. "My men have found you sleeping in our forest. We tried to find clues to as to your purpose here, but besides the fact that you are an ordinary human, nothing seemed to stand out. What is your business in Eskendria?" I am shocked by the sound of his voice. It is the complete opposite of what his eyes were. His voice is smooth, dark, like a dangerous secret.

"Answer woman!" he demands forcefully, turning my head to face him. This isn't anything I would have expected to find in this world.

I swallow hoping for my voice to find its way back to me.

"I was curious about this place, its nature. I read about this kingdom, and since day one I knew that I couldn't live any longer not knowing what it all was about. I had to figure out if the tales the old told us were true." The Prince is focusing his narrowing eyes on me, clearly doubting the truth in my words.

"Then how is it possible that a mortal can pass the Fade!" He hisses.

"Fade?" I ask confused.

"Yes woman, the border between the Natural world and Elfame, the Elf World." He says as if I am foolish for not knowing. "We have made sure that no mortal being can ever cross the threshold to the city in your pathetic world and still here you are. You should have died hours after entering but still ... manage to survive." His voice is dangerously quiet. "Who helped you? The Dark One? Are you one of his spies, woman?" He tightens the grip around my neck and I struggle to get air.

"Nevan!" A rough voice echoes from behind – the High King. Yet, I don't feel the grip loosen around my neck. "I assure you that I am not a spy, I am just a human," I hiss back in his face.

"*Just a human,* would not be able to cross the borders!" Prince Nevan pulls my face towards his. "Who are you really?" This is worse than expected. To be honest, what did I expect? That the people here would welcome me with open arms?

"Speak to me!" Prince Nevan hisses in my ears. This is ridiculous. I may be a human but I won't let people talk to me this way. I hit my head on his nose. I stumble back, gasping for air. Prince Nevan is holding his nose and I can see blood running through his hand. I hear the noise of moving armour behind me but it stops once the High King raised his hand.

"I am willing to talk to you, once I am treated like a visitor not a prisoner. I assure you I am not here to cause any harm but I am able to defend myself in any way if needed," I say, my voice firm.

"I can see the girl has some fire in her blood. After all, her name does fit her." The High King rises from the podium. With a look of satisfaction, I turn towards Nevan who is still trying to make his nose stop bleeding. However, I become irritated once I saw the smirk on his face.

"You make quite the entrance, young lady. Lingering around in foreign woods, injuring a member of the royal family, talking when no one asked you to do so." The elderly man clears his throat. "This could have fatal consequences. I killed people who have done less than you. However, I will let it pass, since I am an understanding person. I am aware that mortals do have problems in behaving and do not understand the importance of manners. Nevertheless, next time I will not show this much mercy." His icy eyes study my presence. "I will not allow you to return to your homeland until we have found your truthful origin. For now you will obey the crown. Understood?"

I look between His Highness and Nevan. I acknowledge the guards present in the room. My chances of surviving an escape is vastly low. This is why I nodded. I will accept my fate, for now.

"You are excused." Two guards are approaching me to take me back where I was coming from.

"Wait." A voice echoes through the hall. "I would like to accompany her myself to her new chambers, if that is allowed." Prince Nevan looks to his father who nodded in approval. *Great.* I am surprised that his touch on my arm is gentle but firm, pushing me out of the room. We walk quietly towards my new room, which I would have never found myself.

The tension was still there. I am unsure what I was here for. Am I a prisoner or a visitor? Comparing the High Kings and Nevan's actions to Salem, I couldn't be more confused. Maybe Finley was right, perhaps Elves really are the dangerous creatures everyone warned me about.

"Why so silent, fire girl?" Nevan says mockingly. His bleeding has stopped and one of the servants has given him a handkerchief to clean his face. "I have to admit, I have not seen the attack you had reserved for me. Made me change my mind about you," he adds once I didn't reply.

"Where am I?" I ask the obvious.

"Eskendria. In the palace." I am surprised that he was willing to answer my questions without anything in return.

"Why did your father not kill me on the spot?" I continue.

Nevan cleared his throat. "Because he has plans and you are the key part in it," he says smugly.

"Would you like to enlighten me with further details about what key role I am supposed to play?" I ask in the same tone he did.

"No, I don't think so." He smirks and we walk in silence up the last steps to my room.

"I demand to know if it includes my life!"

Prince Nevan turns around and looks at me, giving me the feeling that I was the prey and he was the hunter.

"Did you just order me to obey you? *You* shall obey and behave, that is your purpose now and more is unnecessary for you to know," he says firmly, his voice low, all the while squeezing my arm.

"If I am of use to the High King, who I do not serve under, I wish to know my purpose!"

"Don't you dare speak to me in that tone! I am still a prince and what are you? You are just a foolish woman in the territory of wolves!" he growls.

"If I am such an unimportant person, why do I get escorted by the prince back to her chamber and not to a prison cell!?"

Nevan opens his mouth just to close it again. I made him speechless. I give him my sweetest smile and get my arm free of his grip.

I hear his voice behind me once I open the door to my room. "The mortal has fire! I like it. Meet me around six in the evening, maybe I will lower myself and explain your role here."

I close the door to my room and am surprised once I hear a key getting turned. I try to open the door again but it is locked. I am imprisoned. This is ridiculous. I open the window, stepping onto a small balcony. I look below the railing. I am far away from the ground that there is no way I can jump down there without breaking any bones. I scan the upper part of the wall to see if there was an outcrop I can use. Besides some colourful flowers and tendrils there is nothing I can make use of. I let out a frustrated groan and step back into the room. My belongings haven't appeared yet so I search through the night stand drawers to find something which I could use to defend myself, but it is obvious that no one would be that stupid to leave potential weaponry in room with a potential spy. I slammed every drawer in disappointment. A thought crosses my mind and I step into the bathroom, emptying every possible container I can find. With enthusiasm I hold up an alluring golden hairpin. I quickly stuff it into my trouser pocket when I hear someone knocking on my door. I hastily look at the clock hanging on the wall. It is six o'clock, the time is flying.

I hear the key turning and a guard is standing outside with a blank face.

"The prince requested your presence, are you ready for departure?" He looks down at me and wrinkles his nose. I nod and he leads me through the halls of this place I am calling my golden cage. We stop in front of another identical looking door but once opened, it seems to be more compelling than the throne hall or my room. It is darker, cosier, and I realise I am standing in a library filled with books. The smell of paper overwhelms me. I would have never thought that such a place can contain a lovely space.

I see Prince Nevan sitting in a forest green armchair, casually dressed in a white shirt and black pants, nothing compared to what he was wearing just hours before.

"Come on in, take a seat," he says without looking up from his papers. I did not obey but rather wander around the room, soaking it all in. I feel uneasy in such an adoring room. I wish I could read all the novels displayed in this huge room. I try to guess how long it would take me until I would have finished each one. I didn't notice that I drifted off until his voice interrupts my thoughts.

"Aedlin." The way he says my name drove a shiver down my spine. "We looked through your backpack, and found some books on our history. So I believe you are already familiar with the basics," he says as if it is okay to just search my stuff.

"You ... you looked through my property?" I stammer.

"Do not act surprised, woman." He sounds cold. I turn my face away from the book shelves to look at the prince who I caught gazing at me.

"Seeing something you like?" I mock.

"Maybe," Nevan says while looking me up and down. "I believe we have to work on your garments to have you fully fit in the society." I sigh. I walk towards the small reading space where Nevan is still sitting in his chair and I join him. He puts his paper away and put his elbows on his knees and his chin onto his hand.

"I believe starting from the beginning is the best. Do not hesitate to ask questions." Even though I was captured by Elves and kept hostage by them, I catch myself wiggling in my seat, ready to listen to his words.

"Centuries ago, this kingdom was unified, one High King and many lords spread across the landscape. The rules were set clear and people obeyed, until one man sought higher power. He manifested evil by using dark magic and he constructed a deal. A deal that sounded too perfect for it to be faithful. He did not question it which was a mistake. The evil took control of his mind and it manifested its own army, using innocent people."

"The Shadow Legion," I whisper.

"Indeed, the Shadow Legion." He gives me an impressive look. "We do not know much about their soldiers and how this curse can infect others. In the last war fought by the Elves, the Crystal War, we tried to banish this creature into darkness, but not even we, one of the most powerful beings on this planet, were able to stop it. In this war we have lost a Queen." I look close at his face, trying to find any emotion but his face is a wall and he doesn't let anything escape.

"We've lost endless soldiers in this war. We only could weaken it with magical vessels and chains to keep it in place. But it is hard to secure something that is made of shadows. Once we thought it was over, the God Mother spoke to us: *We shall not let fear get close to us if hope is right across the border.* Back then we didn't know what this meant. We searched all around Eskendria and other cities not knowing what to keep an eye out for. I even risked looking around in the mortal Realm but I could not stay around for much long. I couldn't let humans see me. We fled for a reason, the desire to live in peace. Yet, I believe you are acquainted with the tale of human and the Elves." Once I nod he continues talking: "Once my men found you in the forest and reported back the unusual circumstances, I developed hope, faith. I told my father and he requested to see you. He wanted to

91

behead you for being an intruder and a possible spy, but I talked him out of it, for now." He grins from ear to ear.

"Thank you?" I narrow my eyes.

"Once I saw you in person, I knew that you were the sign the God Mother has sent us. An ordinary little girl shall save the Elven Realm. What irony." He chuckles. I stare at him in amazement and shock. This is the role I am supposed to play? The Dark One was right in what he said, about my purpose in this world. I thought this had all been by chance but it actually was meant to be. I frown at his words. How can I be sure that what he is saying is reliable and he is not trying to trick me?

"Knowing that you are human with no special skills makes it hard to believe that you can save the folk," he admit.

"How are you so sure that it is me? You could have mistaken me for someone else." He meets my eyes reassuringly.

"I would never mistake our last hope. As general of the Golden League I am certain in what I observe and declare. I was born with no affinity to the element and had to make my way to be taken into consideration by others. So believe me, if I am certain of something it will be right." He talks about Affinities, could this be that he is the secret writer of the notes?

"Are you familiar with Affinities? I see that your books have covered some of it once I read them," he says.

I am astounded. "You read them? In this short time period?"

"Indeed, I read quite fast – one of the many activities I shine at." He winks at me. I roll my eyes but cannot hide a small smile. I am surprised how the mood could change so fast, first I was threatened by him and now he's flirting with me.

"To answer your question, yes, I am aware of the Affinities and I am stunned by their synthesis," I admit.

"Of course you are," he says. "Aedlin, you are covered in mysteries. And something is in you that makes you very important to us. You might be the key to ending this horror, your visit here was prophesied." He moves his chair closer to mine. "What is it with you?" He looks closely at me, examining every part of my face. I have the urge to turn away but I suppressed it.

"There is no way I can help you, I am a human who accidentally ended up here in this world. There is nothing special about me."

"I agree, you look oddly ordinary, but there has to be something. And I will figure it out." I blushed under his intense gaze. He suddenly moves back in his chair and focuses on the papers laying on his lap. "You are excused." Overpowered by his sudden arrogance, I stare at him. "Leave," he adds after looking up to me. I don't say anything but stand up and march out of the room, ignoring the guards who are patrolling the door.

\-

I slam the door shut behind me. This is insane. I have to leave, now. I won't obey and play this stupid role of being a saint. I want to go home right now! A stupid voice in my head points out the obvious: *Why do you want to go, Aedlin? You could rule the world from here, the saviour is back and wants to claim the throne. No one is waiting for you at home.* SHUT UP!

I look around the room, hoping I would find my backpack, but I was disappointed. I gaze down at my clothes. I am nasty. My clothes are dirty and carry a funny smell with them.

I discover a door to the left on my bedside. Curiously, I open the wooden door and encounter a massive wardrobe. I let my hand slide over the texture of the garments. They are astonishingly soft and kind to the skin, nothing comparable to what I am wearing. I try to locate some clothes useful for what I am planning on doing next. I strip them off and put on some new pants.

I check my door. Once I entered after the meeting with Prince Nevan I haven't seen anyone guarding the door nor have I heard someone locking the door.

I open the door as silently as possible and peer around the corner. Nothing.

It is dark outside, the hallway is barely lit.

I silently move out of the door frame. The halls are scarily quiet. No soul to be seen. I am still overwhelmed by the magnificent furnishing of this building. This is so much more than I have ever thought I would have in my life. And here I am trying to run away back to my wooden hut. My stomach is growling. When was the last time I ate? I curse under my breath. I ignore my craving stomach and walk along the hall, hoping this is the way I initially came from.

In the beginning it was difficult to memorise the different paths and I had to hide from servants in shadowed corners. I got blessed with a fine memory but I did not possess a map of this place and this palace was one of the largest and most sprawling places I've been to. Not even the Golden district could have compared to this.

I hear voices on the end of the hall and quickly dash behind the curtains. I grab the hairpin which I have secured in my belt.

"Isn't it rather curious that the High King has been shut out since the rumours have been spreading?" a female voice whispers.

"I am sure he has a reason to act how he does, we certainly do not want to question his highnesses determination," says the other female voice. I try to peer around the curtains to get a look of the two figures talking, but it is unduly risky to do so, so I stay calmly behind the curtains, focusing on breathing quiet.

"I am sure he has his reasons, but what if it is true? What if they have found them? The person who could save us all. Why would he be so shy about telling us?" They are talking about me, I realise. I try to connect the dots. I am here as the saviour of the Realm, however, no one knows I am here. The King kept it silent even though rumours have spread. Yet, I want to flee back to my home. I know several people will be disappointed, may even die, but is this really my war to fight? I don't know the people, I don't have a connection to them and yet I can feel my heart ache at the thought of dooming all these Elves.

The voices fade away and I risk a glance at the yet again silent hallway. It is clear. I move further until I reach the ground floor. My heart is beating fast. What would happen if they found me trying to escape?

Voices again. I have no curtains to hide behind. The voices are manly and the steps heavy. A patrol. I look to my left and right. No hiding spots besides a door. I don;t hesitate and open the door and let the fresh air touch my skin as a mother would hug her loved child.

I look up, the sky is clear and among the stars the moon appears as full as ever. The shadows it made gives the surrounding a haunting effect. I realise that I am standing in a garden. I can smell the damp earth and the sound of water filled my ears. I kneel and let my hand pass through the grass. Everything is forgotten: my plan of escaping, my fate, my past and my future. I only exist in this masterpiece of nature. The moon was mirrored in the small brook on my right. It looks like it was taken from a novel which I would kill to read.

"Beautiful, isn't it." I snap around at the voice coming from behind me. I see a man standing in the entry, covered completely in black. His hair was brushed backwards giving sight of his pointy ears. He looks as if he'd just arrived. I am captured by his obsidian eyes which slowly narrowed at my sight. This is the most handsome man I'd ever seen in my life – and I was certain this is the man I have seen in the woods. It fit perfectly. The eyes, the garment his attitude.

"Who are you?!" I ask, my voice thin as ice. The mysterious man chuckles.

"I am Prince Alexander, heir to the throne of Eskendria, the question is: who are you?"

CHAPTER EIGHT

I am frozen in place. The empty throne. I thought it was a memory of their mother but in reality, it is his. Everything from his posture to his expression scream 'heir to the throne'. He has a bored look on his face while examining me. I swallow.

"I am Aedlin, Aedlin Orbwood."

"Ah, the human. My brother told me about you. The saviour of the Realms." He surrounds me, leaving me with no chance of escape. "He was quite fond of you and here I am trying to understand what he saw in you."

"Just because I am a mortal doesn't mean you can talk to me as you wish!" I say angrily. I could have hit myself. Who am I to talk to him in this tone? Yet, this was me and I won't be suppressed by some arrogant fool. I am surprised by how gently he touches my cheek to move it to the right, examining my face.

"I can treat you as I wish, my dear. You are in my kingdom," he says in a low voice.

"I am not your dear!" I say determinedly. He chuckles.

"I certainly did not expect the mortal lingering around the palace in the night. A woman should not walk alone at night," he says softly. I frown my eyes at him, confused by his tone. "People can have wrong ideas, my dear."

"I am capable of defending myself," I say proudly.

"I am certain with the hairpin in your hand it will be quite an unfair fight for your opponent." He chuckles. His voice is as calming, as a lovely summer night feels on your skin. Everything in his appears screams 'dangerous', yet, his voice soothes me. I look at my hand which embraces the pin. He is right. Fighting an Elf who might possess an affinity with a hairpin was foolish.

"Given a new room, with comfort and yet, you are trying to run away from your duty." Dark eyes assess me, silently thoughtful. "What would the High King say to his property trying to sneak away? I remember people getting killed for less than that. Do you want to follow their fate, Aedlin?" His voice is as dark as the night when he said my name.

"I am no one's property," I say cold, gripping the hairpin tight.

"Of course you are not, my dear," he says, stepping one step closer to me.

"Don't you dare to come closer!" I say suddenly filled with fear. He is walking with such an elegance it is almost terrifying. He is one of the most powerful individuals in this kingdom. What could he possibly do with just a snap of his finger? He tilts his head.

"I don't wish you any harm," he says as talking to a child. His hand reaches out for my arm and at first I am motionless until his fingers wrapped around it. I lift my arm, turn and hit him with my elbow in his perfect face. He lets go of me in surprise.

"I said do not touch me, *my prince*!" Faster than light he pulls me in and I am captured between his chest and his hand is around my throat. Through my back I believe I can hear his heart beating strong, his breath tickling my ear when he talks.

"I can see why my brother likes you so much, my dear." I try to wiggle myself out of his hold but it is impossible. "You do have fire in your veins, yet, you possess the inability to assess your situation correctly!" He hisses.

"I am not your dear!"

"We will see about that," he says silently, pushing me away from him. "Now go back to your chambers, until I change my mind and throw you to the wolves. I believe my father would not be pleased to hear that you tried to flee." His eyes remain cold on me.

"As you wish, *my prince*." The last words I rather spit out.

"Do not try anything foolish, my dear. My eyes are everywhere." He winked at me while he gave me place to enter through the door before him.

The whole way back to my room I feel someone was watching me.

My prince. I find it utterly weird talking like that. I have never considered anyone my king or prince. In my town, the last royals were killed centuries ago leaving the city divided in the Red and Golden district. Calling this man *my* prince goes against everything I am standing for. I don't crawl to someone's legs and beg for mercy and I will not change now nor in the future.

My room is covered in darkness and I don't bother to turn on the light. Even though the usage of my hairpin is not as effective as hoped, I put it under my pillow and let myself fall frustrated on my bed. Darkness overwhelmed me and I encounter fog and creatures I have never seen in my life before in my dreams.

-

The next morning I wake up on my own. The sun isn't fully up yet but I can't continue to sleep and I am not sure if I really wanted to dive back into these nightmares. I rub my eyes realising that this wasn't all a dream. I am in the Elven Realm. I am soaked in sweat, the last night was a mixture of being awake and captured in a nightmare. The events from the past night are still hunting me. A knock on the door. I don't have time to answer then the door swung open and Salem moved into my room.

"Good morning, Aedlin."

"Morning," I say confused.

"I was sent to check on you, since individuals encountered a figure moving around the palace past curfew. I wanted to make sure that you were in place and have not escaped." She smiles at me knowingly.

"I have never left this place, I can assure you."

"Of course you can." She winked at me while opening the curtains.

"What are you doing here? Are you my prison guard?" I hiss at her.

"If you want it to be that way, I can definitely be this kind of person, but I believe you need a friend here and I am willing to take that place." Her enthusiastic expression does not match her serious words. I frown at her, trying to understand her motives.

"I hope that yesterday was revealing. I even heard the prince requested an audience with you. This is rather unusual. If I were you I would be careful around him," she says. "I want you to understand that you are not a captive here, you are a visitor."

"The locked door does say something else," I point out.

"Precautions," she says as if this explained everything. "You struck the prince in the presence of the High King, either you are the most dense person I have ever encountered or you are brave, ambitious and courageous. You can choose." I am not sure what to reply so I just stay quiet and follow her with my eyes as she moves around my room.

"Coming here and driving us all crazy." Salem chuckles. "To make things clear, I will not be your maid nor servant. I am your guardian, a person you can trust within these walls. So get your ass out of bed and meet me in ten at the library. I think you know where I mean." She winks and leaves the room.

-

After I quickly threw on clothes which somehow were stored for me in my bathroom without my notice, I moved to the library where I met with Prince Nevan. Again, it was breath-taking.

It has multiple levels and was full of people. Filled with life, it is almost more stunning than it was empty. It is alluring. So much knowledge in one place was incredible. I've read every single book in our local archive and it took me quite a while. How long would it take for me to read all these?

My thoughts drifted away from the archive and to Finley. What will he think when he comes by my house and looks for me but no one is there? Would he be worried or would he just turn around and live his life? I shake my head, wanting the thoughts to vanish into the darkness. I try to focus on my surroundings. Books. I can see many Elves sitting or standing, reading them. Talking with others.

"This is the Grand palace library where most of the apprentices work. Right over here we have Master Victor. He is … let's say the boss here so be nice to him." Salem chuckles. Even though I don't trust this woman, she makes it hard to hate her. I'm surprised that none of my guards have followed me. I can easily sneak out from here but then what? Where would my path take me? Back home?

She leads me to a small sitting area near the window, which looks similar to the one I sat in with Prince Nevan.

"Why did you bring me here? Unguarded?" I want to understand her. I feel like everyone can see through me and I am blindfolded.

"To show you that you are not a prisoner. Orders from His Highness," she says calmly. "The High King gave an order to let me out of my prison?"

"Yes, but the guards are never far away, so if I were you I wouldn't try anything stupid. You are not allowed to walk freely within the palace walls, you have to be accompanied by guards," she explains.

"Am I wrong to guess that you are not just a woman who is immensely friendly to strangers?" I smirk.

"You guess right. I am the right hand of Prince Nevan. I am the commander of the Gold Legion," she says proudly. I have to admit I didn't see this coming. I am looking at the beautiful woman in front of me and trying to imagine her in armour fighting for her life.

"So I wouldn't try escaping, I am fast," she jokes, but I can hear the truth out of it.

"What is the plan, Salem? The purpose of my stay?" I ask firmly.

"You will be carefully examined by experts to see if you have magical abilities. Once this is confirmed, the theory that you might be the daughter the God Mother has sent us will be confirmed also. However, you don't have to worry, we are no monsters; we won't peel your skin off your body, this is simply a doctors check by our healers." She smiles but I cannot smile back. "I received informed that you are acquainted with the basics of magic, which is surprising," she adds. "We thought we had vanished each fingerprint of our existence from your world."

"I guess you haven't dug deep enough," I say dry. "What is your affinity?"

"Earth. I am blessed with a double affinity in—"

"Healing, I know." I cut her off.

"Impressed, you do know your stuff." She chuckles.

"I am aware that Elves have Affinities, but not all do. There are also common Elves with no distinctive Affinity. Those who can handle their Affinities with great control may have side Affinities, all depending on the actual Affinity. There are wind, water, earth and fire Affinities." Salem looks at me in shock.

"Where did you learn all this? I doubt all by yourself." I am not sure if I should tell her about the notes.

"Well, I guess I had a good teacher." I know that Salem saw through my lie but she is kind enough not to say anything.

"You learned quite a lot already, good. Knowledge is the first thing needed to acquire to wield magic in the future." She smiles.

I look around the hall trying to guess the affinities of the present Elves, searching for similarity or marks, but they all are different from each other. Nothing can tell me what affinities were present in this room. I wondered if there were superior affinities and if so, if they were divided into regions like it was handled in my hometown.

"Do all Affinities live together or are they separated?"

"In the Elven Realm, we all live in unity. No one is judged by their affinity and no affinity is better than the other. I have to admit there have been conflicts between Elves who possess magic and the ones who do not. Somehow Affinities do prefer certain—"

"Geographical regions." I end her sentence.

"Exactly." She narrows her eyes on me. "Someone was a good student, I assume." Now it is my time to blush slightly.

"In the palace all kinds of affinities are present. I have a huge team of earth benders. We have water runners and wind travellers as well as fire shapers. The Crown Prince Aleksander is considered the fire lord and believe me he deserves his title. The High King himself is an earth bender as well. Queen Elizabeth was a wind traveller." I notice how her voice went down by the mention of the Queen's name.

I guess she was popular among the folk. "And soon we will get your magic out! Trust me!" she says while locking eyes with me.

"My magic? I don't own any of it – I am human."

"And there you are wrong. I can *see* your magic sleeping inside of you, it just has to be activated. It is resting, waiting for the real moment to burst free and once it is freed you will be so much more than just a human," she says with a cocky smile.

"How can you be so sure?" I ask uncertainty.

"Magic sight, silly. I can see all kinds of colours floating around you. You have the tendency of having four Affinities – not like everybody else. Knowing that makes me sure in my belief that you are the gift God Mother has sent us."

-

The next few days passed and I haven't heard from either the High King or one of his sons. Salem told me that the princes had to leave the castle for a political congress in the western city which name I don't recall. I still have to learn so much about the geographical aspects of this world. Salem and I have daily meetings where she tries to bring up the magic, all unsuccessful. She says that having not *Awoken*, as they called it, yet is quite untypical. Normally people lived through this in a young state when something traumatic has happened. It is getting frustrating. I am not sure about my feelings towards this whole magic thing but I catch myself more and more not thinking at home but rather sneaking out of my room to go to the grand liberty to read in books.

Now I don't need to hunt, I have significantly more time which I can spend on reading. I am nearly doubling my reading speed. I've started reading about herbology, remembering that Mother was totally into this. She has always talked so enthusiastically about it so I wanted to have a closer look at it myself. After just a few hours I was fully captivated by it, stunned by what herbs in the right mixture could do. But of course I read further on magic. Read about trigger points, vessels, Affinities. I try to fill my mind with as much knowledge as possible about this world. Fleeing from reality, fleeing from the thought that I am their pet, made ready for war. Every step I make through the palace was carefully watched by my personal guards who never left me out of sight. They want me to feel free but I am still in my golden cage. Once I enter my room and the door gets closed I can hear the key turning in the lock, symbolising that I am a prisoner. Yet, I can ask for anything I want. I feel like a hypocrite. At home everyone is suffering from the cold and hunger and here I am with a full stomach and plenty of blankets.

In the past days I have been trying to get out but I always got caught. I accepted the truth that I wouldn't go home very soon but do I really wish to? As the weeks passed, Salem and I grew closer. She has always been nice to me and I started to like her. We talked about magic, she told me about her life and I tried to open up to her as well. Time passed and life continued and sometimes I found myself crying in my bed over the life I used to have. I woke up in the middle of the night shivering and shaking from the dreams I had. Salem was always there for me in those moments. Holding me, assuring me I was fine. It was comforting.

I feel the gaze upon me once walking the halls of the palace. The word spread that I hit the Prince yet my true identity has remained hidden. Only my closest people knew who I am in here; the rest are making up their own story. That I might have been a mistress to the Crown Prince or Prince Nevan. Some believe I belong to both. I try not to listen to them, yet it was troubling.

I believe I made improvements on my knowledge acquisition. There was nothing going forward in my practiced magic. Believe me when I say I've tried.

One morning, Salem came into my room telling me that it was time to show off what I was capable of. If I couldn't get any progress in magic, maybe I would be more useful in fighting.

Salem leads me to a small court which was surrounded by greenery. We are approaching a tall man who is cleaning some dangerous looking weaponry.

"Aedlin, this is Henry. He will be your combat partner, he is one of my best men if not the best." I nod and she left us alone.

"Hey, little human. I'm Henry. Don't look so afraid it doesn't fit you." He smiles and I let out a relieved sigh. "Do you know how to fight?" he asked.

"I can defend myself very well," I spat out.

"Then the stories are true." He chuckles.

The afternoon passed and the training with Henry was actually very tiring. We tested my balance, my stamina and my punches. I don't remember when I have been that exhausted the last time. Looking at Henry, I realise I really was out of shape. He appears not to have sweat at all, while I am soaked to my bones. I lay myself on the ground once agreed on taking a break. I try to calm my heartbeat by taking slow and deep breaths.

"What do I see here, is Aedlin showing her fabulous fighting skills and I was not invited?" Prince Nevan smirks at me, and my cheeks started to blush. I feel uncomfortable laying on the ground while the prince was standing over me assessing my body.

"Oh no … I wasn't … I can't …" I pant while getting up from the ground.

"But – but – but don't be so shy, don't you want to enlighten me with your acquired fighting skills? I would be honoured to be your opponent." He slowly walks towards me, not losing eye contact with me.

"But my Prince, I would never fight you."

"It is not against me, it is *with* me, like a dance. Every fight is a dance, it can only happen when both opponents are willing to wield the weapon. I perform a move, you perform a move, where are the differences?" He comes closer to me, too close, but I don't want to move back, I don't want to seem weak in front of him. Every move he performs looked elegant and firm, whereas I look like a complete wreck. I stop Nevan with my hand on his chest, feeling the warmth of his skin under the shirt and gently stop him from moving towards me, ignoring that my heartbeat increased in speed. Alright, if he wants to play then I will play but with my rules.

"But my Prince, how would you feel being beaten in front of your guard by a mortal?" Henry has to suppress a laugh. I let it sink in. I can see how his eyes darkened. He accepted my game challenge and was eager to win.

"I guess we then have to find it out, my lady."

"I am not your lady."

"Charming as always." He chuckles, lifting his sword. I am exhausted but I will not make this an easy win for him. I go in position and wait for him to attack. His movements are elegant and he knows exactly what he is doing. Yet, I am faster than him and I nearly stabbed him several times if he hasn't dodged them at the last minute. After some time of fighting, my strength disappointed me and the prince is well trained – I cannot defeat him yet. With his final move he hit the weapon out of my hand and the tip of his sword points at my chest.

"Impressive," he says, tucking his sword back into the sheath. "Thank you for accepting my challenge. I believe next time I won't be such a lucky man." He winks and leaves us.

After I was properly cleaned and dressed, I went on the search for Salem to tell her about the return of Prince Nevan.

"I thought they were still in the cities?" I say while stuffing a delicious looking cupcake in my mouth. On my way to the library, I got overwhelmed with a smell I have never encountered in my life so I had to follow until I reached the kitchen where I also found Salem snuggling some cupcakes away. I didn't imagine that we had enough at home to create such delicious goods.

"Yes Prince Aleksander is indeed, but Prince Nevan decided to come home earlier. You know as the second prince you can basically do whatever you want. No one cares. But as the Crown Prince all eyes are on you. That's why Prince Nevan is considered the *Heartbreaking Prince*. He does as he wishes and everyone likes him. Prince Aleksander is the *Silver-tongued Prince*. We all know that he is doing what he has to do, but he also declares regulations and carries out execution. He is a dark person. They are both pure hearted but life has shaped them differently. And sometimes Elves forget that even the cruel Prince has a heart."

sign. The next morning I notice a letter on my desk with the royal sign.

> *Dear Aedlin,*
>
> *I enjoyed our little duel we had the other day and I offer myself to be continuously present in your training lessons as your teacher.*
>
> *Meet me after breakfast outside, same place as yesterday.*
>
> *Prince Nevan, the Greatest*

I look at the small present placed in the middle of the table. It is wrapped in red wrapping paper. I tore it apart and saw two incredible looking pairs of pants. Unconsciously I have to smile but I quickly wipe the thought from my mind. They are trying to soothe me to get me comfortable until they have used me and I am nothing more than garbage to them. I have to be careful.

I get dressed and go down to the courtyard where Prince Nevan is waiting for me in his normal gown with two wooden swords.

"Hello, Aedlin."

I look him in the face and am again flushed at how beautiful he is without even trying. His face is blessed with high cheekbones and his blue eyes are as deep as the ocean itself. He is wearing his ash blond hair in a ponytail to get it out of his face while wearing a white shirt and green pants. Elves really are beautiful living beings.

"Good morning, my prince.I thank you for the generous gift." I give him my best smile. I am unsure about his motives but I try to convince him I believe his generous side.

He is sliding out a wooden sword from his sheath and hands me the other one in his left hand.

"I believe you are more acquainted with a bow and daggers," he says kindly. "I can tell from your wrong balance. A sword is heavy yet it has to be trained to be right wielded."

"May I?" Without knowing what I agreed to, he already stands behind me. He puts his hand on my tight making me move one foot forward. I am still overwhelmed by his sudden change of mood.

"This stabilises your stance."

He takes my right hand and puts the sword in it, putting my left hand to the side for extra stabilisation. I can feel his breath in my neck while he was moving my face up,

"Never leave your opponent out of sight." With that, he lets go of me. A cold breeze fills the void he had created. He positions himself in front of me.

"And now attack me," he says with a grin.

"With pleasure." I smile.

After endless hours of training and frustration, I concluded that I was shit at sword fighting. When Prince Nevan swung his sword the metaphor with the dance fit perfectly, whereas I looked like I would kill myself rather than the opponent. It was a matter of practice and patience.

I lay down on my back and felt the grass tickling my neck. I still cannot understand how much more intense everything smells here. Nevan sits next to me, playing with his sword in his hands.

"I have to admit that sword fighting might not be your best choice. I believe you shall stick with the weaponry you are familiar with. I bet you are quite excellent with it," he jokes.

"I wouldn't say excellent but it is my preferred choice, my prince."

"I see."

"Why are you helping me?" I ask my question straight. "You know nothing about me. I am an intruder to the kingdom, yet you are friendly to me. What has changed from when I was brought to the throne room until now?" The open expression on his face changed to the freezing cold wall again.

"There are things in this world which are better kept hidden in the dark," he says mysteriously, "You are excused, Aedlin." I am confused by his mood swings. He was worse than a woman in her menstrual cycle. I don't hesitate but get up, bow and leave him sitting in the court. His reply only ignites my curiosity even more.

On my way back to my chambers I stop in the library where I obviously find Salem reading in one of the old books.

"Salem," I whisper.

"Aedlin, what has happened to you?" she jokes.

"I had a fighting lesson with Prince Nevan. And as you can see sword fighting is not my strength." She looks stunned.

"Prince Nevan gave you a private sword lesson?" she asks again while wiggling with her eyebrows.

"Salem! Stop it!" I chuckle.

"No wonder that he is called the *Heartbreaker Prince,*" She smiles. I can only roll my eyes.

"Who is called the *Heartbreaking Prince?*" A male figure appears out of the shade of the bookshelf. I recognise this voice immediately after only hearing it once. I see Salem standing up and bowing so I follow her lead quickly.

"It is nothing for your concern, my prince." I try to help her out. I gaze up and look into the flawless face of the Crown Prince. His black hair was brushed back, the same style when we met the other night. His obsidian black eyes examine every part of the situation. And again he is dressed all in black. Over the past weeks, I noticed that every Elf who was blessed with an Affinity was dressed with its relevant colour. Meaning, water runners were blue, fire shapers red, earth benders green and wind travellers white. But Prince Aleksander isn't wearing any of them; it is as if he has made his own colour.

"I actually do not care about foolish rumours. Yet, Aedlin, I would like to talk to you in private," he says with a firm voice.

"Of course, my prince." He starts to walk away and I look back at Salem who gave me an apologetic glare and I follow Prince Aleksander into the unknown.

We reach a remote room, which after we entered became a smaller office. Prince Aleksander takes a seat and gestures for me to do the same. With his long fingers, he massaged his temples.

"You know, woman, I just came back from an utterly stressful council. It has been rough and now I just want some rest but I have been ordered to keep an eye on you." I stay silent, not knowing what to respond to that. "I read the records Salem has given me over the past weeks on your progress." I feel a sting in my heart. Everything

Salem and I did she documented for him? "And yet, there is no evidence of your magic. I am starting to believe that you are just an ordinary human." He looks up and his eyes focuses on my face. "Salem tells me that she can see your Affinities with her magic sight, but you two couldn't get it activated." He sighs. He doesn't seem to be any older than I am but still, he looks as if he'd had to endure so much more than a man his age should. "This is why I will now be your magic teacher, and my aim is to strengthen you so you will end this goddamn war for real." Prince Aleksander looks at me, waiting. "Have you lost your voice, child?"

"I am no child!" I say firmly. "If I assessed the situation right, I am your last chance so I demand some kindness and respect from your side, otherwise I will not be cooperative."

"I beg your pardon?" He is angry. "I have been nice to you since the moment I did not throw you to the wolves for running away. I have offered you my help and yet you refused and now you *demand* my kindness?!" He stands up from his chair in anger.

"You have offered me nothing. I am a prisoner and I am unsure what your brother is planning but his sudden kindness is obscure," I hiss at him.

"Ever thought that we are no cruel monsters? I guess my brother has started to like whatever he sees in you. You are his toy in this world which will end very soon if you decide to go."

"Could I go?" I ask silently. "If I wanted to go would I be allowed?"

Prince Aleksander cleared his throat. "No, guards have orders not to let you pass the borders of the palace," he says, trying to control his anger. I suspected it. I am imprisoned.

"Why would I even want to help you? I have no connection to this world. This Kingdom means nothing to me!" I spit out.

"You are more entwined with this world than you know. We are soon to be at war and if you won't obey you will die in it, don't you understand?!" He steps closer. Yet, I am too furious to keep my tongue still.

"Did any of you ever ask if I wanted to be in this position? You captured me and even though I am grateful for you not executing me, I didn't want this! I never asked for it!" My voice is strong. I see him swallow trying to calm his anger but his eyes don't lie. His look is intense.

"Then why reply to my notes, foolish woman? You asked for more and here you have it."

CHAPTER NINE

I don't go back to the library but went to the court where I trained earlier with Prince Nevan. I don't care if people saw me, let them talk, let them guess. With the first step outside of his office I feel the presence of my shadows around me. I have to get my frustration out and the best way to do so was for me to shoot some arrows. I would have never expected the notes to be from Prince Aleksander. Why did he care? Why give me the opportunity of knowledge? Even though the strangers' sharp tongue, I felt connected to them. I felt as if they understood me, yet, it has been him all the time. Was he trying to make fun of me? Why reach out to me?

I have plenty of questions with no answer.

I look around and found some cabinets with different kinds of weaponry in it, and after some trial and error I find a bow. I take it and pick up some arrows. I walk towards the training area. I relax my shoulders, close my eyes. I hear the birds, the wind was howling through the branches in the forest. I smell fresh air with a slightly burnt scent. I feel the nature under my feet as if I was one of them. I draw the bow string towards my mouth, focusing on the red dot on the aim. Suddenly, it all goes silent. No sounds, no wind. Only me and the silence. I take a deep breath, and with breathing out I let go and the arrow flies in the centre of the red dot. I continue this play several times. I shoot, score. Again, hit. Again, until the sun makes place for the moon. This game of frustration won't help me any further. I have to understand that this place is real and that the people are probably not delusional and actually know what they are talking about. I sink on the grass, resting my arms and shoulders which ache from holding the bow over and over. With the night fireflies are coming and this place got a magical touch. It is disgustingly beautiful. I hear a crack from behind, turn with my bow ready for everything, but the dim light does not expose its secrets. I get up, noticing that the grass around me is covered with all types of flowers. I swear they weren't there before. Could Salem have been here?

"Salem?" I shout in the night. Nothing. I quickly put the utilities I used back where they were before and drag myself up the stairs into my room. I feel watched. Not by my guards, I sense a presence darker than that.

I take off my clothes and go to the bathroom letting the warm water fill up the bathtub while I am in. I feel like a small child who is playing with water for the first time. At home I usually have no water and if it rained a lot or if it was winter I only got cold water. Bathing was never a pleasure, more a necessity. But right now I feel like I am living my best life. But these quiet moments are also some of the worst. Memories are coming back of running around in the woods, of meeting up with Finley or talking with Mrs Ivy at the market. The disguise. The run. Do I really miss this home or is my heart playing with me?

At home I am no one but here I could become a someone. People put trust in me. Or do they really? Hardly anyone knows who I am.

Hypocrite, a small voice reminds me. I am a hypocrite. Wasn't I the one who declared that I was totally fine with living alone? That I was someone who didn't need the luxury of the rich ones? I shut the voice out. I am no rich one. I am still me, but I am seeking more. Not more power, more knowledge. I have lived twenty-three years in poverty, in a world I could never be my true self. There was so much more to encounter, so many questions that still need an answer. I would rather find the answers than live a life without knowing.

Knowledge is power, and I will try to acquire plenty of it.

-

The next morning I am requested by the Crown Prince. I expect the worst by now. Punishment? Execution? Everything is possible. Guards lead me to the same room I was in yesterday. I open the door and see him sitting in one of the armchairs. He looks as handsome as he was yesterday but his facial expression was as cold as the one the day before.

"Sit," he orders and I unwillingly obey.

"I want to apologise." My jaw drop I don't care how stupid I look but I expected everything but that coming out of his mouth.

"For my behaviour yesterday. I realise that it may not be easy for a human to understand all this so fast and maybe give their life to something that may not be as important as it is for others. I realise that you gave up your rather boring life in the mortal world to come here. But none of that was forced, you have to admit." I look him dead in the eyes.

"But I am not allowed to leave either, am I?" I ask.

"You are asking the right question. Let me ask this: Do you think you would survive going back home? Would you survive the winter? Maybe this one but what about the next one? Do you want to keep fighting for your own pathetic little hut or for the greater good? So tell me, Aedlin, is it worth it?" My silence is enough. "I thought so," he says with a small smile.

"Why write these notes?" I find the courage to ask him.

"To figure out if you are worth my time. If you can save Eskendria."

"Save Eskendria," I repeat silently.

"Yes, my dear. If the God Mother was right, you might have the strength needed to end this war. Excuse me if I do not quite believe that, yet." I sighed. It was quite the pressure I had on my shoulders now.

"I saw you yesterday, shooting arrows," he admits. "Not as useless as I thought you were." I don't know if that is a complement or an insult. "You noticed how the grass reacted to you, am I right? The flowers bloomed right at the spot where you stood. Tell me, what did you do?"

"I just shot arrows," I say stupidly.

"Woman, don't play games with me, I don't have patience. I know that you shot arrows but what did you *feel?*" I try to remember the night. How the fresh air filled my lungs, how I felt connected to the ground, as if I could hear its heartbeat under my foot.

"I felt the ground. I felt its beating heart under my feet," I admit.

"No, Aedlin, you felt its magic because it was responding to your magic." I look at him in shock. It sounds ridiculous, that I suddenly should possess magic, yet, hearing it out loud is scary. Having the truth in front of you is frightening. My whole life I have been a human but now they tell me differently. This is too much. I can feel my head becoming dizzy.

"It's impossible," I whisper.

"Knowing that you really have magic in your bones, I came up with a theory about how to activate your magic." I listen carefully. "Affinities cannot hurt the person who is wielding it." Prince Aleksander pulled up his hand and a red flame surrounded it. I instinctively create a greater distance between his fire hand and myself. "My magic isn't hurting me. I can't die from burning because I *am* the fire. It is more like a tickle on the skin rather than a burning sensation. For what I am asking you, you have to trust me." I am quite unsure about this. But maybe it would help, maybe I really could activate my magic.

"I would never trust you," I say numbly. Aleksander sighs.

"Of course you wouldn't, what do you want me to give you to show you my words mean the truth?" he asks slightly annoyed.

"I want to be free, no guards." I smile triumphantly.

"Ridiculous. Can you hear yourself talking? Have you ever thought that the guards may be there for your protection?" I am silent. To be honest, I haven't. For me they have always been my prison guards. Figures that didn't talk nor show emotion.

"You are in danger. If the rebels or black legion would encounter your presence here in the palace, they would try to attack," he hissed.

"Rebels?" I ask.

"Yes, my parrot, rebels. Fighting for a democracy," he says annoyed.

"I bet, with this heir I wouldn't want to be under his control either." I snort.

"Be careful what you say, woman," he growls.

"I say what I want."

"Fine, be the dense child. I allow it. Yet I cannot agree on letting you walk around without guards," he says dangerously quiet.

"Is the prince worried about my wellbeing?" I mock.

"I rather be dead than be worried about *your* wellbeing," he hisses.

"I want answers." I sigh. This fighting would lead to nothing. If he is the only one skilled enough to help me I will put my trust in his actions even though I despise the man in front of me. "I want you to answer my questions, doesn't matter how stupid or how many. I want to understand this world." This is what I want – knowledge.

"Okay." He sights. "I promise to share my knowledge with you, as much as I can."

"Then we have a deal," I say.

"I believe so."

He leads me through dark pathways which I believe were not taken by many people in the past centuries. It is hard for me to see the next step but Aleksander walks firmly forward. The air smells mouldy with a hint of salt. The steps are wet, but as we walk higher they become less slippery. A breeze makes my hair go wild. I thought the steps would never end until I hear the sound of waves crashing at stone. Is it what I think it was? Prince Aleksander is already far ahead of me and I try to close up, wanting to see what he sees. By the time I stop, I feel dizzy from going up in height. Once I reached the last step of the endless tower I try to grasp for air once my gaze crossed the endless ocean. I am speechless. Prince Aleksander slows his steps and comes to a stop in front of the railing. I put my hand on the cold metal and forgot what I am fighting about just some minutes ago. It is just me and infinity. That's how it looks. An infinite pool over different blue ocean. I can barely figure out where the water touched the sky. It is astonishing. The sound of the waves crushing onto the shore is alluring.

"Beautiful isn't it?"

I jump around to see Prince Aleksander slowly approaching me. I'd almost forgotten he is here, almost.

"It is stunning," I admit letting the wind greet me.

"Follow me." The wind increases in strength but not enough to make it dangerous to be up here.

"Come," he orders again, and I oblige.

The view takes the breath right out of my lungs. We stand on a small balcony, barely large enough to make room for two. It feels like the top of the world. I can see how the castle is throning over the world, its many tears cascading down the mountainside and into the capital. It is an endless ocean. If I stretch my vision towards the horizon far enough I can see the flickering light of another city. There is still so much to discover.

"What do you think, Aedlin?" He has moved behind me. Even at such close proximity I can barely listen to his words, still captivated by the view.

"It's amazing," I breath, ignoring how close he chooses to stand behind me. "At home we don't have anything this beautiful. I have never seen an ocean in real life." I breath.

"I have heard that this ocean is great for swimming." His words barely registered as I looked upwards at the sky. It is an engrossing scene, it is as though I am at the very place where the earth and sky met. I take a tiny step forward, sweeping my gaze back to the rocks below me. Perhaps it was my enchantment with the wonder surrounding me. Or perhaps it was the sound of the sea. Whatever it was, it disguises his last footsteps. The prince placed his hands lightly upon my shoulders giving me goosebumps.

"Trust me," he whispers, his lips barely brushing over my ear. I don't even have a moment to turn my head before he effortlessly puts his hand under my legs and swings me over the railing, letting me fall into he empty space beyond.

Chapter Ten

I fall through the air as though I was as light as a feather. My eyes are focused on the always closer coming waves and I try to prepare myself for the contact. I attempt to fill my lungs with as much air as possible, yet, the incredible pain which struck my body on impact draws all of it out again. I hope to die on the stones close to the palace, yet, I have luck to fall into the deep water with no way to grab onto something. I feel how I am heavily forced to the ground of the ocean. I try to get to the surface where the water seems to have a far more welcoming shade than what is waiting for me. However, not even my limbs are obeying me at the moment. Panic strikes me once I realise I will not make it and in addition a burning pain establishes itself in my lungs.

I lived a risk-filled and dangerous life, and I have heard that if you are on the edge of death, you will see your life passing before your eye – but this never happened to me since I always made my way out, I had a plan. Yet, I am clueless. All I can see is the sky and its fluffy clouds starting to blur as I am drowning. In a land with no lake or sea, people didn't find it necessary to learn to swim. My mother and father couldn't swim themselves, neither could I. I stop struggling and let the water surround me, outside as inside. I am going to die. I am shocked by how fast I am accepting this fact. I am weak. I should fight! I should try at least. But I cannot force my body to do as I wish. My thoughts go dull and my heart slows. My head feels heavy and my vision dims. I feel the water surrounding me carrying me to their cemetery. I feel light, the water was warm and put a soft hand around my body. Suddenly, I feel a tingle in my hand and feet. It quickly fills my whole body. Bubbles are spreading from under me as if they are trying to bring me up to the surface. I let out a voiceless scream, once a pain stroke through every part of me.

-

An explosion rings out through me and I sat upright. Awake. Alive! I instantly regret opening my eyes in such a hurry. The room looks off. Too many colours. I have trouble focusing on anything in it. I turn quickly to the other side of the bed, reaching for something to fill with my stomach liquid. The process of vomiting causes my abdominal muscles to contract, leading to more pain. I let out a cry of pain as I fall back into the bed. My body feels wrong. As if someone has replaced essential parts of myself with something strange. I check myself with my fingers, finding nothing unusual. Laying on my back hurt but moving hurt even more. I squeeze my eyes tight, then open them, trying to identify where I am.

I find myself in a room nothing like my old one. It is small but looks more adorned than my room. I try to lift myself up which ends in having a coughing attack causing my lungs to burn.

I turn my head towards the door, muffle voices and quick steps are approaching on the other side of the wall. The door burst open and two figures approach me. There is a man with red curls who I have never seen before. I had to blink again to make my vision clearer.

"Salem?" Even my voice sounds like trash. I hear a similarity with Miss Ivy's voice. The man quickly leaves the room. Leaving me and Salem alone. Suddenly, I feel scarred of this place and the hinges they can possible do to me. Did she know? I should me dead. How am I alive?

"He tried to kill me" My rusty voice croaks. "Did you know?" I ask in fear.

"Aedlin." At the sound of my name, I try to move.

"You have to get down, and keep down, you need to rest." I am so confused "I am fine." I hiss, "At least I did not die!" My voice grows louder.

"Please Aedlin."She begs .

"Why?" I can barely form the words. "Why should I ever trust you again?"

"I did not know!" Salem says firmly. "Prince Aleksander has brought you here after you have awoken."

Awoken?!

I hear footsteps approaching, and the Elf came back holding a bucket and a mop. I have missed the pail on the floor. I feel ashamed when the Elf begins to clean up the mess on the floor.

"Willow, the green bottle please," Salem demands. He nods and obediently leaves the room. I move to the edge of my bed. As far as possible away from this woman.

"No Aedlin, stop this!" Salem tries to reach my arm but I dodge her hand. "What have you done to me?"

"*Aedlin!*" The firmness of her voice reminds me of another man's and I instantly have the urge to puke again.

But I allow Salem to help me drink the suspicious liquid and gulp down the syrup with a cough.

The liquid flows through my body like fire and then someone started to scream as the bottle fell to the floor. It wasn't until I find myself in the arms of Salem that I realise I am the one screaming. And then the screaming makes place for sobbing as the burning slowly passes and my body goes numb. I cast aside all decency and simply weeps against her chest. I can faintly hear how Salem is talking to someone but I am too exhausted to figure out who it was.

"… is weak now. I tried everything … has to learn … body has to heal … not sure if it worked." The fog in my mind clears away. I feel more alive. I can feel my limbs moving. Salem Looks down to me as she feels my movement.

"You had severe lung damage. You needed to have help for the past days to breathe. They almost shattered under the pressure from the water" I laugh slightly against Salem's chest. "You will be alright," she assures me. "But it will take time. Don't force your body too much," she says calmly. At this moment I don't care about what they are all plotting but I need someone. Salem moves my pillow so I can comfortably lay back. Willow gives me another bottle filled with a lilac syrup. "This one is next, but don't worry, it shouldn't hurt." I frown at her words but took the bottle. What else was there to lose?

Her words were true. The liquid passed my paper dry lips and I had no immediate reaction towards it, it only scratched in my throat.

"Water," I gasp and Salem nods, handing me a glass of water. She wanted to bring the cup to my mouth but I took it out of her hand. I am no child. I can drink on my own.

"Aedlin, believe me, this isn't how I wanted to see you," she starts, placing the cup back on the nightstand. "Prince Alexander didn't know how to help you in your current condition so he brought you to me ... four days ago."

I choke on the remaining water in my mouth.

"Four days?!" I manage to say out loud even though my throat hurt.

Salem nods. "We weren't sure if you were going to make it. You were all screwed up. Basically you should have not survived. It took the best healers to fix all this again. We had to let you sleep because you were screaming and fighting against us. It would have harmed you even more," Salem states dutifully, "but letting you sleep hindered your magical healing, making it almost impossible to heal your body from your Awakening."

"Does that mean ..."

"Yes Aedlin, you got awoken, you manifested your power. I was right, wasn't I? I knew you were full of magic." She gives me a sad smile. "However, under normal conditions the 'manifesting of magic' is a bit gentler. This was rather dangerous and stupid." She admits.

The next time I woke up, it is already dark outside. My room is empty except for some food and a cup of water. I slowly move myself into a seated position. My vision stayed steady and my head doesn't go dizzy. The world shifts a little but overall it is alright. I am alright. I consider that a small victory.

My gaze is captured by the small fruit stack, beautifully arranged on the nightstand. My mother used to do that when I was small and when we had some extra money. She was able to create something beautiful out of ordinary things. What would she have done? Would she have left or stayed? I don't know. I know barely anything about them. They disappeared almost twenty years ago. I had no real chance of getting to know them. I realise that a few stray tears dripped onto my palm. I am still not quite sure how I should feel about this change. But what does it mean for my life? Will I ever be free again? Or will I be bound to the High King forever? Exhaustion consumes all of my emotions. I swallow my cry and took a bite from the fruit basket when I hear mumbling from across the door. The resonance of one voice was unmistakable, causing me almost to choke on my bite. I get up and stumble towards the door, pressing my ear against it hoping I can understand what is being said.

"Aleksander, what were you thinking?! By all saints!" Salem asks, furious. It is weird to hear her talk like that to the crown prince. However, she is high in rank as well. Yet, hearing such familiarity between them is off putting.

"I do not owe you an explanation, *woman*," the prince sneers.

"She could have died! The only hope left in this world to save us! And you pushed her off the tower. Are you out of your mind!" Salem voices my inner fears.

"There was no way I could have killed her," the prince assures , utterly confident. As Salem told me, the prince had a *silver tongue* but right now I believe I can hear that he is truly hurt by the thought that he would kill somebody.

"Why did you do it?!" Salem demands to know.

"You told me that she is the one we were looking for. I trust your word more than anything," the prince comments.

"What if I was *wrong*?!" she says frustrated. "There was no way I could have been a hundred percent certain. She has only been here for a couple of weeks and has not yet shown signs, there was no way that you could have been sure but yet you risked her life!" I can hear that Salem is furious.

"You underestimate my powers." I can hear the sound of boots racing the room.

"Certainly! Next time you know something or assume something, you will come to me, tell me! I don't want to be called to see a friend lying half-dead in front of me!" she cries. *Friend.* She sees me as a friend? Hearing Salem's worry warmed my heart. Maybe I didn't want to accept that Salem had been my friend here all along. I barely know anything about her.

"Is that an order, Salem?!" the prince asks quietly.

"Of course not, *my prince*. Only a suggestion," she says with the same dangerous quiet voice.

"Do you really think I care about her? I couldn't care less if she gets hurt or breaks some bones – if it helps the Realm, in the end it's worth it. You think I would lower myself to trouble with a plain common mortal?"

"You troubled yourself enough to write her notes," Salem points out. It was indeed strange that the crown prince sought out me – a plain common human as he liked to phrase it.

"She is the key for the Realm to rise again. Of course I would trouble myself." His tone had turned cold and calculating. "I had to see for myself if this woman was capable of bringing us victory!"

A long silence signalled that the prince is done with the conversation.

"I confirm that she has magic in her blood."

"You really are a jerk, you threw her off the palace tower into the ocean where she drowned, and you still had the need to confirm the obvious."

I can almost see him rolling his eyes on that comment.

"However it seems like she has only manifested one element, not all four at once. She won't be ready – I should tell the High King …"

"No," he says firmly. "I will deal with my father, Salem. I do not want to catch wind of you telling the slightest bit to the High King about her."

Do I hear worry in his voice?

"Very well," Salem sighs. "Aleksander, I can only theorise what your plan is with the girl but remember, the stories were true. What we've studied—"

"Salem," the prince growls dangerously.

"We hoped for decades to find someone like her," Salem continues, ignoring the warning tone of the prince.

"Don't ruin it—"

"She is not your concern," Prince Aleksander snaps. "I will oversee her training."

I growl escaped my throat and I rested my forehead against the door, reminding myself to breathe and that I will survive this. He will never be able to come close to me again. I won't let my guard down.

"You will be her shadow and report to me, to no one else, understood?" he says firmly.

Why me? Why did the prince choose me as his puppet? Willing to kill me? What is his plan?

"And now if you excuse me, I would like to check on her myself," he says.

"My prince, I am not sure if you are the right person she wants so see at the moment." Panic rises in me. I quickly depart from my spot at the door to my bed.

It was at the right moment because just as I fall back in bed, dark eyes met mine. I look up uncertain of what to expect.

"You are awake," he breaths and his eyes softened as he spoke. Is that a look of relief? I am sure I misread his expression.

"It looks like it," I comment dryly. I am relieved that my voice has found its origin again.

"I am glad," he says softly.

I narrow my eyes on him. All the anger I refuse to feel came back in one shot hearing this stupid dark voice of his.

"You. *You* are glad?" I scream, furious at him. "You pushed me to death! I trusted you and you pushed me!" Anger fills my words as I glare at the tall man dressed in all black.

"I am, Aedlin—"

The prince takes a step closer to my bed and I slide further away.

"Don't you dare come closer. Never come near me again!" I am surprised by the roughness of my voice. I have never talked like that to anybody before. Right now I don't care that he is a prince and the second most influential person in this world, I don't want to be in a room with him, ever again.

"Aedlin." The prince has the audacity to smile at me. Who did he think he is – he sad I was the child but right now he acts like a spoiled kid. "We should celebrate, that's not the time for anger."

"Oh, maybe you didn't hear me but YOU! PUSHED! ME! OFF! A! TOWER! I drowned. Have you ever asked yourself if I could swim?!" I ask. By the look of his face I know that he didn't. And then he laughs. I wish so badly to have the strength to strike him right into this perfect cheek.

"You are fine. You are healing quickly and you can breathe. Now with your manifested magic, I will teach you how to use it properly." I couldn't believe what he is saying. Should I feel honoured to be taught by him?! Should I fall to my knees and thank him for his grace and mercy? This is definitely not gonna happen.

With all my strength I get up from the bed standing right in front of the Elf.

"What didn't you understand, *my prince*? I don't want to see you again. You disgust me!" I hope this would look more dramatic but given the way I looked, it possibly seems stupid.

"Stop with the nonsense," he says, his deep voice gentle. "You should sit, Salem did not quite agree with my coming in so if she finds that you look worse than when she left *she* will execute me. Let me help you." His sudden kindness makes me want to scream and puke at the same time.

"Do not touch me," I say firmly.

"Aedlin—"

"Do. Not. Touch. Me!" I cry, pushing his hands away. "You threw me off a tower and now you want to *help* me?!" My voice turns nearly into a shrill. "You could have warned me! You didn't warn me!" I notice that tears are falling on my cheeks.

"If I warned you, it would not have worked. If I warned you, you would not have done it." He crosses his arm over his chest.

"You don't know me. If you would have given me a proper reason, I would have considered it if it would benefit us. I would have done it if you had asked me!" I cry. "I trusted you to be my teacher, I shared my thoughts with you in those notes. I would have trusted you with my life even though you are not *my* prince but a stranger. I trusted you because you asked." Saying it out loud makes the situation even more complicated. I would have risked my life for a civilisation I have nothing to do with it. I realise what could have happened. I could have died. But I am familiar with the risk, yet, my hands start to shake.

"Your trust was put right, I have helped you manifest your magic." His voice grows cold and distant.

"I didn't want it to happen like that!" My voice trembles from the pressure I put on it.

"You asked for it!" Now his voice grows loud as well. The door flies open, and Salem and Willow step in. "My prince this is not—"

"I didn't ask for this! I don't know what I expected to be honest. You say I am a foolish woman but you have the audacity to use this foolish woman for your ambitions." My rage grows bigger every second I see his face. "You changed me without my consult!" I say.

"You are something far more greater than you were before."

"I was fine the way I was, no one had the right to threaten my life. Not even a foolish prince!"

"You were boring. You were human, normal. I gave you the chance to become something greater." He looks at me harshly.

"What would have happened if Salem had been wrong and I was just a human? What would have happened?"

"I do not have to obey you. Don't forget who you are and who is standing in front of you."

"Do not use me like one of your puppets. Tell. Me."

He stares at me for a long time. "If things would not have been as expected, you would have drowned in the ocean. You would have died. The earth would have one less useless human." Prince Aleksander shrugs as if he doesn't care.

"You bastard, this is all just some sick game for you. Taking a life? Who cares if it benefits you, why not? Am I right?" The words are out before I can rethink them. After saying them I do regret them.

"*What* did call me?!" Prince Aleksander growls.

"You, *my prince*," I say mockingly, "are the world's biggest egoistical self-centred, selfish, narrow minded, narcissistic, self-absorbed, stuck-up"—I feel that my anger has reached its climax—"*bastard*!" A loud shatter focuses my attention on the now wet chest of the prince.

The water can on the nightstand shattered in a thousand pieces. I am shocked by what I had just done but cannot hide a smile. I see that he had to fight for his self-restraint.

"Calm down," he growls, "or you will regret it."

"You can't tell me what to do!" I shout.

"I can tell you whatever I want. I *am* your prince, my dear." I can see how he is slowly losing control of himself. Small flames are licking around his arms. He steps closer to me.

"Remember this position. Stay where you belong, pathetic little rat who refused my help when I gave it the possibility to turn into something magnificent."

"My prince," Salem says firmly. I completely forgot that they are still in the room.

"I have chosen you, and you refused my help," Prince Aleksander snarls.

This is the prince everyone feared. Not the mysterious, intellectual stranger and certainly not the sudden kind man who had first entered this room.

"Maybe you should go back to your filth, what you call home!"

He storms out of the room. My body feels numb. Salem wants to reach for me but I want to be alone.

"Salem, please go," I whisper and she follows my wish, letting me alone with all my thoughts. Have I done a mistake in trusting them? Should I have fled? This was the last thought I had before I collapse under the pressure of this new life I am faced to life.

CHAPTER ELEVEN

I am trying to leave this narrowed chambers, yet, I encounter the locked door which becomes my obstacle in reaching freedom. I hear mumbles from my guards of a rebel attack in town and something about that it would be too dangerous for me to be out there which is why I am locked up in this room. Pathetic. Three days have passed and the only freedom I feel is once the windows are opened and the wind goes through my hair. Yet, it only ignites my curiosity of what lies beyond these prison walls. I pick up the shattered pieces of the can which are placed on the sideboard next to the huge window. I turn it around, examining its composition. How dare he? How could he have threatened my life like this? Yet, I believe I survived for a reason, I have to stay, I need to fight.

I had to smile once the image of Aleksander being wet crossed my mind. Why can I do these things now? What has changed?

Salem has visited a couple of times but never stayed long. I have tried to activate my "magic" again, but besides the incident with the water can a couple nights ago, I feel normal. I don't feel as if my magic has manifested. But how am I supposed to feel? One time Salem visited, I couldn't contain my questions any longer and asked them. I said to myself I have forgiven her, since she didn't even know but in times like this it is rather hard to forget what has happened. But she has always been nice to me. I don't see any hidden intentions in her actions.

"Salem, I was taught my whole life that Elves are something dangerous, that their magic is evil. My town detests them. I will never be able to go back, am I right?" Salem looks at me in sorrow. Her black curls fall around her flawless face.

"You can do whatever you want but you will have to live with the consequences," she replies cryptically.

"Why do you care about me? I mean when I first came here? I am a mortal," I ask, my voice almost like a whisper.

I came here with the hope of finding answers to my questions but instead I got dragged into this place, was threatened and humiliated; however, I was their only chance. It was hard for me to trust people, especially strangers. I trusted Aleksander, and he used it for his own will. I may become soft in my view of this world but I still have to be on guard. Elves are insidious beings.

Yet, looking at Salem and remembering that she took care of me when I was on the edge of death soothed my anger.

"You know, the civil war between the mortals and the Elves has affected more mortals than Elves, I believe. We settled in that village to secure our entrance to the Elven Realm but with the purpose to make allies along the way. The humans were the first kind and we celebrated their holidays and they celebrated ours. It was peaceful, yet, they eventually saw us as a threat, I don't know why. It has been too long. I wasn't born then. The only thing I did was read books, diaries about this event hoping they would help me to understand." I stay silent, listening carefully to every word she is saying. "As horrible as it may sound, we forgot about mortals; we are superior to them and if they ever tried to attack us in the Elven Realm they would be utterly disappointed – their weapons would fail them. You learned to fear the Elves, we learned to forget the humans. There is a difference.

I always wanted to become a soldier. I felt like I had to protect the Realm with everything I could offer. My parents begged me to become a library apprentice or a maid in the palace. Yet, I have found my own way and besides the two tremendous princes, I love my duty." She looked past me through the windows as if memories appeared before her eyes. "When you first came here. I saw myself in you when I came here, years ago." Salem swallows.

"I was born in the west. As we already discussed Affinities prefer geographical regions, and the west was known for their Earth-benders. I came from a poor family who could not afford me anymore. My parents worked on the field day and night to feed me. Their backs were bent and their skin burned from standing too long in the sun. I wanted to help them. I wanted to give them a life where they didn't have to worry about anything, but this included me applying for the most dangerous job in the Realm. Soldier. I left home with the promise of coming back and looking after them once I have finished my training. I kept my promise." She swallows hard. "One day after I got promoted to Lieutenant I went back home, my pockets full of essentials, excited to tell my family what had happened over the years. I reached my hut and I had to face the truth. I'd been gone for too long. They died. I couldn't be the daughter they wished me to be and I cried over their deaths, over the memories I had cherished over the years. I had lost the people I was doing all this for. I had lost hope and faith yet I had to continue my life. I had a duty to fulfil so I kept fighting for them, for a better kingdom." She smiles sorrowfully. I am unsure what to reply, shocked by the intimacy of her words.

"I am sorry, Salem." She just nods being far away with her mind.

"On the night when Prince Aleksander was here. I heard you two talking. You two seemed quite … familiar," I say, dying of curiosity.

"Someone was eavesdropping, I see." She chuckles. "The Prince and I have a special relationship, I would say. We were close friends. Prince Aleksander never had a close relationship with his brother and there were no further children in the palace. Once I arrived, he demanded to teach me. But not in a prince-and-his-subject way, more in a friendly way." I try to imagine Prince Aleksander younger, actually being nice. It is rather difficult.

"I was his friend, however when the pressure on his shoulders increased, our friendship suffered from it. There was a time where not even I could go to him. It was a dark time in his teenage years. It hurt me to see him isolated. I wanted to help but still, I am just a soldier. Once we grew older, no one cared anymore that we were best friends. They saw him as the Crown Prince and me as a subject to the crown. However, he was always kind, in his way." I can barely believe that Prince Aleksander had friends. He seemed to be a lone wolf, wanting to do everything on his own.

"What he did to you was utterly ridiculous and could have harmed you in many ways. I have told him and I believe he understands it. I believe he did not think of you getting hurt, rather that you would benefit from his action. He is a calculated man but he is no machine. He told me that you were bright. That you were surprisingly smart for a mortal."

I snort. "Of course only he would phrase a compliment in an insult."

"He meant it," Salem assures me. "And getting to know you over the past weeks I think he was right." With these words, Salem gets up and leaves me alone in the hospital room.

I stretch my sore limbs out. The things Salem has told me about Prince Aleksander won't change that I hate him, but I maybe will understand him someday.

-

I decide I cannot be in this room for any longer. I have to get out of here. I push myself out of bed. It is working. I walk towards the door, put my hand silently on the doorknob and try to open it. I hate myself for stealing the key form Salem's pocket. I just cannot be in this room any longer and once I saw the opportunity my quick fingers didn't hesitate. I peek outside, looking for possible people who will make my life harder.

I sneak out and went slowly towards the library. If I cannot shoot arrows, I can at least poke around some books. After only a few minutes I feel like I am being followed. I turn my gaze across the room and see two guards patrolling behind me. I will never be alone anymore. Yet, they don't hinder me from continuing my journey so I walk towards the library.

I find a cosy place right under the window where barely anyone can see me. I lift my face into the sunshine and take a deep breath in. Days ago I didn't know I would do that ever again. The smell of old books fills my lungs and I sighed. If someone had told me that I would end up in the Elven Realm, enjoying the smell of books, I would just have shot them with an arrow, not bothering to hear anymore lies.

"Welcome back to the living." And silence vanishes. Looking at the Elf's face who helped Salem to take care of me makes me smile. I never had the opportunity to talk to the blond man. He has always been so quiet and distant so seeing him walk up to me was special.

"Hello," I reply.

"I am glad to see you doing so well. I am sure you have lots of questions. Don't hesitate to ask me. I'd be happy to help. My name is Willow by the way." I have to smile at the torrent of words coming out of his mouth.

"It's nice to meet you, Willow. I am Aedlin, as you probably already know." I smile. He is more energetic than on the other days I saw him hustling about my room. "You work here?"

"The master of the library is standing in front of you." He poses like a proud statue. "No kidding, we don't really have one. Some people say that it's Viktor but to be honest he is so old he would barely realise if anything was going on." I look over to the elderly Elf and see him starring into his mug, I cannot suppress a small giggle, it is the first time I laughed since my 'almost death' experience. Looking at Willow, he reminds me of Finley. Clumsy but always kind and cute. What was Finley doing right now? I ignored the thought.

"How many libraries does the palace have?" I ask him. He takes a seat opposite me.

"Two: this one where all the books are based on magic, and another one in the left wing of the palace filled old documents and agendas, which if you ask me is very boring. This library is private, you see? It got some great stuff in here. Barely any non-palace beings know of this place. Here we have stored the originals. Books written by the God Mother and the saints. Quite astonishing." He speaks it as if it is nothing. I am practically hanging on his every word, waiting for him to tell me more. Mortals have believed for decades that all Elves are evil and now I am here seeing the complete opposite. Some Elves are more closely related to human than to Elves. What are Elves with no magical abilities? Mortals with pointy ears?

"You want to see them? They are stored separately."

"If I may?" I ask.

"I mean, you are already here. A being obviously possessing magic, so gladly." He smiles again.

Willow takes my hand and places it on his arm, escorting me to a table that stands against a tall wall in the back. I look eagerly at the book secured behind a glass wall.

"So considering what has happened the other night with the Crown Prince, I assume that you are a water bender, currently. I have read stories about your prophecy. That a being will come filled with such a pure heart, able to wield all for elements." He picks some books off the surrounding shelves.

"Yes indeed, the signs show that my affinity for water manifested, however, I don't feel any different. And if I ever have to endure such pain again just for some stupid magic to manifest I don't want it," I say without turning around. It's getting easier to accept the truth. That my life will now be here amongst the Elves. Yet I've been wondering how I lived for so long without noticing what lay dormant inside of me.

"You know, I imagined you to be different," he says. "For all the centuries Elves have looked for people in their Realm to be our saviour, and now I stand in front of her, looking at her face and feeling sorrow for the life she had to leave behind and for the duty she was born for." His voice is firm and my heart hurt from his examination. It is the truth I was scared to hear all along. I can only give him a small smile in return.

"You know, I believe there is one book in particular that you would enjoy." There are no rolling ladders and Willow is left to find a nearby food stool. "There's not much written down about the prophecy but there is this one book. *The Story of the Immortal Soul.*" I look at him in confusion. "I won't be able to explain it well, it's better if you read it." Willow hands me the book. "Here."

I look at the old manuscript he has given me: *The Story of the Immortal Soul.* It is an old book. I am almost afraid to open it.

"Thank you." It is like holding the gate to my new self. Once I open this book, I will fully accept my true being. I will be the one everyone expected me to become. I will save this world. Or I can give it back to Willow so he can store it somewhere far away from me. I take the book and walk back to my seat at the window. I sigh, open it and start reading the first page. Before I can dive into the story a small text caught my attention. I frown and trace the words with my finger. I tuck a fallen-out strand of hair behind my ear just so it can fall into my face again.

The writing is utterly familiar. It is a beautiful handwriting, soft. This was written by someone I know. I have seen it before. But can it be? It is impossible. I blink at the title page.

The Story of the Immortal Soul.

Let this be your Introduction into this world, my darling.

Written by Amidala Orbwood.

CHAPTER TWELVE

*A*midala *Orbwood.* The name has to be a mistake. It is probably just a common name here. Why else should my mother's name be the author of this book? My mother who died decades ago. Why should she have ever written a book like that? We were taught to fear the Elven Realm in my world.

I put the book aside, afraid to damage it. My hands are shaking. My head is dizzy. What is going on?! I pause suddenly, feeling very small. This whole time I was fearful of Elves, even though my own family had business with them. They lied to me. Or did I just not ask? I lean against the shelf, trying to calm my rapid breathing.

"Aedlin?" the library boy asks softly

"Yes?" I blink at him a tingle went up my arm and suddenly my vision becomes blurry.

"Hey, Aedlin. Are you okay?" he whispers worryingly and places a hand on my shoulder. "You are very pale." His touch offers me an oddly welcoming feeling.

"Sorry." I can barely whisper the words. My thoughts stuck in the memories.

"Don't, Aedlin, this has to be a lot." His voice is gentle. I have to get out of here. Now.

"Willow, I am sorry," I say and storm out of the library, leaving the book there. Eyes are following me, I hear whispers. I hear loud steps running behind me – the guards. This just motivate me to move faster, running away from the truth, running away from who I am. I don't know where I am heading until I find myself in the small garden again where I stumbled into Prince Aleksander the first time. I sink to my knees and let out a scream. Why have I been so blindsided the past years? Emotions crash over me, hope, sadness, anger. I cannot control it. It all moves so fast.

I draw my hands in the grass, feeling the dew from the night. My whole life flashes in front of my eyes. The pain, the suffering, the waiting for them to come home. I mourned them. Became a killer in the hope that eventually I would find a stack of bones. I believed they were killed by an animal attack even though it made no sense, but for a small girl who wanted revenge, killing animals was the way to find it. My life is a lie. My existence is a lie. I can feel how the wind increases in speed. Have the Elves something to do with their disappearance? Water droplets are crawling up my arm, defying gravity. I take a deep breath but the sobbing won't stop. My voice turns into a shrill cry. I thought I am over their deaths. I thought I have grown stronger, but seeing the handwriting of my mother destroyed everything I have built up over the years. I press my wet palms against my eyes trying to stop the tears from falling.

They lied to me.

They left me in this world.

They knew who I was and they hadn't prepared me for it.

Anger fills me and with a last scream I press my hands into the ground and the surroundings flooded with water. I am soaked, not knowing where all the water has come from. My only focus is the betrayal of my parents. I start to see black dots and collapse into strong arms which were holding me from behind. I don't question it. I don't ask, I don't hesitate. I let it be because I am a foolish woman. I can feel how I am picked up and I settle my hand on someone's chest, trying to hide my tears. Their grip is soft but firm as if they want to make sure I won't fall and hurt myself.

"What are you up to? Making me soaking wet, again," I hear a deep voice say but I can have misunderstood it since my mind drifts away into another world filled with darkness.

-

I suddenly woke up. I am in my room again. I look down at my body. I have been changed into new clothing. I scan my room and see a figure sleeping on my chair. I clear my throat. Green eyes open immediately.

"Oh Aedlin, you're awake!" Willow says, gets up and walks towards my bed.

"How long have you been here?" I ask.

"I have waited here since Prince Aleksander left." Even the sound of his name sends a shiver down my spine.

"What?!" I open my eyes in shock.

"You ran out of the library. I didn't want to go after you, I believed you needed some time. So I looked at the page you left open and then I understood. I was looking for you when I ran into the Crown Prince. I told him what had happened and he immediately helped find you. He said he knew a place you could be. And there you were." Willow looks at me with his big eyes. "The scene we found was … amazing. You were kneeing in the grass surrounded by a huge wall of water. I could have cried. The Prince did not find it as amazing as I did, however. It seemed like you couldn't hear us so the prince didn't hesitate and went right through the water wall and grabbed you out of your trance. He carried you up to your room and left to inform Salem, who came back to check on you a couple of hours ago. I stayed because I didn't want you to wake up to an empty room." He smiles shyly as he finished talking.

"Thank you," I say. "And I am sorry for making such a scene."

"It's fine, going through the process of manifesting is troubling. I believe it can be a bit overwhelming, which is why I thought you should read it" He takes out the manuscript from behind his back.

I swallow. "My parents died years ago, I grew up on my own. I was alone, you know. And then I opened this book." I point my finger on the manuscript. "And I read my mother's name. Apparently she's the one who wrote it."

"I am sorry for your loss. I will let you read it then, if you want to. I just wanted to make sure you were okay."

"Don't." I grab his hand. "Don't leave me." Willow has only been kind to me and to be honest, I am afraid of facing her words alone. This will be the least words from her dedicated to me. Goosebumps spread around my neck thinking of it. I don't want Willow to go.

"Okay, I will stay," Willow agrees. He sits next to me in the bed and goes silent once I start to read. The story started centuries ago once the Crystal War had started. The Shadow Legion penetrated Eskendria as they thought they would lose. On the night after several soldiers died the people sat together, praying to the God Mother to give her a sign of hope. A sign that they should not stop believing. The God Mother herself came to them that night telling them that hope was just across the border and that they should never lose faith. The next day they thought harder and deadlier than they ever had, knowing that hope was right behind them. This belief made it possible to capture evil for the time being. This was done with the help of the God Mother who died in the war alongside her subjects. The whole civilisation was looking for the forsaken child who could replace the God Mother as consequences has arisen from the fall of the Sorcerer Supreme. People questioned the right to rule over people. A rebellion started and as the Shadow legion began to rise again. Without the magic of the God Mother, it was impossible to fight the Dark One. The Elves became desperate and the High King ordered a search for the child spoken of the prophecy. Without a Sorcerer Supreme, everyone was suffering. However, the High King and his closest guards weren't always kind. They took children from families, experimented upon them and killed them if they weren't the Sorcerer Supreme. This continued for centuries but nothing was ever found. The shadow creature slowly came back to life but hope wasn't found yet.

When I saw you, my child, I knew you were special and your father and I tried our best to keep you safe even if that means leaving you alone. We wanted to save you from this War, from this Life. But apparently we weren't good enough. Please remember that we loved you. You were our everything, our star in the starless sky. Our special gift. I know you can do this, even though it may all appear too much. You are our warrior and we know you can fight like hell. So give them hell on earth, my darling.

The world belongs to the ones who are courageous.

Love, Mother and Father.

I wipe away some tears on my cheeks. I see my life now in another light. They tried to protect me. But somehow, they knew I wouldn't listen to the warnings because I was stubborn. It is heart-warming reading something from them to me. It is personal.

"Willow, can you teach me?" The blond-haired man is startled by my question. "I am no Elf but a sorcerer, right? I can use magic, as you have seen. How do I do it willingly?" I ask eagerly. "If all this is true, I am supposed to become the next Sorcerer Supreme, yet, I cannot even control my magic."

"I am no teacher, Aedlin," Willow cautions. " You should ask his high—"

"No." I say firm, "Try your best." I give him a weak smile. I remember the last Elf I considered to be my teacher. Wasn't I taught not to trust Elves and here I am begging for one to teach me … how life changes.

"Are you sure you feel ready for that? You just collapsed after you used your magic. I should probably get Prince Alek—"

"No," I say firmly, "I asked *you*." He looks at me not convinced so I add a small "Please"

He takes a deep breath and gets up from the bed. "Fine. I'll try my best but I won't promise anything. Affinities feel different to everyone. My affinity is wind," he says and on his mark, the window flies open and a soft breeze comes in. "Again, I am no magical teacher, so I am sorry for any bad advice." He smiles gently, yet, am captured by how easily his magic responds to him. "When I was smaller I was taught that wielding magic is composed of two things: Visualisation and Allowance. You have to visualise what you want and then you have to allow your magic to do so. I know, best explanation. But does it help a bit?" he asks.

"Maybe?" I say honestly.

"I don't know how it works with the future Sorcerer Supreme." He smiles. "But I believe it has to be the same because the magic is the same. Try it," he says. I do my best to visualize the water cup standing on my nightstand. I imagine letting the water flow out of it, suspending it in the air as a solid liquid. I try to locate some feeling in me. A feeling that might be associated with magic. I pinch my eyes close. Thinking about creating something like a mantra in my head.

I open my eyes, examining the room to see if something has changed.

"It's not going to work."

"You call that trying?" Willow chuckles.

"I tried!" I say determinedly.

"Maybe, but your magic won't respond to you in mere days. Normally Elves learn to do that when they are younger. Being young always helps to acquire new skills faster." I look at him with narrowed eyes. "You are still young compared to me, don't get me wrong, but it needs more time." He gives me a apologetic smile. This is all so frustrating. I take the cup of water in one of my hands and put the other one in it. I don't care if it looks stupid but maybe the connection to the water would help.

Hesitantly, and doubtfully, I try to visualize the image again.

It is as if the water is listening to me breathing. I see the picture as clear as if my eyes were suddenly opened.

There was *magic* in me, somewhere deep down.

I was kidnapped by Elves who put all their faith in me. Faith that I would be their key and it looks like I am fine with that. I am fine with living here. I am fine with doing something for a purpose. I am fine risking my life for a world I have never known to be true. My thoughts drift away to a prince. I used magic then. If he can bring out my magic, I can do it as easily without him. My magic has to obey my will, not his.

I open my eyes at the right moment to see the water splashing back into the cup. My mouth is open in shock.

"You did it! You used your magic!" Willow smiles, and is clapping his hands like a madman.

"Yes I did it," I admit hesitantly. I did it. Wow, an exhilarating feeling fills my body.

The door flies open and Salem scurried in. She looks confused upon seeing Willow dancing like a crazy man but her eyes scan me looking for injuries.

"I am sorry for interrupting whatever this is but Willow we need your help. Rebels have invaded the west wing!" she says hastily.

"Rebels?" I ask. "Can I help?"

"It's best if you stay here until we clear the area."

"But—"

"No but." Her voice is cold as stone. I can see the young woman behind the mask. The woman who fights for this kingdom for her family. The general shone through the kind face. I just nod and watch both of them leave. I try to focus on what was in the room but my thoughts drift away from them. I cannot just sit here and wait for them to survive. I have to help.

I get up and quickly move to the door where I seek out the guards patrolling my door. To my surprise I encounter Henry standing next to my door.

"Hello, Henry," I say quickly.

"Aedlin." He nods. I move past the door and walk towards the right wing.

"Where do you think you are going?" He suddenly stands in front of me. He has the special skills of an Elf, which I barely now.

"Just to the library," I say as innocently as possible.

"Sadly, I cannot permit it. I have orders to keep you in the room." He looks sad at this.

"I am sorry too," I say and he looks at me, confused. As quickly as I could I kick him in the kneecap. He is so surprised that he goes to the ground immediately. I slung my legs around his neck and squeezed tight so he cannot escape my grip.

"Do you know how it feels to be trapped in a room? Always followed by people because they are afraid of your actions?" I hiss.

"Don't get me wrong, I like you and I am thankful for the training, but I have to help them. I am no child who had to learn her lesson alone in her room."

I am surprised that Henry appears to immediately weaken, not fighting back in any way.

"Oh no, you have defeated me. I am completely lost. My weapon is out of reach and there is no way for me to prevent what is coming next," he says loudly. At first, I am confused by his words until I realise. He is allowing me to leave. I get up and look back at Henry on the floor. He winks at me and whispered, "Go." I grab his weapons and run towards the west wing of the palace. I put a sword on my back and equip each hand with a dagger which I have found on my way.

-

I hear voices echoing from the walls. The smell of blood lingers inside my nose. I see a black figure fighting against three rebels. I sneak around from behind but still the person has heard me and turns towards me. His black eyes stare at mine. This will have consequences. He lets down his guard and a rebel who got back his strength tries to hit him from the left. I have to resist the urge to throw the knife into the prince's face, but I throw one of my daggers as precisely as possible in the Elf's head and he falls backwards. The expression on Prince Aleksander's face is one of both surprise and anger.

"Good afternoon, *my prince*." I say sweet.

"What are you doing here?" he hisses in my ear and grabs my upper arm.

"You are welcome. It was an honour of saving your life, your highness," I mock. "I still have one knife left, so don't you dare touch me ever again." He lets go of my arm and I walk past him.

"You should not be here," he says from behind me.

"Nor should you, your highness. Go back to your safe room and let your subjects do the dirty work," I say not even bothering turning to him.

I don't even see him passing me but suddenly he is standing tall in front of me.

"Don't you dare talk about things you have no idea about. This is none of your business."

"Really none of my business?" I say, outraged. "I am the future Sorcerer Supreme and I am willing to fight until the last for my people. So please if you would let me pass so I can stop more deaths from occurring, I would be very much grateful."

He steps aside and lets me pass. "I am coming with you."

"Whatever you wish, my prince." I roll my eyes.

We follow the sound of swords clinking together. People are laying on the floor. Ours and rebels. Blood is everywhere. I try to focus on Salem and Willow, they are still alive. I feel the presence of the prince behind me. In the edge of my eye I can see how Nevan is wrestled down my a Rebel. I hear myself scream but firm hands prevent me from jumping into the scene.

"He is capable of defending his life" I hear Aleksander hissing at my side. And he is right. With the next sword collision Nevan manoeuvres himself up over the rebel and brutally slices his throat open. I let out a hiss and are focused on the scenery. He lifts his sword and our eyes meet. He gives me a wink and slices the next Elf's back open letting him fall over.

"If you are not ready for it yet, we can go back. I could tell the servants to let you in a hot bath, my dear," Aleksander whispers in my ear.

"Never!" I hiss and storm into the crowd.

I let out a scream when I stab my dagger into the stomach of a rebel who didn't see me coming. My brain switches off and all I can see was the enemy. I am dancing through the crowd, dodging strikes and swords. I know Prince Aleksander has never left my side. I feel the heat emanating from him. We are working as a team, he protects me with his flames and I protect the Crown Prince with my daggers. It is odd yet acceptable. I still haven't forgiven him for what he has done and I am unsure if I ever can but we are a good team if necessary.

I am not sure how much time has passed but eventually the rebels are all cleared out, only one is kept alive for interrogation. The Crown Prince saw the situation and orders everyone to leave and to take care of themselves. I look down at my hands which are covered in blood. elf blood. I just killed several Elves. I thought I would have become acquainted with killing but shooting an animal is different to killing an Elf. Pulling a dagger through their chest so their heart stops beating so you can continue living. My breath increases in speed.

"Salem and Willow. If you are not hurt please bring Aedlin back to her room," I hear Aleksander saying over the crowd.

"Aedlin! I told you not to come." It is Salem's voice.

"I thought you would know me, for me to be kept away from a fight I have to be chained." I chuckle, still focused on my palms.

Slowly strangers' hands cover mine and I look up to see Willow's face which is covered in blood as well. "Don't look, Aedlin," he soothes me.

"I am fine, you do not have to bring me back to my room." I am trying to appease them but they are stubborn.

"You just had an intense fight and killed Elves. No one should be alone after such a thing," Salem says firmly. I start to wonder. How many Elves has she killed already? With those tiny hands? She looks so delicate, nothing like a ruthless warrior and even Willow looks better stored behind books than fighting on the battlefield.

"Do you want to join us for dinner?" she asks.

"Oh yes, Aedlin, please!" Willow begged, leaving me with only one option so I nodd.

-

I sit between Willow and Salem in the dining hall. I am surprised to see so many Elves eating here. Nothing remembers of the rebel attack. "Why have the rebels attacked?" I ask Salem.

"They believe that the High King is not ruling as fairly as he is supposed to rule. After the last God Mother left this world our fields became dry and the economy broke down. They believe the High King should give more to his people rather than keeping it all to himself."

"What do you think?" I say in curiosity.

"Sometimes what we think should be kept silent," Willow says and Salem agreed, nodding.

"So you believe they are right?" I am shocked.

"We only say that we are loyal to the crown and words should be considered once spoken out," Salem says. "Now eat, you look like you haven't eaten in days."

It was true, I have not eaten much lately. Yet, I am overwhelmed by the diversity of food they have here. I have the opportunity to eat delicious food from all over the country. From Eskendria which is in the south and where I was staging.

From Alastas in the North, Cilest in the West and Silicenen in the East. Each dish is stunning on its own. I am not used to eating so diversely. Normally it was what I hunted on my daily walks. I couldn't remember the last time I ate something because I wanted to and enjoyed it. Yet, I couldn't forget what Salem had told me about the rebels' ambition. The thought is planted in my mind and each time I take a bite I had to think about the poor Elves out there struggling to survive.

The longer I have been here, the more eyes are looking at me. More people are mumbling words under their breath. I know they were talking about me. But in all those Fairytales where it was said that Elves will eat mortals in one bite upon first sight, no one ever had something towards me. No one threatened my life, despite the Crown Prince. I thought the folk were rather sceptical species. Sometimes I wonder who they think I was, yet there hasn't been a public statement made about me, unless I wasn't aware of it. I am lost in my thoughts once shrill women voices interfered with my inner monologue.

"We are really sorry to disturb, my lady." I turn my head and see two Elves. One is taller than the other one. The taller one has blue hair and her skin has a light green shade, yet the other was the complete opposite. She has orange long wavy hair beautifully assembled in a high ponytail. I can see how Salem goes stiff oppositely of me.

"We were wondering if the rumours are true?" The fire head asks with a curiosity in her voice.

"We are not here to—", Salem starts but I interrupt her.

"What rumours are you talking about?" I ask. The two woman share a look and I know it would have been better to stay quiet. As if I invited them to dine with us they squeeze themselves in the bank I am sitting at. I can see that Willow and Salem exchange a knowing look.

"People are talking you know, my lady?" The blue hair one says, "Rumours are spreading of your sudden appearance." She clears her throat before she continues. "Is it true that you sudden appearance in Eskendria and your hidden stay in the palace is the result of a secret engagement?" I have troubles to contain a straight face. This is what the rumours are about? That I would be a potential wife to the royal family?

"An engagement?" I troubled finding words.

"It is okay, you can tell us, my lady. Has Prince Nevan chosen his wife?" If I wouldn't know better these two seem to be disappointed at the though of Prince Nevan being engaged to someone who is not them.

"How come you think I'd be engaged to Prince Nevan and not his brother?" Once I have the chance to talk with others I had to use it. I feel a kick at my shin but ignore it. The expression on their faces is priceless. The orange haired one with the freckles is looking at me with big eyes.

"Oh we are desperately sorry for assuming your private life. It just never occurred to us that Prince Aleksander has ever had interest in finding a wife. He barely shows up to seasonal events... We assumed you and ..." She gets interrupted by the other one, " So I assume that Prince Nevan has then not made up his marital plans, my lady?" Her eyes sparkle. I look at Salem and Willow and see that they had to contain a laugh.

"I can assure you that the rumours are only rumours. I am not engaged to anyone." I state.

"I do not want to be direct but why are you then here? You are clearly no Elf so ..." The blue haired one looks shocked at her friend. "I apologise for my sisters behaviour. Lexa sometimes does not understand the etiquettes. It is not our business to know your stay, my lady." She gets up and pulls her sister with her out of the hall.

"That was rather strange." I chuckle. How will they react to a mortal as their answer to the prophecy? No, I won't be a mortal. Neither will I be an Elf. I am the future Sorcerer Supreme. I will stand above the High King in the hierarchy.

Chapter Thirteen

I am in a hall, I cannot remember ever walking in. Two figures are standing in the middle of it. The moon is shining on the woman's face, family features caught my attention. I try to get closer, yet, the shadows make it hard to identify the person. She looks shocked. The woman has dark brown hair and her face seems to be too familiar.

"My prince, please you have to promise me!" Her voice I stop in shock. The situation seems desperate, the woman looks desperate. I move closer to the scene and the woman looks me dead in the eye.

"Did you hear that, my prince?" I stumble backwards. These eyes. The same blue my eyes were – the similarity was striking.

They are my mother's eyes as if she has heard my steps.

I try to calm my breathing. Breath in, Breath out. I look again. Yes, I am certain. She looks different than she was in my memory.

If this isn't shocking enough, the other figure turns around, entering the moonlight and I am out of my mind. I never thought that she meant my crown prince. Aleksander's eyes look around the hall searching for something or someone lurking in the shadows. He looks younger. As if he has just hit puberty but he still radiates an air of authority. He acts like the future High King, however, he looks more innocent, not yet drowned in responsibility.

"Amidala, there is no one do not be foolish. I need you to calm down," he says. His voice is soft but firm. Her gaze goes back to the Crown Prince. "Aleksander, you have to promise me, you understand?! You owe me!" Owe him what? What was going on between them?

"Do not forget who you are talking to."

"Of course not, I would never, my prince," she adds quickly and lowered her eyes.

He takes a deep breath. "I promise," he says and my mother's eyes lift and fill with tears. "Thank you, my prince. I will never forget that." He chuckles and vanishes into the darkness, leaving my mother there in the hall.

I woke up, soaked in sweat. The moonlight shines through the window onto my bedsheets.

My mother knew Prince Aleksander?! She was here in the palace and begged him to do something and he agreed. What happened between them?! What is there left I have no idea of?

I get out of bed and put on something quick. I have to find him, something tells me that the Crown Prince has not yet made his way to bed.

I lurk out of the room, finding my sleeping guard. No one would expect me to leave at this time. I have a strong feeling where exactly to find the Elf. I sense that he won't be far. I make my way to the office he once led me in.

I take a deep breath and open the door, without knocking.

-

Dark eyes assess me in shock. He is sitting at his desk, all casual. His hair is messy and his black shirt is open around the collar. This is a bad idea. But I need answers. He looks so relaxed, so calm. He could have been anyone, any ordinary person at that moment, not the Crown Prince.

"Aedlin, did no one teach you manners?" he asks while looking back at the papers laying in front of him. I make no effort to answer but moved towards him.

He sighs. "Then I believe I have to teach you myself," he says, while looking at me under his eyelashes. I try to hide my blush. Besides all the horrible things he has done, I cannot stop myself from admiring his beauty. He doesn't look fearsome at all. He looks like a normal man who is under a lot of pressure. He looks tired, exhausted, and sad. I almost feel pity. *Almost.*

"You should go back to bed, Aedlin. The day has been long."

"We have to talk," I say.

"Oh you do the orders now, how fresh." Is there a hint of a smile in the corner of his mouth? As fast it appeared it vanishes again. He places his arms on a table in front of him and rests his chin on them.

"What is it you want to talk about at dawn? What is so important, Aedlin?" His eyes pierce through mine. "Is it the fact that I pushed you? Or that I kidnapped you? What is it *this* time?" His tone makes me want to hit him right in the face but I have myself under control.

"My mother," I say coldly. The Crown Prince raise an eyebrow.

"Why do you think I can tell you anything about your mother? Don't you think you are too old to have childhood trauma?" he says dryly.

"I saw it." I swallow. "I saw you talking to her, you promised her something. You *knew* her. Earlier today I read a book written by her. It is oddly strange to see my mother's name, who was *mortal*, written in one of *your* books. " I see that he did not expect to hear this coming from my mouth. He draws back leaning into his chair.

"What do you mean you *saw* it?" he asks calmly.

"I first thought it was a dream. But then it all looked so real. And when I saw her eyes I knew it couldn't be a dream, my prince. It was real." I swallow. "As if it was a memory from the past." He tilts his head trying to find anything that revealed that I am bluffing.

"Interesting. You manifested your magic not long ago but are already able to wield side Affinities." He looks at me. "How impressive." Hearing a compliment coming from his mouth confuses me.

"You still haven't answered my question, *my prince*."

He got up from the chair. Even this early in the morning, he looks majestic.

"Yes I knew your mother," he says quietly. *Knew.* "She made me promise her something. And this promise I will keep. I am a man of honour." He looks at me, seeing that this answer does not satisfy me. He takes a deep breath.

"Let's go somewhere else. I am sick of being stuck in this room. Would you follow me in the rose garden?" he asks kindly.

"If you promise not to throw me off something high," I say.

"No, Aedlin. I won't." The crown prince chuckles.

I am surprised when I feel his hand on my lower back leading me through the palace until we arrive at the decided spot.

His hand lingeres a second longer upon me. I feel somehow empty there when he takes his hand away but told myself it isn't important. I look around and even in the dawn I can see how much care was put into this place. The smell reminds me of my mother. I take a deep breath and try to hide the memories which fill my mind and focus back on the crown Prince, who wanders off and picks up a rose which he gently twists around with his fingers.

"Such beauty, destined to die." He says almost too quiet as for me to hear it.

"I knew your mother for a long time and she knew me," he starts. "We grew up together. She was … a friend." I try to examine his face, what he is feeling right now but it is impossible.

"Time is different here. People age faster in the human world. I believe the magic here is keeping us young. That's why I am still in my twenties even though your mother died in her forties." *Died.* A small spark of hope has embedded itself into my brain, telling me they might not be dead but hearing the Crown Prince's words made it disappear and leaves a void in its wake.

"You remind me of her. Curious, eager, foolish at times. She never listened. She did what she wanted, which wasn't always the best thing." He chuckles at the memory. "Once when she came back from one of her trips, she rattled on and on about this place she had found. This other world, with people who do not look like us. People who are normal. I tried to forbid her to go there anymore. I tried to explain to her how dangerous it could be but she did not listen to me. She ran off. And I was worried to death. I thought I had lost her. So I made my way to find her. I only heard stories about mortals. I was scared and young. I went to the human world and I looked for her. I asked around until someone could tell me where she was. I found her in a hut. A shabby one. Not one the houses I could have offered her as a lady of my court. I opened the door, I still thought she needed my help. And I saw her. With your father, sitting at the campfire in the living room. She was pregnant. I wasn't prepared for such a scene. I was prepared for war. All the years I thought she was abducted by a stranger but she was enjoying her life. She was living her dream with the man she loved." He looks at me and I am certain he sees her in me. "I looked her in the eyes, the same one you are blessed with and I knew it. I knew she was happy. I should have left her alone." His voice grows thin. I am afraid of what was coming next.

"I went back and told Father. Told him that she had betrayed our trust and fell in love with a mortal. I felt horrible after saying it. But I was so furious. She left me for him!" I listen closely, hanging on to his every word and the meaning behind each one.

"I did not mention the child. The High King ordered them both here and made them soldiers, to fight in the Crystal War. And they fought like hell. I saw them die, together. Even in the end they were united." The crown prince swallows. "I … I made a mistake. I know that but I promised her to keep an eye out for her child. I owed her for everything I had done." He looks me in the eyes.

"Aedlin, I am the reason why you have no parents, my actions killed them." He looks away. "When Amidala intercepted me in the hall that night … It was the night before we headed out for war. She told me about you. How amazing you were. How much she loved you. And she told me about your secret, your ability. She made me promise not to tell anyone about you. Not to mention that you were the one we were looking for all along. She wanted you to have a normal, safe life. I put her wish before my duty to my people.

"All the years I checked on you. I helped you survive. Because of me you *had* to do it on your own. I was there. And each day you became more like your mother." He stops and I am speechless also. All the anger I felt towards him vanished into confusion. His words make nonsense but at the same time explained everything.

"You loved her, didn't you? And you felt hurt by what she did," I assess. He looks at me and I can see that he has closed up again.

"Oh Aedlin, don't be foolish. I could never. She was meant to find your father. You were meant to be born. I was just a side character in the prophecy. She was my … friend." I reach out my hand to touch his shoulder but the way he looks at me with his cold obsidian eyes makes me quickly regret my action.

"In the woods … it really has been you." I whisper. He nods, "I have been keeping an eye on you, you were never alone." He steps closer to me, " You grew up to be a woman. I was shocked seeing what you had to endure because of me." He shakes his head, trying to remove the memories, "This lies in the past now, Aedlin. You need to be trained. Trained by someone who is capable of doing so." He turns his body, facing me. "And this somebody's me. Tomorrow afternoon in my office" He turns around, ready to go.

"Is that an order, my prince?" I ask.

"No, Aedlin." He turns his face so I can investigate his perfect profile. "It is an advice from someone who promised to protect you."

CHAPTER FOURTEEN

The Crown Prince answered a lot of questions but I have even more unanswered ones now.

He was the one who looked over me? What has he done? Where has he interfered? But most importantly: Who was my Mother? I feel betrayed, I knew her as the woman who stood in the kitchen, cooking, working with herbs, waiting for father to come home. Did father know everything about her when they met? Had she told him right at the beginning who she was? But who was she? A sorcerer like me? Or an Elf?

That would make me a changeling. The stories she told me when I was smaller might not be made up ones, maybe they were real. About fairies, treasures. Maybe those were the stories she listened to when she was younger. Why did Salem never mention her?

After walking around in my room I decide I need some air.

I step outside and the wind welcomed me as a long-lost friend. The sky is soaked in orange and red-ish colours. The start of a new day. I can feel the first sunbeams on my forearms. I am stunned by the magic humming around me as if I was a part of it. It feels like it is talking to me.

My steps bring me to the court where I first trained with Prince Nevan and Henry.

Speak of the devil.

"Good morning, Henry."

"Good morning, Aedlin," he says, his voice rough. He probably woke up shortly after me.

He still has his cheeky grin and rabble-rousing manner, however.

"You look like you need a good fight." He smirks.

"Oh, how kind of you, but I don't know if you are up to losing in the morning," I joke, not expecting him to accept the challenge.

"I say: let's find out."

He directed all his martial arts against me. Even though the sun is low and the temperature is close to twenty I sweat in my airy clothes. I don't know how long we were fighting but every breath caught in my throat hurt. The muscles in my arms and hands burn intensely, and my pinkie is shaking uncontrollably. I see how it wiggles back and forth while Henry walks towards me and grabs my hand.

"That happens because you are hitting with the wrong angles. Index and middle finger, with them you should hit. If you hit here," he says and tips his calloused fingers on the sensitive sore skin between ring finger and pinkie, "you will cause more damage to yourself than to your opponent. You are lucky that you won't have to win this war entirely in a fistfight." Henry is joking, but I cannot join in.

For an hour he tried to teach me the basics in combat. It turned out that my left side was as good as useless. I was as uncoordinated as a new born baby that was trying to take its first steps. Hitting with the left body part and simultaneously dodging was almost impossible for me, and I stumbled against Henry more often than I could actually hit him.

"Go grab something to drink," he says finally, "then we will work on your balance. It makes no sense to train punches, if you can't stand on your own feet."

I follow the noise of clashing swords, which is coming from the other training area opposite from us. Surprisingly I notice that Prince Nevan and another guard, I don't know his name yet, are sword fighting. Even though the temperatures are dropping, Prince Nevan has put off his formal gown and is left with only a white tunic which is soaking wet from his sweat. His sleeves are curled up revealing his pale, slightly shimmery skin and I see how soft tattoos covered his right underarm and disappeared under his shirt.

"We get this tattoo after we get accepted in the Willowfall circle of soldiers. It is supposed to be a lucky charm and bring fame and honour to the battlefield," says Henry who followed my gaze. However, I doubt that Henry saw him with the same eyes as I did. I admire how handsome Prince Nevan looks even though he is soaked in sweat and my cheeks immediately turned red at the thought.

Henry nods at the two fighting Elves.

"Prince Nevan is not in great shape but won't admit it and Kenneth" – that's the other guy's name – "is too benevolent to force him to the ground." Prince Nevan is not in good shape? I think differently.

My knees are shaking when I walk to the stool, where Henry has put a bucket of water and two glasses. I pour myself a glass of water, and realise that my pinkie starts to shake again.

Henry pours himself a glass of water, and clinks his glass softly against mine. He seems to be a new man: gone is the brutal fighter, who has taken blows and dealt them so hard that I struggled not to fall on my knees and whine for mercy.

"So," says Henry and takes a huge sip from his glass. Behind us Nevan and Kenneth are fighting tirelessly. Swords are clinking.

"How do you feel being a potential last hope for the whole folk?" This question hits me unprepared. The clinking of swords stops for a moment as if everyone is waiting for my answer.

"I am ready to accept my fate. I believe now that I was born for this," I reveal. Henry nods.

"Why have you let me go, the time the rebels have invaded the palace? You have against against your orders, why?" I ask curious. "Because I see you are special. You are worth the risk of bringing the High King's anger upon me." He smiles, "Even if I would have forced you to stay back, you re too stubborn to let it go." He chuckles. I don't know what I should response this this so I am thankful once he forces me back to the training area. "No balancing exercises, only fist punches I remember you owe me," he jokes.

And so goes the morning, with me always being the loser, however, I can see my improvement: my movements become faster and I am able to observe Henry's tactics in order to better dodge his punches.

"You will get better, it is quite unfair to fight against a trained soldier, I am just too good." He laughs, and I join in.

"We are done for today are we?" I pant and put my hands on my knees to calm my breath.

"Yes I hope you will get sore muscles tomorrow."

"Ha ha ha, very funny! Next time you will have sore muscles, believe me!"

-

I drag myself back to my room seeking a hot bath trying to smoothen my muscles. Before even going into the bathroom I collapse on the big bed. The mattress under me feels like heaven and I can immediately sink into a world of dreams. It is still too early to go see Prince Aleksander so why not just fall asleep?

"Exhausting day?" I jump up, and see Prince Nevan standing on my balcony, his normally excellently styled hair is messy and he is only wearing his shirt with his sleeves rolled up. No part of his body indicates the brutal fight he just had. With his sleeves rolled up I get another closer view on his tattoo. It looks beautiful, dark ink stretching itself along his arm. I would have to ask him about it later.

"Good day to you too, sir, what's the problem? Want to have another fight? Henry said you seem to be in not great shape so I could easily kick your ass." Prince Nevan turns around while saying,

"If you invite me to a fight in this room I can't promise that the furniture stays safe," he says with a smirky smile. I roll my eyes and press my lips into a slim line.

"I don't want to be rude to you, my prince, but I seek a warm bath, either you join me or leave," I say provocatively, raising one eyebrow.

"Oh, woman, if I wouldn't have so much to do currently I definitely would join, I will keep it in mind, my love." He winks and my cheeks catch fire. *Heart breaking* prince. I get it.

"Why are you here?" I am a bit annoyed.

"Isn't it allowed to just seek out some company?" he soothes.

"Not when it comes to you, my prince."

"Ouch that hurt," he says tragically.

"I only wanted to tell you to prepare for the Midsummer festival. This is an important event for our social season at the end of summer. We are going to present you to the folk," he says enthusiastically.

"You will *introduce* me not present. I am no object," I correct him.

"Of course, Aedlin." He winks. "I want you to understand that this event is essential for future collaboration among the Realms. As well as you have to be cautious about what you do and say. All eyes will be on you and we don't want you to become the target," he says as if it would be nothing.

I sigh. "Okay, understood."

"Delightful."

-

Right on time I knock on Aleksander's office door. "Come in," he says in his deep voice. His hair is brushed backwards and he is properly dressed. Nothing could be seen from the man I was talking to hours ago. He gazes up at me, "You seem tired."

I straightened my back a bit more, "I couldn't fall asleep anymore after this morning, I had some training lessons with Henry in the court." I say in a monotone voice. "I see, I see." He gets up from his chair, looking me up and down. I feel uncomfortable being under his examination.

"I am sorry." It is so soft that I could barely hear it. I look at him in confusion. "Aedlin, I am sorry." I turn my head, inviting him to talk more. "I should not have lashed out at you like that." A spark in his inky eyes is pleading for something I am not sure I can give. He steps closer, "I believe you have heard the stories about me and my existence, I assure you they are all true. I am not versed in … in." He pauses looking for the right words. "Developing a relationship with people?" I finish his sentence.

"I have hurt you with my words … and actions. I am sure of that. I do not believe that it means something to you but … it was not my intention." He sighs and looks away.

"How can I be sure you mean it?" I ask.

"Because I gave your mother my word and I would rather die than break that promise, Aedlin. I promised to protect you and said I would not want to harm you … on purpose."

"For me it seemed like you don't care if I live or die."

"You are so wrong, Aedlin. I am cruel but I don't kill for entertainment or because I am bored. I care for you." The words are spoken and a strange feeling establishes itself in my stomach. I choose to ignore it.

I suddenly am hit with a moment of realisation. "You threw me off the cliff because you *knew* I had it in me. You knew it because my mother told you. You trusted her." I throw my hands in the air.

"That's why you could not explain it to me earlier, in front of all these people, because they don't know about your relationship. That's why Salem has never told me about that, because she doesn't *know*." I look at him, wide-eyed. The Crown Prince cannot look me in the eye.

"Yes, it's true," he says. I look at the man standing in front of me, risking his honour for my mother.

"Fine. I am willing to work with you but do not think that I forgive you for what you did. I almost died because of you and I had to grow up without parents. That's all on you." He looks up and our eyes met.

"I will do my best to make it up to you even though I understand how you feel. Forgiveness is the hardest thing in this world."

A strange silence establishes between us. Then he claps his hands and grabs a notebook from his desk. "Let's begin."

"Water affinity manifested. In the last few days, did you have any strange feelings towards the other elements?" he asks.

"Not particularly strange. I have the feeling of being drawn towards them. When I am in nature it feels as if the elements are talking to me," I admitted.

"I believe that your magic is manifested in all elements. You have magic inside you which we can see, and I don't believe we have to *unlock* each element individually." I let out a relieved sigh. The thought of experiencing the same pain three more times was too much.

"May I try something?" he asks.

"If it doesn't include me dying," I joke. The Crown Prince steps closer. But still kept a save distance between us.

177

"I am going to touch you, with my flames." I flinch back. "Let me finish. You are blessed with all four elements. Your own element cannot hurt you. This means my flames cannot hurt you. Because it is your element as well. If it doesn't hurt you, we know that your other affinities have not yet manifested," he says slowly. I take all the information in.

"Do it." He nods and raises his hand. Flames are dancing around his palm and fingers. It looks stunning. With so little effort, he manages to manifest his flames. I have the urge to touch him. I want to know how the dance of fire would feel on my skin. I stretch out my hand and touch the skin of Prince Aleksander. The flames tickle my hand but don't burn me. They dance with the same intensity of red and orange on my hand.

"They can feel your magic, they are drawn to it," he says quietly, not removing his hand from mine.

"It's stunning," I breath. And then the fire is out and my hand is normal again, suspended in the air. I quickly put it behind my back.

"I see improvement. It's good to know that you have manifested more than one element. You need to train in order to use them." I look up at him. "And I will help you." Then, he sighs. "But not now. I will let you know. I have to leave for the counsel."

"Why helping me?" The words were out before I realise it. He turns around and looks at me. "We are at war, and as a Crown Prince I have to obey rules. You're not the only one who feels locked up, Aedlin," he says, casually walking out of the room.

Chapter Fifteen

The next few days were rather monotonous. I woke up, had breakfast with Salem and Willow, read in the library and had fighting lessons with Henry in the courtyard. I hadn't heard from Prince Aleksander since the day I was in his office.

Salem and I met in the library to bring me up to date with my history lessons.

"We covered the geographical part, the economical part, so what is left is you." I look up from my book.

"Me?"

"Who are you? Isn't that a question you ask yourself often?" She was right. Since coming here I was constantly wondering who I really was. Knowing that my mother and father were a part of this world caught me off guard. If they were from here, what would that make me?

"The Sorcerer Supreme has the ability to wield all four elements which makes you almost unkillable. Being able to have all four elemental affinities makes you resistant to all possible threats since your own magic cannot hurt you," she explained. Prince

Aleksander said something similar. It explained why his fire wouldn't hurt me.

"People call you "Diamond" because the person who will end this war should be rough but wise. A diamond is strong because it is made out of carbon and forms a giant covalent structure which makes it the hardest element in the world. You are our diamond. Rare but beautiful, strong but weak," Salem finishes.

"This means that if I manifest all four elements, I can be a weapon in the wrong hands?" I swallow.

"Yes, it would be fatal to have you in the wrong hands," she says and confirms my fears.

Someone clears their throat behind me. "My sincerest apologies for interrupting this quite lovely history lesson but I have to talk to Aedlin," Prince Aleksander says.

"Of course, my prince." Salem stands up and bowes her head. I sigh and get up. It is weird seeing him standing next to the bookshelves so casually. I look back at Salem who gives me a look that says that I definitely have to explain something to her. I haven't told anyone that the Crown Prince gives me lessons in magic. I am already the centre of attention. I don't want to have any more eyes on me. I nod to Salem showing her I understood her sign.

I follow the Prince to his office. I can smell the scent of ash and wood after a heavy rain. It is welcoming.

"Aedlin, you mentioned that you feel magic around you, is that correct?" he asks while taking a seat on his desk.

"Feel magic?"

"Yes, my dear, feel magic. Every Elf has this feeling inside of them. Some say it is a spark, others say it's like a fresh wind." He looks at me waiting for a response. I take a deep breath and feel into myself. I attempt to feel the warmth of the sizzling magic. Yet, nothing responds to me. I open my eyes and draw a breath in once, noticing how close Prince Aleksander stands next to me, examining my being.

"It didn't work," I whisper.

"That's what you called trying?" He snorts and pulls himself back. "We cannot continue like this. There is a war waiting at the border. More and more people are getting infected. We are all waiting for you to *decide* to wield your magic."

"Well, I am trying. It is not as instinctive for me as it is for you, my prince!"

"Then try harder, or do you want your parents do have died for nothing? Do you want to go back home? Where you do not have to worry about any of this?" He raises his arms. "You need to *want* it, otherwise we cannot continue, foolish woman."

"Do not talk to me as if I am some dense child!" I say, furious.

"Have you forgotten who you are talking to?" he says mockingly, stepping closer.

"I don't know, tell me, are you a blind, fooled hypocrite or will you finally teach me!"

He looks shocked at me. "You did it."

"I did what? I am tired of people talking to me as if I am a child. *Explain*!"

His eyes leave my face and gazes down. I follow his stare and look stunned at my hands which are covered with flames like Prince

Aleksander's hand was yesterday. I lift my hand examining it in front of my face, remembering the feeling. "I – I did it." I say, astonished.

The Crown Prince takes my flamed covered hand into his.

"Isn't it beautiful, how your emotions trigger your magic?" His coal dark eyes look into mine, full of joy. And gone was the angry Elf. The feeling of his hand touching mine brought up goosebumps on my skin. I don't like this.

"However, we have to change that. Having your emotions lead your magic can be dangerous, your instinct has to take over," he says quietly. The flames have vanished by now but he still has my hand in his. I watch him with big eyes while he said, "Try to manifest it again. Think about the feeling. Imagine what you want to create in your head." His grip is firm but soft. I try not to overthink this. I need fire.

And there it is. A small sizzle, a spark and I have a flame hovering over my palm. Astonishing. I look up to see his face. The colours of the flame are dancing, lighting up his face. They are mirrored in his eyes, making it seem like he is made of fire.

I close my eyes. What am I doing here?

I hear the movement of clothes and when I open my eyes again I see Prince Aleksander writing down in his notes.

"What are you writing, my prince?" He looks up.

"I am recording your improvement for my father." I frown at him. "He requested records on how you are progressing with you magic, understandable considering the current situation. It is objective and formal. I am not including the times when you discover you have the same sharp mind as I was blessed with," he says and I can see a small smile developing on his face. And I don't hide mine.

"What do you mean with *more people are getting infected earlier?*" I ask out of curiosity. He looks up wide-eyed.

"Did I say that? I think you misinterpreted my words."

"No, it was loud and clear. What is going on?"

Aleksander sighs. "The Dark One is surrounded by soldiers. Yet, these warriors are neither Elves nor mortals. They are something else. We call them Syrivis. Beings created from the shadows infecting innocent Elves. Once a Syrivis has taken over the system of an Elf or human it is impossible to turn them back. They are destined to die." He swallows. "Yet, the 'sickness' is spreading throughout the country and more and more Elves get infected and fight for the Dark One. Which means we have to be fast before his army exceeds ours." I examine him while he is writing down notes. The power this man has over the country but still he feels trapped. Has he heard about the rumours spread about his father? And if so, what does he think about them?

He looks up and our eyes met. "You may go now, Aedlin." He puts down his notebook. "I will see you soon."

I lower my head and walk towards the door. "Thank you for the help, my prince." I grab the door knob but stop when I hear his voice.

"Call me Aleksander." I turn around to look at his face. "In private." He looks back down at his book not noticing my surprised smile.

CHAPTER SIXTEEN

A room, no a hall, appears in front of me. The light is
dense, it seems to be night and my eyes need some time
to adapt to the darkness. Where am I? The hall is magnificent, the
floor is covered in glass and the ceiling is a mirror where I can see
myself. I am wearing normal clothes. The ones I believe I had worn
before I fell asleep. But this isn't part of the palace. It feels like death,
lonely, empty.

"Aedlin, finally we meet again."

The voice immediately brings up the goosebumps. It is the
same I heard when I first entered the church in the forbidden city. And
again, there is no one around. Just me. I cannot locate the direction
the voice is coming from. It seems to be everywhere and nowhere.

"We have a lot to talk about, my little princess, so pure and
innocent. Though you are here. In this chaotic world. Isn't it hard to
adapt to a world you think you don't belong to?"

I turn around, trying to find the body attached to the voice. "A world I don't belong in?" I ask, trying to get them to speak again.

"I see ... someone feels comfortable here with the attention. You feel wanted, not something you felt back in your hut. Such a tragic story with your parents—"

"Leave them out of this! This is clearly between you and me and don't dare bring them into it!" I feel a breath of air at my neck and turn around to see something had appeared out of the darkness. Two shapes.

"And here they look so innocent, your mother and your father. Such a shame that they had to die in such a cruel way."

I start walking towards the shapes. The outline of my parents. They look different. No joy, no life. They look dead.

"You know what happened to them?" I ask, quietly, frightened of what the answer would be.

"Knowledge, what is knowledge? It is such a meaningful word. Maybe I do, maybe not. But hey who am I kidding? I killed them. I turned them into my slaves." A cruel laugh echoes through the empty room. I turn around, wanting to walk away but the room disappear, only darkness is left.

The shapes of my parents become clearer and change. My mother is holding now a baby in her arms, Father is looking at her with great love. The baby smiles and laughs at them. A beautiful family.

"Your parents loved you. They did quite a lot to protect you. Even sacrificing themselves for you."

Darkness again. The pictures are gone. I am all by myself, the darkness gives away to my bedroom. I am alone, on my own, as nothing has changed.

My night wasn't long, I am already up when Salem knocks at my door.

"Didn't sleep well?" she ask in concern.

"No not really, if I am honest." I rub my eyes red and try to get energy in my bones. I will have to tell them about my dreams. But not today. Soon.

Salem sits next to me on the bed. "Maybe you would like to join me in the city, I need to get some herbs for my potions."

The more I get to know her sweet side the more I start to like her. I agree to join her. I make myself ready, while Salem is packing some "essentials" I need for the small trip. After we were done, we make a small stop in the kitchen to get our hands on some of the delicious food they have stored.

"Salem, is it just me being weird, or does the food here taste different?" I ask her on our way to the carriage which is parked in front of the palace. "Oh no you are definitely right, the fairy food does taste better, or humans believe so. I have never tried mortal food before, but people tell stories. You have probably noticed that everything, the smells and tastes, are different compared to your home town." How can you possibly compare a palace and a shabby village?

We walk towards the main entrance. This is actually the first time I have seen. When I was brought here I was unconscious.

I draw in a breath when I see the carriage standing in front of me. It is a beautiful construct out of a shiny material I cannot name.

Finley probably could. To my surprise I see Henry standing outside at the carriage who also joins us on the trip.

Salem enters the carriage and I follow her.

"Hey girls, you haven't forgotten me, have you?" a familiar voice shouts across the court. I have to laugh when I see Willow running from the entrance, struggling to put his jacket on.

"Of course not, how could we?" Salem jokes and rolls her eyes.

"How come that I heard from Master Viktor of your delightful plans?" he says, looking judgingly at us.

"I didn't think you'd like to buy herbs with us in the city and I thought it would be nice for Aedlin to see the city she is living in." Salem looks at me with a soft smile.

"This is all so fascinating," I admit and stare out of the window while the carriage starts to move. "The colours and smells. It is so different from home." My voice is going dull.

"Do you miss home?" Willow asks. Do I?

"I am not sure. Not particularly the life more the ... people," I admit.

"The people or a person?" Salem asks while wiggling her eyebrows which makes me laugh. I hit her arm softly. "Stop that! It is not like that. We were friends." *Were.* What would he think of me if he sees me right now? Would he worry about me?

"We were close. He helped me over the years but people change and sometimes you realise that you don't know the person you considered your best friend," I say calmly.

I can feel how Willow put his hand on my knee. I look up and give him a soft reassuring smile.

"You know, you are not a prisoner here. You could check on him if that is what is keeping you back. Sometimes it has to be done in order to move forward, and the High King does not necessarily need to know from it." Salem chuckles .

"I would even come with you!" Willow says full of joy and gone are my sorrowful thoughts. How can these two people make my life so much better?

-

While driving through the countryside of Eskendria I appreciate its nature and wildness. Even a normal farm looked magical as if there were treasures hidden underneath. The people all seem to do normal work as I would have expected humans to do. But I do notice the long looks they give us as we drive past. The sun is high up in the sky but the weather is not hot. The wind is playing with the leaves of the oak trees and the birds are singing their favourite song. Yet, the fields seem to be dry. The people are full of sorrow, trying to hold it together. I see children looking thinner than they should.

Upon entering the city, the troubling atmosphere from the country makes place for the hassle and stress. I see Elves kneeling, sitting, and crouching on the street, begging for money or something to eat, their eyes piercing through me. How could I not want to help them? I used to be them. I used to be begging for money begging for other charity for my survival, yet, this has not turned out pretty well. We cross a woman sitting on paper, partly wearing weather appropriate attire. I can see that she has troubles silencing her crying child. It is way too cold for them to be out here. I look at her and call for Salem, "Do you happen to have some change with you?" She moves to where I am standing and hands me over some gold coins from her purse.

"This is for you." I say to the woman. Her big green eyes lock with mine. "My lady, this is too generous … I cannot take it." She almost whispers. "I insist," I say, " And this is for your child." I take off my cloak. "The temperatures are continuously dropping no child should freeze." Once my eyes reach hers I see how tears made their way up. "Thank the God Mother for you, my lady."

I drag myself away from the image and follow Willow and Salem deeper in the hollow city. If we weren't the centre of attention before we are certainly now. Some Elves give me long looks and whisper under their breaths. I could feel how Henry moves closer from behind. I try to seem friendly, I wave towards a small child which stopped in front of me before his mother could pull him back. I couldn't really read their expression but mostly it has been shock.

"Who is she?"

"She is no Elf."

"Escorted by the Royal Guard. Could it be?"

We stop at a small herbal store. As we open the door, scents, pungent, and sweets, tingle in my nose and bring a secret smile to my lips. It reminds me of the smells of my mother sorting her herbs in the kitchen. After that, the whole house would smell like that for days. I welcome the warmth, since I have started o freeze outside. The Winter is coming closer. I am surrounded by bundles of craggy roots, leaves and strange plants. A grey-haired woman, who looks like the reincarnation of joy, is standing behind the corner crushing seeds, leaves and petals. I immediately feel welcome. Salem Starts an intense conversation with the old woman but I only have eyes for the thing in front of me. I bring the small tubes to my nose and absorb their scent. It is as if I am smelling Home.

I don't know how much time had passed but at some point I get caught in my thoughts.

"Young woman," an old voice calls. I turn to face the lady at the counter. She draws in a deep breath. "Saints. You look just like your mother!" I walk up to her.

"You knew my mother?" I ask.

"Oh, I did my child. She was a warrior, and you just look like her. The eyes, the nose. It is as if I look into her eyes. After so many years." A tear rolls down her cheek. I can feel her hand on my cheek. Normally I do not let strangers touch me this easily, yet, this woman has something on her that soothes my mind. She maybe has answers to some of my questions of my mother.

"Oh no, please there is no reason to cry," I say, grabbing her wrinkled hand. "Is it possible, that we have met before?" I ask her. "My child, it's no time for this right now." She sniffs, "Come back once you have dealt with your demons." She smiles , "Go, my child, help the Realm finish what you mother has started," she says.

I look at her strangely as if I look in the face of a familiar person. I withdraw myself from her grip. It seems as if she doesn't want to let go of me.

Outside of the store I turn around to look at the name of the herbal store so it would be easier for me to find it again. I freeze in the middle of the street.

Orbwood, Herbs, Scents and Sweets.

This cannot be a coincidence. *Orbwood*. My name, my mother's name. The old lady, could she be a relative of mine?

"Aedlin?" Willow asks. "You alright?" I turn to him.

"Orbwood, is it a common name here?" I demand to know.

"No, you are the only one I know who has that name."

I point to the sign above the shop. I can see the moment he understood.

"First the book and now this? I get the feeling there is more about my family I don't know yet."

Willow couldn't answer my questions so we try to catch up to Salem and I wrote a note in my head to ask Aleksander the next time we met.

-

The moon is already high up when we finished every single thing on Salem's list. I am exhausted and my leg hurt as if I have been climbing a mountain for the past hours. I would have never categorised Salem as being this energetic. She is so fragile but has so much power. I lean my head on the cold window of the carriage, gazing into the woods, which look so beautiful. The moon light shimmers through the tree crowns giving it a mysterious atmosphere.

However, the darkness hidden in the woods has a strange feeling. As if it is watching me. Suddenly, the carriage stop and I hear someone talking outside. I look confused to Salem and Willow but she shows me to be quiet.

"Oh have mercy, I am an ordinary salesman who got attacked by this furious creature in the woods. Please, I can't feel my leg anymore." It is hard to understand them. I want to look outside and see what is going on, so I lean forward when Salem pulls me back in my seat and puts her finger to her lips.

"Man, if you are who you say you are, where is your waggon, or did the creature take it with it?" one of the guards jokes.

Then, a scream!

"Protect the carriage!" I hear a voice cry out.

"Sam, are you okay?! Can you stand?" I hear an anxious guard ask one of his friends. No response. I look shocked at Salem who slowly moves to the floor of the carriage trying to make as little noise as possible. I can see how her grip around her sword tightens. Footsteps are approaching, I cannot tell how many. Swords clanging, men growl, screams.

Their voices do not sound human. It is more a growl and a shriek scream.

The door is kicked open, leaving it hanging broken at the side. I couldn't suppress my scream. This man had no face. It looks horrific. He takes my foot and pulls me out of the carriage, another one gets hold of Salem who tries her best to fight back. I kick and bite but nothing seems to work. I see how the guards are fighting fearlessly.

One of them, Sam I believe, hacks away but he is fighting to stay conscious. The Syrivis is pulling me towards the woods. I feel like a potato sack. I try to grab something on my way so I scan the wooden floor for potential weapons. A stone. Nice. I throw it at the creature's head. He screams, but it is not a human cry. I try to reach for my knife in the pocket of my dress but I can't grab it.

He gets hold of me again but I kick him with all my strength away from me. I try to remember what Henry has taught me in combat.   Yet, my mind is blown empty. I need to get time, and distance between this thing and myself. From behind I can hear screams and cries I have no idea what these things are planning on doing with me but if they want me dead, I would be already. They need me alive. Facing the creatures I have to suppress a cough, his face still looks disgusting as if he should have been buried in a coffin and not be standing here alive. I start to run not knowing if this is clever or not, but I need time. I know the Syrivis are following me, I hear heavy footsteps on the leaves which blanket the ground. Magic, come on! Suddenly, they grab my shoulders and pull me to the ground. They are hoovering above me only inches away from my face. I pull my hand into a fist and slam it into their profile, hearing an unhealthy crack coming from their jaw. They let go a shrill scream and toss me against a tree, hitting the floor roughly.

"Oh you didn't just do that!" I growl. The creature just screams at me in response.

"Saints. Ever heard of mouth wash?!" I get up, run towards it, punch the creature in the stomach and take advantage of their recovering by taking their feet off the floor. A scream again! Oh boy, they are angry. I see more creatures are approaching me. They are calling for help. I am surrounded by death and decay. I focus on my inner self. Aleksander told me to focus on the feeling of the sizzling, but I don't feel anything. I take a deep breath. Remembering what he said his voice in my head. His breath on my skin. The flames dancing on both of our hands …

Suddenly, I hear nothing except the pulse in my veins. I can hear the blood rushing through my body. I feel warmness spreading through me. I am angry, yet, I dug into the wound of my heart, which is full of sadness and anger and pour it all out. The tears which are running down my cheek feel on fire.

I feel the sensation of one of the creatures touching my arm. I open my eyes and extend my left hand grappling the creatures neck. The instant our skin touches they dissolve as if my fingers are acid. The screams are horrible but fill me with joy.

"Let the party begin!"

The remaining monsters are running towards me. I let myself slide over the forest ground splitting the floor underneath the Syrivis, letting three of them fall into their deaths before closing the gap again with a stomp of my foot, crushing their remaining bones. I look shocked at the scenery of what I made happen.

Goosebumps establish on my back, warning me from the next intruder. I let my instinct take over and hit the side of my fists together creating a water snake that fills the creature's lungs with water, letting it drown. Two remaining. They are surrounding me. I lift my hands in the air, crossed them and pull them down in one go, creating an air wave which threw them in the air and struck their bodies against the trees. Just to make sure they are dead, I burn them. I try to catch my my breath. Slowly my head returns to its normal state. I turn around seeing the faint lights of the carriage. I feel a sudden but overwhelming tiredness. I run out of the woods, seeing Salem crouching over a guard's body, trying to heal him. It is probably Sam. Willow is sitting on the steps of the carriage and his eyes meet mine.

He gets up, wide-eyed but my knees collapse under me and I fall to the floor, taken in by darkness.

CHAPTER SEVENTEEN

Voices. "She needs more rest. Maybe giving her more of the serum might help …" I drift away into the shadows again. Feeling numb. Feeling trapped in my own body. I feel how people are around me, the presence of the other individuals is as clear as an image. But I could never stay conscious long enough to reach the surface of the ocean into which I always get pulled down again, fighting for every breath.

The light is dimmed in the room. I fully open my eyes, surprised that the deepness of the ocean isn't calling for me again. Why do I always have to get drugged here? Nothing a Camille tea couldn't fix, no need to black me out every time I got hurt.

I support myself with my hands while trying to sit straight. The windows are shut. Only an inch of light could go through it. In the corner is an armchair with a sleeping figure on it. I clear my throat, hoping to wake the stranger.

A head moves, an eye opens, looks in my direction and closes again, only to reopen in amazement. I have a feeling of Deja-vu. The last time I felt unconscious, Willow was looking over me.

"Aedlin, you are awake, thank the saints!" Salem stands up and rushes towards me, checking my head for any other possible injuries. "How are you feeling?" she asks.

Salem looks tired, but seeing her calms my heart but then I remember what has happened.

"How are the others?!" I look around in horror hoping they would be somewhere.

"Aedlin, look at me." She holds my chin with her hand so I focus on her. "Sam didn't make it. He was brutally attacked and our best healers couldn't bring him back to life. I am sorry. But the others survived."

I didn't know Sam personally, but knowing I will never have the chance to get to know him hurt my heart. He probably had a family and he died because of me. Because I was in the carriage. Without me the drive back would have been normal and safe.

"What do you remember, Aedlin?" Salem asks me.

I try to recall my memories, it is harder than expected. But then a bunch of pictures fall back into place.

"I killed them," I say quietly. Salem takes my hand in hers.

"I killed these monsters with magic. I … I was able to use all four elements," I whisper.

Silence.

"How is Willow?" I ask, trying to lead the conversation into another direction. I don't want to think about what has happened. I know these things were not considered much alive but I made their hearts stop same as I made the rebels stop living. What has happened with me?

"He stopped by, I had to force him out of the room to get some rest himself. I ended up falling asleep here." She chuckles. "Someone else was looking for you as well," she says knowingly, "and he was quite worried but couldn't stay." I nod. I am not sure what else to do.

"I will leave you alone," she says and rise from the chair.

"Thank you."

I do not move, I stay in bed I have to process what has happened. I killed people. Sure, they would have killed me but I ended their lives. I was used to killing animals. It was no pleasure but this is how I had survived in the last years. Killing people is a new level. I don't know what happened to me at that moment. I feel like a different person. High on the feeling of magic.

Then, I hear footsteps approaching my room.

"You cannot enter, she needs rest."

"I can and I will," a familiar voice demands. "I am your Crown Prince, I want to see *her*."

No response. I hear a soft knock on my door, nothing left from the furious anger in his voice. The door opens and he walks in, dressed all in black, as always. His coal eyes are focused on me, trying to search my face and body for any injuries that he doesn't know about.

"You are alright. You foolish woman, how could you have gone alone?" he asks, but in his voice there is no hint of real accusation.

"I didn't choose to. I got dragged out of the carriage and got pulled into the woods. And suddenly I was surrounded by eight or nine of these … these things," I say. Aleksander approaches my bed and lets himself down on the corner of it.

"I managed to kill them with my magic. It felt so natural. As if it has always been there. Not only water but also the other elements," I say looking down at my hands.

"You did well. I am proud of … your improvement," he says hesitantly.

"How about now? Can you summon your magic?"

I try to recall the feeling from yesterday but it feels like my magic is sleeping, as if it needs some rest.

"No, it is a strange, dense feeling. I know it is there but it doesn't want to be bothered."

Aleksander has to smile a bit. "Understandable. We will continue our lessons tomorrow. I have read your health report and have been assured that you will be alright."

"Wait." I call. He turns and raises his eyebrow waiting for my words. What was I going to say again?

"Do you have any idea of how miserable he folk is living in the town?" I ask. he looked me in the eyes not moving and inch.

"Have you visited your people?" I ask again.

"Time never made it possible." He admits.

"They need you! It is getting colder. There are children on the streets of your kingdom, sleeping, fighting to survive. Please do not let them suffer." I begged. Aleksander swallows.

"I will see to them." I nod.

He gets up ready to leave. On the door he stops.

"Aedlin, I was worried about you," he said, turning his head back. "Not only because I promised your mother to keep you safe." In his eyes lurks a secret he isn't ready to reveal yet.

"Thank you, Aleksander." It is the first time I have said his name out loud. I can see how he tightens his shoulders but he doesn't say anything against it. He nods and leaves me in the room.

Nothing big happened in the next few days. I attended my magic lesson. Salem and Willow helped me to get up to date with the news and drama. Willow was excited about the upcoming midsummer festival. I had never heard of such an event before, yet, it was praised like Christmas.

"We dance, we eat good food and enjoy the weather change to the colder days. It is a goodbye festival." Willow explains.

Indeed, the weather is slowly turning to autumn but not the grey and cold one I had experienced for too long in my world. It is an autumn filled with red and orange colours. The woods look even more fabulous than in summer.

When I sit on my balcony and drink my tea, only then do I realise how long I have been here now. How much time has passed in the human world? I try not to think too often about Finley but sometimes he creeps into my thoughts and dreams and it is hard to let him go. I tell myself I would go back one day to check on him and his family, but I am fairly sure I could never live there in his world anymore.

-

I find myself in Aleksander's office for my next lesson. In the past days we made great improvement on my manifesting skills and he reported this to the High King who requested insight in my progress. For him I am a weapon to bring him victory and I see that in Aleksander as well; however, I increasingly think that he has, perhaps, stopped seeing me as a weapon and instead as a person, but maybe this is part of their plan as well. However, this world is suspicious.

"Who was my mother?" I ask out of the blue. He is eagerly writing down notes but by the mention of my mother he stops.

"I mean, who was she here? I know her as a human but when I visited the city with Salem and Willow, I met this woman who had a herbal shop with the same last name as I had. She acted rather strange around me and ... could it be that she is related to my mother?" I ask hopefully.

Aleksander sighs. "Your mother was an Elf of low birth. Her family owned a herbal store in the city. There was no reason why we should have met. Our worlds were far apart. But someday the High King got sick and even the best healer could not help him. Your mother's mother claimed she could do so ... and she did, she saved the king. She was granted one wish and she chose to give her daughter a good education in the palace. This is how we have eventually met."

"So the elderly lady ... is my grandmother?" I ask, stunned.

Aleksander nods.

"This would make me ..."

"A changeling," he answers. "Half human half Elf. Normally changelings are not blessed with magic, maybe with only a little, however, you are different."

As the lessons continues, I am able to manifest my magic faster than before. It is more stable. I don't want to admit it, but Aleksander has been a good teacher. He has taught me how to focus on my magic without relying on an emotional outburst. He has written down every possible information useful for the High King. I want to figure out the true nature of the man who was leading this country.

"Are the townspeople satisfied?" I ask Aleksander one day during our class. He stops what he is doing and looks stiff.

"We are facing tough times and the townspeople could have a better life. We hope once all this is over, the village life will go back to normal."

"I am the so-called property of the Crown and I want to understand the goal the crown is seeking. I heard rumours and if these rumours were true I would not feel at ease with myself killing the rebels."

"What are you pointing out, Orbwood?" Aleksander faces me and lifts an eyebrow.

"I am just casually asking if the High King's achievements serve the society as a whole or just himself."

"You could be hung for the words you just said," he says calmly.

"I know I could, but I won't, am I right?" I look at him. "The rebels are fighting for their survival, we are living in excess of food and drinks. Next is the midsummer festival, isn't it rather pathetic to celebrate and feast while there are people starving in your kingdom?"

"So what you think is that I should do? Side with the rebels who wish to extinguish the royal bloodline because you believe they are right?" he growls.

"I am just pointing out my doubts," I hiss at him.

"Yet, your doubts include the betrayal of your locality to the High King," he says back angrily.

"Aleksander, you have to see it as well. This Kingdom is under a wicked King. The people suffer. I saw it with my own eyes." I sigh. "This Kingdom needs a faithful leader, someone who believes in the good, someone who listens to people but also can be strict if needed. Someone like you!" He looks shocked at the words I have just said.

"What makes you think that I will be a better High King than my father? I am nothing of the person you described," he says determinedly. "I beg to differ. You might seem cruel on the outside but once someone took the time to listen to your motives you would be a pretty good High King," I say looking at his wide-eyed face.

-

I ho back to my room wanting to read on my balcony, enjoying the sun on my face. It is only early noon and I am already done for the day.

A knock on the door.

"Yes?" A handsome blond-haired man walks into my room.

"There you are, my love, I was looking all over for you," Nevan says enthusiastically.

"You were?" I ask doubtfully.

"My brother told me where to find you." He walks to the balcony where I do not make an effort in getting up for him.

I look up to see his blue eyes. He bents over so our faces are only inches apart. I can feel his breath on my cheek.

"Is something on my face or are you this close for no reason?" I roll my eyes.

"I just wanted to appreciate your beauty," he jokes. "You know we had a fun discussion in today's council. Aleksander brought up some interesting topics which I assume came from you." He raises one of his eyebrows.

"I am sorry but I don't follow."

"Of course you can't, my blossom." He touches my chin with his warm fingers. "Thanks to you we will open our doors to the townspeople for tomorrow's midsummer festival, to celebrate all together as one unity." He smiles. "You should have seen the High King's face once Aleksander has presented his idea." Nevan chuckles.

"This seems to be a great idea, but it's not coming from me," I say with my sweetest smile.

"As humble as ever, Aedlin." He swallows. "The people are going to love you. You care for them even though you were not born into this world. They will appreciate your kindness and strength. You will achieve great things, Aedlin Orbwood."

"Thank you , my prince." It is odd to hear such compliments from the man who once threatened my life. But I believe threatening someone's life is like requesting friendship here.

"I assume that you don't already have a date for tomorrow's festival, am I right?" he asks, his eyes sparkle.

"No, no one in particular, my prince," I answer confused.

"Lovely. I want you to join me for the midsummer festival, as my partner."

"You and me?!" I am even more confused. "Why do you want me to go there with you?"

"Don't you find the idea appealing that I want to get to know you more? The next Sorcerer Supreme, a mortal. A woman who can easily change a man's mind with just the right words. This is fascinating." His words make me blush.

"Alright. I will go with you as friends. But I don't think I own something nice enough to wear for such an event to be accomplished by a prince." I say. I don't want to think about the image we would make together. The next Sorcerer Supreme accompanied by the Prince of Eskendria.

"That is why I requested the presence of my favourite stylist." He smiles like a boy.

"So you invited this lady before asking me if I wanted to go with you?" I ask.

"I couldn't imagine why you would not want to go with me." He points at himself. "I believed you would need suitable attire for the night."

"You're sure it won't be a problem?" I ask.

"No one will be bothered, it rather shows your commitment to the situation." Nevan nods. "And it is rather suitable showing up with a partner to such events, I believe my brother is looking for one as well." At the thought of seeing Aleksander at the midsummer festival with someone at his side, a strange feeling settles in my stomach.

"What happens if people don't like me?" I shift my weight uneasily from foot to foot.

"No one will not like you." It isn't the answer I am looking for but the best I can get. "And if so, since when do you care what others think of you?" He winks at me. "Let's dance." The prince extended his hand to me.

I do not have time to object before the prince has pulls me in and leads me into the middle of my room. It is immediately obvious by the first turn that I have no idea what I am doing. My feet are more often upon his than they are on the floor, when could I have ever imagined I would need to know how to dance? The prince laughs, assuring me it is okay. His laugh is different to Aleksander's. I realise that I have never seen him genuinely laughing. The crown prince chuckles but laughing, smiling from ear to ear? Never seen before.

The prince is, surprisingly, a gentle and encouraging instructor.

"You need to calm," he soothes. I am very well aware of his palm on my hip.

"Why are you doing this?" I mumble.

"What do you think people do at a festival?" He smiles.

"How should I know? I've never been to one." I am stubbornly focused on my footwork.

"We dance." The prince laughs. He takes a step back and twirls me again. This time, I remember the steps. Prince Nevan leads me so gracefully and I tried my best to do so equally.

"You are getting it."

"Barely," I mutter, my eyes still on my feet. I hear a chuckle.

"Now look up," he says. I lift my head and look into his ocean blue eyes. Only now I realise how they are sprinkled with small brown sparkles. He is a handsome Elf.

Slowly, under the prince's hand and motivation, I begin to enjoy myself.

This is simpler than I would have ever expected. It is as if his eyes promise me only the truth. There is no cruelty, no anger. I stumble when his lips brush my cheeks.

"You are beautiful, you know?" the prince whispers thoughtfully.

"You are making fun of me, aren't you?" I smile.

"No, you are since I first saw the fire that lingers underneath this skin, I was captivated by your being and I wish to ensure everyone sees it at the midsummer festival." Sliding his palms down my forearms, the prince steps away from me with a kiss on my knuckles.

My heart is beating a bit faster than it should have.

CHAPTER EIGHTEEN

Prince Nevan leads me into an empty ladies room which looks as if it has always been used for fittings.

"Nazizza might scare you but she is the best. Even my mother got her dresses done by her." He winks at me.

The inside is full of different fabrics and textiles. A middle-aged lady comes from the back, her black hair is up in a ponytail and red glasses frame her ink black eyes. Believe me, there is no colour, only black.

"Hello, my prince, I see you are not alone, you have brought me the mortal." The woman comes up to me and gives me her hand. "I am Nazizza. And I will help you to look exquisite for the festival. Come with me, darling."

She takes my hand and pulls me into a separate room with lots of dresses and a stand in the middle.

"Please would you be so kind and get up there." Nazizza shows me the little stand and takes my measurements, while Prince Nevan is leaning in the door frame, his eyes eagerly on me.

Before I can ask a question, fabrics are held up against me. I stand there overwhelmed with so many colours.

"Is it possible to wear red and black?," I say suddenly.

"Pardon me?" Nazizza asks. "Maybe you want to consider something more lively, more colourful."

I look into her ink black eyes.

"I want to wear it this way, Nazizza, no discussion," I say firmer than I have intended to.

"Aedlin, maybe consider this light green. They are Elves colours and I think would be more suited for such an event—" Nazizza is back to her talk.

"Let her wear what she pleases," Prince Nevan says suddenly. "It definitely has a reason, and as the designer you should respect the customers wishes even if they are not yours, Nazizza" His eyes catch mine and he winks at me.

"In that case I will have to get additional black fabric. But just that you know. If the High King is unleashed with this outfit it was not my fault!" Nazizza says and excuses herself.

"I hope I did not offend her." I walks towards Prince Nevan.

"No you certainly did not, however, why are you so persistent in wearing these particular colours?" He smiles.

"Red has been my mothers favourite colour." I simply say.

"Whatever you wear may it be velvet, green or obsidian you will look stunning." He puts a loose strain of my hair behind my ear. "Just remember to save a dance for me when every man on the court is begging to dance with you."

"I don't think this will happen, have you seen my dance skills?" I joke looking up at him with a slight smile.

"Then I will have a dance?" Prince Nevan asks again as we step into the hallway.

"Actually, you already had one." I press my lips together in a little grin. He turns around and his face is too close to mine again. He looks me in the eyes but then drops his gaze to my mouth. "Another?" he whispers.

"How could I refuse?" I say quietly and blush at the intensity of his glaze. I laugh, getting used to his normal state. The casual prince.

Then Prince Nevan's eyes focuses on something behind me and he straightens up, make some space between us.

"Hello brother," Prince Nevan says sweetly. Aleksander looks confused between us. He swallows a few times and then his icy mask is on again.

"How did the council with father go?" The blond-haired prince seem to be pleasantly unaware of the tension in the room.

"Very well," Aleksander says. His voice is as cold as ice itself. I want to open my mouth but there is nothing I could have said.

"I will need help in planning this nonsense of a festival, would you like to meet me in ten minutes in my chambers, *brother*?" he says casually, as if it is something normal to say. Aleksander leaves us.

"Always in such a good mood, my brother." Prince Nevan laughs.

The Prince leans in, kisses me on my red cheek and leaves me standing in the hallway room.

-

The next day started soon enough. The whole palace is occupied with servants running around trying to finish setting up the festival.

A knock on my door.

"Come on in!" I shout from the bathroom. I hear tiny footsteps approaching me and I know it is Salem who entered my room.

"Are you insane?" she asks. "Attending the midsummer festival side by side with Prince Nevan?!" She takes a deep breath. "How all saints did you end up in this position?" Her expression changes to curiosity.

"How do you know?" I ask.

"There is a reason why I am the general of the Golden Legion, nothing slips through my glaze. I noticed that Nazizza was here in the palace and it doesn't make sense for her to come again. Unless there was a visitor coming shortly. I knew that Prince Aleksander would have nothing to do with that, he despises such things. So the only person who would have the power to ask Nazizza to come back to the palace was Prince Nevan. He told me ... and gave me this." She steps outside the bathroom. I follow her into my bedroom and a red gown is placed on my bed. It looks rather majestic. Nazizza owned her name of being the best dressmaker.

The fabric is soft but shimmered in the light. She has created a red silk dress from where a shimmery back skirt goes until the floor.

"Now get ready!" Salem drags me out of my thoughts.

"I know, I am probably late, aren't I?" I ask her while brushing my hair.

"Desperately late, Aedlin."

What a fuss. I would have to hurry. I let her help me with my dress. The fabric is as soft on my skin as it looked. I believe the quality was only the best of the best. I think I look weird wearing such things. Going to events like this. Who have I become?

"You look delightful, Aedlin, like a warrior queen. Trust me every single person in this room will stare at you." That really helps to calm me down. The red dress reaches my ankles, the texture feels light as if I am barely wearing anything. The red silk is covered with black glitter making it look as I am on fire. Nazizza has done magnificently.

"Will you also be there, Salem?" I ask, hoping she will be by my side. I have to admit I am extremely nervous, entering a room full of important High Elves, me the only human.

"Sadly, I did not get an invitation from the prince but as the general I will be present at the event as well." She squeezes my hand, which probably is quite sweaty. I am glad she doesn't say anything.

A knock.

Prince Nevan.

Salem opens the door and I don't know what to say. His hair is down, not as he usually wears it in a ponytail. Instead of wearing his usual dark green colours, Nevan has switched to dark blue. It would rather be simple if not his vest is decorated with small patterns of fabric, yet, it suits him very well. He is a handsome Elf.

Our eyes meet. He opens his mouth but closes it again.

"Is his royal highness out of words?" I joke while walking towards him. It is rather difficult to walk in such high shoes. I curse slightly under my breath once I nearly trip over my dress.

"His royal highness didn't expect to see a queen," he replies making me blush. Damn it. He holds his arm up waiting for me to link in.

"Seeing you now I am not quite sure if bringing you today was the right choice," Prince Nevan says. I quickly look down at my robe hoping everything is alright.

"I believe I cannot follow, my prince," I say.

"I hoped I could dance with you the whole day but looking at you, I think I'll be lucky to get at least one dance." He chuckles.

"You are too kind, my prince."

"You do look like a queen today, I have to admit I wasn't ready to see you like this."

"Like what?" I ask, curious.

"Like an Elf."

I don't know what to say to that. We approach two guards who are standing at a huge door. They exchange a confused look between them. I believe they did not expect to see Prince Nevan in company, but is it such a surprise?

"My Prince," both of them say while bowing. "And..." They look at me, not knowing my name.

"Lady Orbwood," he says with a calm voice as if I am his new toy to play with. But for today I don't care. I let it happen. Today I am Aedlin Orbwood, the next sorcerer. No little girl who hides in her hut. By my name they immediate widen their eyes as if it is known among the folk. It is funny to watch once they realise.

We step into the light, and I draw a deep breath.

"Presenting His Royal Highness Nevan Lèfevre, with his company, the future Sorcerer Supreme Aedlin Orbwood."

I am nearly blinded by the intensity of the light in the room. This is not a hall, it was a ballroom, its walls covered in mirrors. Yet, I can spot plants and trees everywhere. It reminds me of a magical forest in the dim light of the moon as if I am entering a wonderland. We walk down a long stairway which is challenging since I am not used to walking in high shoes. I am thankful for the subtle support Prince Nevan gives me.

People stop talking. I can only hear hushes and whispers, even though the lovely music continues to play. It seems like there are thousands of people present in this ballroom due to the mirror's reflection. I am unsure where to look first.

I suddenly feel small under the gaze of all of these eyes. *Future Sorcerer Supreme Aedlin Orbwood.* I will be the people's hope for the night. I would make them believe that I can save them all. If I don't believe in me they will never.

I walk slowly but steadily next to Prince Nevan trying to take in every detail of the room. I quickly notice that the people aren't only whispering about my name but about what I am wearing. I look around and see various shapes of sapphire and velvet, but I am covered in ruby red kissed by darkness. I am well aware of the low cut back of the dress.

In addition, I am in the company of the prince. This might be just as overwhelming for them as it is for. It is if they are shocked at not knowing their prince's up-to-date dating list.

I scan the crowd until I meet obsidian eyes. Standing with the royal family, there was a prince. Aleksander's face shows so many emotions at once that I have to smile. He doesn't notice or care that his jaw has dropped. I grin brightly at his wide eyes as I stride over to the royal family arm in arm with Prince Nevan. I feel a triumph having overwhelmed the Crown Prince.

The crown prince stares at me blatantly the whole way.

Chapter Nineteen

The whole room vanishes. I curse under my breath for my heart is beating faster than it should. His eyes never leave my side and I can feel how a blush establishes on my cheeks. This feeling is dangerous. I reach the small podium and try to dip into a graceful curtsey, which is not possible.

"Welcome to our midsummer festival Aedlin Orbwood," the High King says warmly but I know his words are lies. "I see you brought company, my son." He turns his attention towards his younger son.

"Indeed father," he sneers. The High King looks at me and I lower my head. I have to play this role of being the High King's pet, even if I despise it. Here are way to many meaningful Elves to create a scene.

"I am pleased to see that you have finally giving up on sleeping with various woman but please do not invite *her* in your bed room," he mocks. I am troubled with not letting him see any type of emotion but I am shocked by how easily these words come from his lips. I can feel how Nevan tightens under my hand. My gaze moves to Aleksander who carries a shocked expression on his face while looking between his brother and me.

"I hope you will enjoy the celebration," The High King adds.

"Thank you, my lord," I reply, keeping my head down.

"My son has a sense of fashion, maybe you should have listened to him. Your attire is rather atypical for an Elf court" I open my mouth unsure what to say. It feels like my tongue is numb.

"She looks beautiful," a far too familiar voice says. Aleksander's voice is soothing and deep, sending a shiver down my spine. The High King rolls his eyes and dismisses me. I can feel how the eyes are on me of the present Elves once I make my way to the little seating are under an Oak tree. Prince Nevan excused himself and joined the podium to properly greed incoming guests. I try to ignore the presence of my guards around me but it is inevitable . I try to paint a picture of his face in my head while I was walking down the stairs.

I pretend to be interested in the greeting and the other noble Elves entering but it is just an excuse to look at Aleksander. He looks amazing in his black coat that falls right above his knees and has a slit in the back. It is unbuttoned at the top making it possible for me to see the collar of his white shirt. The black jacket has stitched flames on the sleeves. Comparing him to some other Elves in the room, Aleksander does look stunning. While the others exaggerate their wardrobe and look like parrots, he looks elegant. I am well aware of the sensation in my storage once I acknowledge his presence. I should despise him. He almost killed me, his actions killed my parents, I should hate him but I realise that I grew fond of the Elf standing there in black.

I notice him glancing over at me from time to time. I cannot stop but gave him a small smile occasionally. My cheeks darken when faced with the intensity of his gaze. His expression is unreadable once our eyes cross. Does he has the same strange feeling or just his normal disgust in human?

I cannot fully ignore the people's gazes around me. Occasionally, people come up to me and thank me, even though, I haven't done anything yet. I try to act as normal as possible but sometimes I catch my fingers trembling. I notice several guards to the left of me who are involved in a heated discussion with Salem. She's managed to tame her black curly hair into a lovely smooth wav, and she looks absolutely stunning in her sunset orange dress which was kept simple, yet, looks breath-taking on her.

After an eternity, the High King calls for the Midsummer to begin. I fight with my fingers, unsure what to do now. The musicians have changed the opening music to something quieter, like a ballad. I have never heard such instruments played in harmony. At home, you barely even heard music, because no one could afford it and we barely had time to enjoy our free time with things like this. I am lost in trance that I haven't realised that Prince Nevan is standing in front of me.

"Lady Orbwood, will you grant me the honour of this dance?" My heart is beating a tiny bit faster when he dips into a half bow. I take his hand hesitantly. I promised him a dance, yet, faced to be dancing under the gaze of numerous High Elves make me nervous. His hand is rather soft, nothing I would have imagined from a Prince of War. I look over his shoulder and see Aleksander staring at us. We lock gazes for only a second until he turns around and continues his conversation.

Walking towards the empty dance floor a thought crosses my mind,

"The first dance," I hiss in his direction, suddenly aware of how many eyes are focused on us.

I try to calm myself and remember the steps he's taught me in private. Prince Nevan had years of experience and I am just stumbling clumsily around the room. But he navigates me effortlessly. His hands are soft as they guide me and his arms are supportive to prevent me from falling.

"Why the first dance, isn't there someone else you want to charm?" I whisper.

"Maybe it is you I want to charm." He flashes me a dazzling smile.

"But everyone is watching," I protest while looking over his shoulder and seeing all the Elves watching.

"Let them watch. Just enjoy this moment. Try to forget the others, it's just you and me, dancing," he says close to my ear so I can feel his breath in my neck. He pulls away, and I look up at him. The rest of the room disappears. My head become empty and I focus on the man in front of me who is guiding me steadily over the dance floor.

"Smile, Aedlin. You look beautiful when you do so," he says and my cheeks flush unintentionally.

We continue dancing for the next two dances until someone taps the Prince's on the shoulder.

"My Prince, may I?" A gentleman gives a small bow.

I am not looking forward to dancing with a stranger but I guess I have no say. I dip into a courtesy and the Elf starts to dance with me through the room. He is talented, for sure. But not as skilled as the Prince himself. I cannot stop myself from looking across the room, trying to find a familiar pair of dark eyes. My gaze stop when I see Aleksander talking to some ladies of the court. I know I shouldn't but the image gives me a feeling I do not like. But what did I expect, that he would be the odd one out who is standing alone? He is the crown prince after all and the most desired bachelor in the kingdom. I cannot stop thinking if he would have asked me for a dance if Prince Nevan hadn't.

Prince Nevan is right. I don't remember how many people I danced with. After each dance there was another gentleman who would be *honoured* if I danced with him.

Luckily, none of them asked me serious questions. I kept up the facade of the gifted human who was grateful to be chosen to fight in this war.

After listening to thousands of different stories about how honoured they were to finally meet me or how beautiful I was, I finally excused myself. I do not want to believe Prince Nevan but he is right, I am the centre of attention. Yet, I am delighted to see some faces from the town in the halls of the palace. Aleksander really kept his promise. He would be a great High King – he just needs someone to support him in every way possible. He could not do this alone.

I have to get some fresh air so I move towards the balcony. I welcome the breeze through my hair. The sun has made place for the moon on the star-lit sky. The temperatures have defiantly dropped over the past days but it is not uncomfortable to be outside only dressed in light attire. I look over a garden which resembles a huge labyrinth. The moon is displayed on the water surface underneath the terrace. I cannot stop myself from admiring the beauty of this place. I take a deep breath in through my nose and out through the mouth trying to calm my trembling hands. Why am I afraid? I have accepted my faith, why am I hesitating?

"Fear is nothing people should be ashamed of" I hear a deep voice.

I turn to the side where it comes from and see the Crown Prince coming from the shadows.

"I am not ashamed," I say sweetly.

"I am just pointing out that everyone now and then is afraid," he says calmly.

"So you are afraid as well? Afraid of what is coming?" I almost whisper.

"There are things I am afraid of, yet I do not consider it a weakness. Fear is a resemblance of strength. Fear indicates that you have acknowledged the danger of the situation." He steps beside me, "Yet too much fear can hinder us from acting as we should and to little will make us reckless." I listen to his words trying to understand their meaning.

"What are you doing outside?" I ask

"The same as you, escaping this chaos of people." He admits with a small smile. I am confused of how to interact with the calm Prince.

"Shouldn't you be inside dancing with the ladies of the court? I can see they are all staring at you," I point out.

"Even though they are delightful I am not interested." He chuckles.

"Why is that?" I ask curiously. "Shouldn't you secure the royal bloodline?" I add boldly.

"Oh, Aedlin, I indeed should but I do not wish for my children to grow up in a world as dark as it is currently. I am eager to change it all, yet this will take time," he says with sorrow. "And despite that I am not a lover of these women's fashion trends. All these colours and scents. It feels pathetic in these dark times." He swallows. "I am looking for a certain someone who can understand me, someone who will be my equal because we have a lot in common, not because I am the Crown Prince."

"I am certain she will be out there," I say.

His eyes meet mine. "I am certain of it as well, Aedlin." I feel how I blush but am thankful of the dim light so he cannot notice.

"I am delighted to see the towns people filling the hall." I swallow, "Thank you for taking my advice." He looks at me with a face I cannot sort out.

"I have focused greatly on the development of the war, that I have forgotten how much my folk has suffered. I cannot even remember the last time I have visited the city." His eyes drift away from my face and scan the garden. "I have initiated a rescue missions for all the Elves who have suffered greatly from the war and offered them to stay in the palace." I cannot believe what I am hearing.

"Do not look at me like that, my dear." Aleksander said with a small smile, "It makes me believe you have thought so little of me."

"As mentioned before, I am not your dear and I am just surprised by what you are willing to do for the folk, yet, people are not talking about you with much delight." I add in sorrow.

"I am aware of my status in their conversation. I believe they would have preferred to have Nevan as heir and me as their useless Prince." He said stiff.

"I don't think that is true," I face him, "I believe the people deserve to see the true Aleksander. The true man behind the facade who cares and risks his life." I swallow.

"A true man? I believe that is the first time you called me like that. No Elf, no creature but a man." He moves closer to my face, "Have I grown attached to your heart?" He smirks. I am confused of the sudden change of atmosphere and my loud heart beat makes it hard to think straight which is why I take a step back. "Don't be foolish, my prince. I just want the best for the Kingdom." I say loud but my voice sounds dull. I can see how his expression has changed to the cold Prince.

"Seeing you with my brother today," He swallows and turns towards the railing, "Reminded me of your mother and how she has found the person she would die for." I look confused at his profile.

"I want to assure you that even the High King has declared you as property of the crown you are still a woman and may do however you wish … with whoever you wish to." I cannot contain my laughter and bust out.

"Aleksander, what are you saying?" I smile at him.

"I am just pointing out, that he can make you happy. My brother has a great heart. This has always been easy for him, people love him." His voice grows thin, nothing left of the intimidating Prince.

"Aleksander, I can assure you I am not interested in finding my soulmate here. I am risking my life, who says that I will survive all of this. Who says that I will have a future. You are having thoughts I haven't allowed myself to have." I say with sorrow.

"Then why are you his company? Do you have any idea how this looks to the other Elves? Opening the midsummer festival with you?"

"I am his company because he has asked me." I say numbly. "You could have asked me, and I would have said yes, but you did not" I add. A silence establishes between the two of us. I can see how he swallows.

"Would you prefer me over any Elf in the room to dance with?" He steps closer to me.

"Is this an invitation?" I whisper.

"Maybe." His voice is as quiet as mine. It feels like this moment is not allowed to exist. He holds out his hand and I cross the remaining space between. His right hand is placed on my waist and my right hand is placed in his left one. I put my free hand on his shoulder admiring the texture details.

He dances differently than his brother but I enjoy it even more. He guides me through the gentle push of his hand and the movements of his hips to the faint sound of music coming from the inside. The closeness of him makes my head dizzy. I can smell his scent of ash and burned wood. I close my eyes and feel his touch, his breath, his smell. I feel him with every sense I possess.

He pulls me half a step closer in the next turn. It is now impossible to move without touching each other. A warm feeling settles in my stomach. When his hand shifts from my waist to the area of my lower back, gooseflesh dots my arms. I look up and he meets my eyes. I don't know what to say.

"I am envious of your friends and of my own brother," he says quietly.

"Why?" I ask, not looking away.

"It seems so easy for them to be around you, and here I am struggling to ask you for a dance. What kind of man is that?" he says, pulling me an inch closer in the next turn.

"You are the crown prince, you can have whatever you want."

"Indeed, but sometimes I would like to be a normal man. Someone who does not have to think about politics and regulations." A shadow covers his face.

"Maybe tonight, you can be a normal man," I say.

A fire ignites behind his eyes. I can feel his breath on my cheek. We are standing too close for this to be a formal dance. I don't move but I should have. This isn't right, but on the other hand, I am shocked by how badly I want this.

"Ah, there you are Aedlin."

Aleksander immediately pushes me away, creating a safe distance between us as if nothing has happened. I am still too overwhelmed to realise that Prince Nevan has stepped outside on the balcony. He locks eyes with Aleksander,

"Hello brother, didn't think to find you out here," he mocks. Nevan's attention moves to me. There is something in his eyes I cannot really understand.

"Lady Orbwood, you are missed inside," he says monotone and turns around on his heel. I look back to Aleksander whose face was a mask of ice.

Over the remaining hours of the festival, I haven't had the chance to talk to either of the brothers. I want to demand an explanation for their weird behaviour. I am frustrated and hungry. The buffet has been untouched by me and I have to change this. I meander through the dancing bodies, trying not to stumble into them.

I am again overwhelmed by the variation in food and colours here. This is incredible. I cannot tell what anything was by looking at. I shovel a variety of foods onto my plate, grab something to drink and take a place on the designated tables. I decide to take first the … weirdly shaped chicken leg?

"My lady!" I hear to familiar voices shouting through the crowed. I focus on my plate hoping they will let me alone.

"My lady!" Blue hair covers my sight and suddenly I am in the presence of the delightful sisters from lunch the over day.

"You are remembering us, don't you?" The blue haired Elf asks, "I am Jane and this —"

"I am Lexa, my lady!" The orange haired woman interrupts her sister. "We are delighted to meet you hear and have never thought of your true identity to be this important for our future, my lady." I take a deep breath and prepare myself for the upcoming conversation.

"I am delighted to see you here as well, are you enjoying the Festival so far?" I ask.

"Oh indeed, my lady. It is perfect. Yet, we are a little confused by the presence of the towns people in the palace..." Lexa admits. I have to prevent myself from rolling my eyes.

"It has been my wish to have them here as well, symbolising the unity of the kingdom." I try to say as easy as possible so they understand.

"Of course my lady, how considerate of you." Jane says in her high pitch voice.

"So my lady, you are indeed human, aren't you?" He eyes widen with curiosity, "How is the mortal world? Is it similar to the Elven Realm?"

"Yes, my lady, please fill us in." Lexa adds in excitement. I let my cutlery down, I won't be eating anytime soon.

"The mortal world is far to huge for me to summarise it in only a few words considering I myself have not visited it all." They are hanging on my lips as if I would share with them my darkest secrets.

"I would love to visit your home town, one day, my lady." Lexa says with eyes wide open. I smile even though I can hardly imagine these two fragile Elves in my village.

"I believe once the time is right you may visit." I smile at her.

"My lady, I am mesmerised by the attire you have chosen for the night, I need to know the sewer. No wonder you have grabbed the attention of both of the Prince's." Lexa admits. I am surprised by the sudden change of topics but am thankful for not talking about my past life anymore.

"Don't be foolish, I have only grabbed people's attention because of who I am for them." I say calmly ignoring the feeling in my stomach.

"Yet, are you not considering at all, my lady? An alliance between the Royal house and the Sorcerer Supreme would be quite a statement for the world." The blue haired Elf wonders.

"I am open for what is good for the kingdom, yet, I am wandering of into realities that cannot be real. I am here to fight to risk it all no need to dream." I say a little too harsh than expected.

"But my lady, above all the pressure you have to carry on your shoulders, isn't it nice to dream just a little bit. To have something to fight for." Jane whispers in thoughts.

"Something worth risking it all." Lexa adds and I cannot stop myself to lift my head and look at the man dressed in black.

"I believe some dreams are allowed if they make you stronger." I say cryptically.

"Aedlin?" I hear a familiar voice calling for me. I turn my had and look into the grey eyes of Willow walking towards our table.

"Ladies," He nods his head towards the sisters. "Aedlin, would you like to dance with me." He says while bowing in front of me. He tries to keep a neutral face but cannot hide a smile. I look at the two Elves who are frozen in place by the picture. Do I maybe see a blush establishing on Jena's face. I look again to Willow examining his presence. Sure he is handsome. The suit looks exquisite on him. He is wearing a turquoise blazer with a crème button up underneath. On the jacket you see small gust of winds similar to the flames of Aleksander's jacket. And his smile might take other women breath away.

"Of course, it would be a pleasure." I smile at him and get up from my chair.

"It has been lovely to talk to you two." I say while turning away from the ladies.

"You know what, my feet are killing me. Would you like to go outside with me?" I whisper so only Willow can hear me.

"Of course, whatever the lady wants," he says mockingly. I link my arm in his and we leave the crowded hall and enter the balcony where I have met Aleksander not long ago. However, we don't linger long here. We continue going down the stairs into the palace gardens.

All the time I have spent in this world and I have never really investigated the beauty of the palace garden. During the night, the moon fills the garden with a mysterious light. You can almost consider it being romantic. I have no idea where we are heading but I follow Willow through the labyrinth.

"Thank you for saving me." I joke.

"My pleasure, I could see how much you enjoyed the presence of them." He replies with a smile.

"Have you seen how Jena was looking at you." I mock him.

"I believe you have misinterpreted, she might has seen the Prince." He says quickly. I decide to let the topic go.

"You look stunning in this dress. I envy you." Willow says and makes me blush.

"I have to say, I grew fond of it as well." I swallow, "First, I wasn't sure what to think of me wearing such garments when at home I made clear that I despise people who wear such things." I turn around and look him in the eye, "But someone has told me today that dreaming is not wrong." I say.

We walk towards a bench which was situated in front of a fountain. I feel how my pulse calms by the sound of the water droplets.

"You have made quite an expression on all of us." Willow says while taking a seat next to me.

"So I have heard." I almost say to myself.

"I know this whole situation is probably quite scary and overwhelming, I want you to know that Salem and I will always be there for you." He says while locking eyes with me. I can feel how my worried thoughts sooth under his words. We don't talk. We just exist and I am thankful for the calmness of his presence. I have never thought that I would count these Elves to one of my closest friends by now but I couldn't imagine a life without them.

Suddenly, I hear screams.

My face turn to Willow who looks to the palace balcony from where we have stepped outside. People are running around and screaming. What is going on.

"Willow?" I whisper grabbing his arm.

"I believe we have visitors." His says dangerously quiet. He gets up and looks around, moving like an animal.

"Aedlin, we have to get you out here." He whispers. "I believe they are coming for you." He wants to grab my hand but gets burst back from shadows lingering in the dark.

"Willow!" I scream and try to get up but I get grabbed by my shoulders and by the smell I am sure that the Syrivis have surrounded us. I try to get rid of them but their craws are too deep in my flesh. I let out a scream of pain by my movement. Willow gets up and nocks out the one Syrivis who pulled him back. I can feel how the wind increases around me.

"Aedlin get down!" He screams and I obey, ignoring the pain in my shoulder. I hear a gust of wind and the craws have been ripped out of my shoulders. This will leave scars. I cry out. I see how Willow runs towards me. "You have to run!" He says determinedly.

"No, I am not leaving you!"

"Don't be foolish!" I look at Willow's face but hear the voice of the Crown Prince. I get up and lock eyes with the Elf man. His eyes are black but a fire lingers behind his facade. I try rolling my shoulders which feel stiff but it ended in feeling a massive pain shooting through my arms, I smell blood.

"I am staying!" I say dangerously quiet. "They are here for me, and I do not wish any one to die because I have fled. I am no coward. You are the one not belong in here, my prince!" The Crown Prince moves dangerously close to me, his eyes have changed they are even darker. "I am here because I made an oath of protecting you, Aedlin!" He says furious. " And now stay out of danger!" He pulls me away so the Syrivis which was creeping up from behind gets burned by a flame which magically came from his hand.

"Leave!" he pushes me away and I can see the please in his eyes. I move a few steps back to focus on my breath and my magic. I am watching Willow and Aleksander fighting off these creatures with pure beauty. Their magic obeys them as it is a part of them. It looks amazing in the dim light.

I try to focus on my inner self but also try to keep an eye on the surrounding. There can be more lingering in the dark. I thought I have overreacted when I first encountered them in the woods, but indeed they look horrific. For some, their scalp is only covered with some scraps of skin, others are missing the flesh around their cheeks, looking like decayed meat. I have actually read that *Syrivis* means *walking shadows* in the old tongue, which sums up the creatures pretty well.

A smell of decay fills my nose and I turn around to see some are slowly stalking towards me, like they are a pack of wolves and I am their dinner. I get my dagger out of my dress and try to balance my feet. A creature to my right is sprinting towards me. I quickly jump to the left, turn and stick my dagger into the man's back, letting myself slide down and open up his back. The smell is immense and the scream is unbearable. It is an inhuman, high-pitched shriek. The first Syrivis is down.

I wipe away the blood spatters on my face, only to spread it even more as the blood from the dagger run down onto my hand. I choke. Suddenly, two Syrivis are attacking me at once. I try to remember what Henry has taught me in our daily lessons: balance, dodge, attack. I say as a mantra in my mind: balance, dodge, attack; balance, dodge, attack; balance, dodge, attack.

I don't see the one coming from behind me. He put his claws on my shoulder in the already existing wounds, pulling me back and I fall to the floor. The pain is immense, I see black for a second. I try to focus again and turn around, his claws still in my shoulder. I ignore the pain. I scream and stick the dagger into his stomach, causing it to vomit its body fluids on me. I don't know what it is made of but to be honest I don't want to know. The Syrivis collapses on top of me. I feel how I have reached my human body limits. With my last bit of strength, I push the dead body off me and get onto my feet. I feel sorry for the beautiful dress but right now it is incredibly inconvenient. I take my dagger and cut off the long skirt, giving me more leg freedom.

I feel how my knees shook. The Syrivis bare their teeth – well, some still have them, others don't – and run towards me. They deal more blows to me than I do to them. I feel my movements getting slower. My reaction time decreases. With the next attack I sink to my knees, gasping for air, trying to breathe away the pain. I cannot strain my right ankle any longer, if I do, an immense pain will shoot through my leg. I can hear the creatures surrounding me, not sure what to do. This is it, isn't it? I hope the others are okay.

I can hear them growl, yet I cannot move my body. A Syrivis traps my neck and pulls me up slicing my cheek open with its crawl. Its face is too close. I have to close my eyes.

A heat wave brings me back to consciousness and I open my eyes to see the Syrivis burning alive. A fire wall has been created in front of me and through it a fire lord steps. I am shocked to see his face, even though he is covered in blood he looks beautiful. I cannot tell what he feels in the moment, anger? Relief? Worry? I gasp for air and give him a thankful nod. I cannot manage to stand up.

My head is empty again. I can only focus on how Aleksander manages to keep the Syrivis away from him. His fighting is elegant, majestic. He is a born fighter. Behind him, I can see that Prince Nevan is fighting side by side with his men and Salem. Her beautiful black curls flying through the hair every time she goes for a hit. I have to be better. I have to be stronger than this. I clear my head and focus on who I am. On who I have become. I am the gifted one. The last of its kind. I am the prophecy.

The fire rises in me, it crackles in my veins, fingertips. This feeling scares me. I do not try to fight against it, my instinct is superior. Suddenly I feel a pulsation, a pinch, and the scent of smoke. My magic surrounds me now.

A Syrivis attacks me out of the blue and strikes me against a tree. Now the magic burns on my cheek, magic that is trying to get the upper hand. I feel like I get hit in the stomach. I try to fill my lungs with air but I have a hard time breathing. I am focusing my breath on the sensation of the magic flowing through my veins.

I get up again.

The fire comes out as blue flames and races to the Syrivis, covering the surrounding trees in red. I have to control the elements. I extinguish the fire on the trees to the right with water. Water that I have summoned out of the fountain. Slowly but carefully the Syrivis are still coming towards me: I can smell them, I can hear how the shadows pulsing through their veins, I can hear their breathing. They don't know that they are walking into a dangerous volcano which is about to erupt.

Energy is pulsing through my veins. I give in to the sweet promises of the magic. It is screaming for me and I give it everything I have.

The creatures are only inches away from me when I look up at them. I smile.

"Let the party begin," I say and open my arms, releasing a huge fireball, firing it toward the frozen creatures. I thrust my arm which is blazing with fire through the chest of one of the Syrivis, feeling joyful. It is just me and them, I forget everything else and let the magic control me. I take my dagger, turn around and slice the next one's throat open. I am covered in blood. I make eye contact with a monster, at least, I try to since it doesn't have eyeballs anymore. I feel the wind through my hair and the flames surrounding me rise higher. The Syrivis back away, trying to not get burned. I lift my hands in front of my body. I raise them and clap' forming a huge whirlwind once I slowly open them again. It wipes out the Syrivis coming towards me. I look to the right and see Aleksander's shocked face. He isn't the only one. I cannot believe I have just done that. I have not trained in this elemental power but still I manage to summon it as easily as the others. It is thrilling! I listen to my inner self. I do what feels right. It feels like the night in the forest, all seems to be natural. Suddenly, Aleksander's eyes widened but not in amazement.

A Syrivis has appeared behind, and thrust its crawls through the chest of the crown prince. I hear myself scream. The Syrivis smiles at me with its remaining face. I lift my hand and toss the Syrivis with a wind blaze against the nearest tree, away from him. I run towards Aleksander who has collapsed on the floor.

"Hey! Aleksander! Open your eyes!" I cry out, hoping he will obey. I put his head in my lap, ignoring the screams of soldiers around me. It is only him and I.

I look wide eyed at the crown prince's face. He tries to move but stops due to the pain. I shake my head trying to symbolise him he should hold still.   I press my hand to the wound on his chest. I go quiet once I pull it back and see how much blood coats it.

"You are stunning while you fight," he says while his eyes flutter.

"Aleksander, don't leave me, understood?! We need you!" I lower my head over his, whispering, "I need you." I press my hand again to his wound. I press as hard as possible, hoping it would help, hoping the bleeding would stop but it didn't. In this moment something changed in me. Facing the fear of loosing him. I will dedicate my life for him. Fight for his cause, fight because he has to survive. Only he can bring the Realm back to his origin. Without him I cannot win this. I check his pulse, it was faint but I feel it. His skin is still warm. I realise that I have never touched his skin besides is palm. I am confused by my feelings but I know I don't want him gone. I take his hand in mine, squeezing it tightly. Assuring him he is not alone. Nothing in response. His hand becomes limp in mine. I checked for his pulse. Silence.

I don't realise how I am gently pulled away from his limp body. Arms hold me in place once the healers brought Aleksander back to the palace. My hands are covered in blood. His blood. I let out a sob. I feel empty, as if the oxygen I need to breathe is gone. I sink on my knees, gasping, hoping the air can find its way back to me. It floats into my mouth, hissing through my throat. I grab it greedily, ignoring the pain. I will kill them all. I will wipe out the Dark One and kill them by myself.

A faint voice whispers the painful truth in my head: It should have been me, not him.

CHAPTER TWENTY

I refuse to be taken to the medical wing. I am fine, at least physically. I am thankful that no one speaks to me on my way back to my chambers. I assured Willow that I would be fine. He needs more help than I do. He got badly hit. His arm looked far from healthy.

The halls are empty. I haven't heard anything about Aleksander's state but I guess I will be the last one to know since it is none of my business. Right now, I just want to get out of my ruined clothes. I haven't seen Salem, I hope she was is okay.

I storm into my room which is empty. No lights. No Salem. I was secretly hoping to find her waiting for me. I don't want to admit it but I want company. I have … I have killed and I have enjoyed it. I am afraid of myself. I rip off the clothes which are soaked in blood and throw them in the corner of my room. I don't have time for a bath. I go for a shower.

I let the warm water wash away my sins and blood. I hope it would erase the memories but it doesn't. I cry. I scream. I let it all out. I let my emotions take over. I sink to my knees, the water flowing over my head. I don't know how long I have stayed in this position without moving, but I know I needed it. I have held it all together for so long but truth is that I miss the old me. The me who wandered off into the woods to hunt. The me who was the shadow of the town.

Once the water is cold I get out and drag myself to the bed where I cover myself in blankets and fall into a restless sleep.

I am in a field. Lots of people are gathered here to see ... what? There is a stage, made of wooden pallets. I can hear people shouting.

"Thief!"

"Liar!"

"He deserves worse!"

Who are they talking about? I try to squeeze myself through the crowd to get to the front. I stumble. I see the High King with not as many wrinkles as he has currently. And I see a young prince, undoubtedly Aleksander. He looks like about fifteen or sixteen but Elves do age differently. He doesn't look as terrifying as he does now. He looks like a child who has been forced to give up his childhood too soon.

"We have gathered here together to bestow justice upon this. He is a thief and a liar, once a well-known soldier in the Royal guard, now a nobody," the High King says firmly. "This man doesn't deserve to be killed by my hand which is why the honour of this kill belongs to my son, Aleksander."

The crowd is celebrating as if this was a joyful event. I can tell from Aleksander's eyes that he is not doing this freely. He is being forced to take this man's life. Forced to kill him.

"My son?" The High King steps aside leaving enough space for the young crown prince. He takes out his sword. I see that his hand is shaking.

Is this the first time he has to kill someone? The man isn't begging for mercy or pleading his innocence. He looks the boy in the eyes and nods. Assuring him it is okay. Assuring that once this is done nothing would change. But for Aleksander, everything will change once he has cut the man's throat. I don't want to look. I don't want to see the moment he finally broke. But even though this is just a memory, I want to be there for him. Aleksander lifts his sword with both hands and lets it slide through the soldier's neck as if it is butter. He doesn't look away. His gaze is locked upon the limp body of a former soldier. The audience is cheering and the High King is smiling. This is some sort of evil joke. This is entertainment for them. I could puke at the sight of it. Aleksander slowly tears his eyes from the dead body. His expression is numb.

Born is the Cruel Prince and the Wicked Kingdom will rise.

I wake up soaked in sweat. I try to recover from what I saw in my dreams. I come back to reality – to the realisation that our Crown Prince is in danger, living on the edge. But I cannot stop wondering what the dream meant. Obviously, they have a connection. I have gained insight into a memory of Aleksander's. Why now? Why this memory? I let out a frustration groan and press a pillow over my head. I hiss. I forgot how painful the movement is with my sore muscles.

A knock on the door. I don't have time to respond until the door flies open and Salem storms into the room.

"Good saints! I was looking all over for you. You weren't in the hospital wing nor were you in the wounded area." She comes to the bed. "I couldn't ask anyone due to the troubled circumstances we were in. They … we were all busy … saving him." I take her hands in mine. They are trembling. I feel guilty for sleeping, seeing her now so restless and tired as if she hasn't closed an eye for the whole night. She was out there helping people who needed help and what did I do? I cried like a baby. I should have helped them, been out there.

I am afraid to ask the real question, the question which haunts my thoughts.

"How … is he?" I ask. Salem takes a deep breath. It is nerve wracking.

"He lost a lot of blood and the healers were trying their best. According to them he shouldn't be alive, he should have been dead." *Should have*. Should have. He is alive!

"They were suspicious about his wellbeing so they examined him, looked deeper. They found magic." I move closer to her, not letting go of her hands. "Magic?" I repeat.

"Some strong magic helped him survive. It healed him. Magic is like a signature of the Elves. Every Elves magic is different and individual. However, this magic was different, stronger, not yet registered in our folders. But I checked myself, I used my magic sight, it seemed so familiar." I note in my head that every Elf has a magical fingerprint.

"You were the one who saved him, Aedlin!" she cries. "It was your magic I saw, we all saw!" She is almost shouting now being energetic. Probably the aftermath of her long working hours. But me? I saved him?

240

"No this cannot be. I … I tried to help but I couldn't. This was my fault." Now it's her time to take my hand.

"Don't be stupid, whatever you felt at the moment he died … it created the need to save him. You wanted to save him with every bit of your body and soul. You wielded an immense accumulation of magic in your sorrow. He is alive because you saved him." I let out a breath I haven't realised I was holding. This feeling is odd. I am relieved, of course, that the Crown Prince is safe. Shouldn't we all be? But there is something else, deep down inside me. I shut the door to these emotions. This is a problem for the future. I listen to my inner self and found that the troubling feeling vanished into nothing. I feel suddenly very calm.

"That's amazing and terrifying at the same time!" I say.

"I know right! Half the palace knows what you did and due to your credibility, the High King himself wants an audience with you," Salem says, speaking nervously now.

"The High King wants an audience?" I whisper.

"Yes, I am sorry, Aedlin. I tried to explain but … he strongly believes that you acted out of order." Saints.

"Now?" I ask hoping she would say no.

"Now."

—

I am nervously walking through the halls of the palace. Too quiet to be normal. Knowing that Aleksander is alright relieved me, but I am unsure what consequences I would be facing.

Guards open the door to a congress room I haven't yet encountered. I take a deep breath in.

I will take the judgment with pride. He cannot make me small, make me feel worthless if I have saved his son's life.

I enter the room. A massive wooden table is in the middle of it. The High King is placed at the head of the table, to his left Prince Nevan. He would defend me, right? He would have told his father that I had no intention of killing the Crown Prince.

"Aedlin Orbwood." The High King's voice is deep and firm. "A festival is dedicated to you and still you managed to give yourself special treatment." I look into his face, trying to hide my shocked expression.

I want to avoid it. Whenever I look at him face to face I am terrified he would be able to read me. Read my mind, see my thoughts, know my fears. Even though we are meeting privately, the crown is firmly placed on the King's head. It is as if he has to remind each and every one of his status.

He is intimidating and cruel in every aspect.

I don't know where to start, how to explain myself. Is it useful to justify myself in front of the law itself? I look to Nevan, hoping he would defend me but apparently, everything is more interesting than me. Of course. Why would he help *me?* The realisation is surprisingly hurtful. I thought we are more than this. I thought I am more for him than just a tool.

"How can it be that a *servant* to the country was found at the scene of my son's accident?" The King speaks quietly. "Sneaking through the folk and risking the life of hundreds of innocent Elves." I try to interrupt him but he continues to talk. "After your little display in the gardens, they know for sure now that you are here. You endangered several guards; in fact you endangered everyone present, *including* the royal family. The Crown Prince could have died because he was stupid enough to risk his life for something so … so pathetic as you. You are a tool, Aedlin. You may not be a human but you are also not one of us. I need you, I will use you. You shall not enjoy yourself in the palace, you shall practice and work TO WIN THIS WAR FOR ME." He screams the last words. I try not to flinch. I hate appearing vulnerable.

"My lord …" I try to speak up.

"Who gave you the right to speak? The fact that you apparently saved my son? This had nothing to do with you, it was luck. Do not feel special or hope for special treatment. Because you won't get any. He only got hurt because of your existence. If you were not here, he would not have got hurt—"

"If I was not here, you would not have the slightest chance of winning this war. You're lucky that I was there to save the Crown Prince. I may be a pathetic human but I am still the future Sorcerer Supreme, and if my studies are correct, the Sorcerer Supreme stands above the High King. And if you want to have me on your side, I demand to be treated with respect from your side because without me, you are dead." I see how the High King opens his mouth just to close it again.

"How dare you raise your voice to your High King?!" he growls, rising from his throne.

"I offer you the same treatment you give me. We are equals and I wish to be treated as one, *my lord.* I am no subject of yours who you can treat as you wish!" I hiss.

"The only reason you are still standing on my grounds alive is because my son is breathing."

"And he is alive because of me not because of you. You, my lord, did nothing for this kingdom!"

The High King walks towards me. I will not step back. I do not flinch when he put his long cold fingers around my neck. "If this happens again, I will order my son to kill you himself." I know that he isn't talking about Nevan, he means the son I have saved; the son who knows something I don't even know. Has he seen the tension between us? Impossible. There is nothing between us. His grip strengthens around my neck and I have trouble grasping for air. He let me go and I move my hand to my throat, trying to get more air in.

"You are excused," he says in disgust as if touching me burned him. My eyes meet Nevan's and I could see the excuse in his eyes. He cannot help me because he is under the authority of his father. Of course. He doesn't hate me. I walked out of the room with as much pride as possible and promised myself one thing.

I will bring down the reign of the High King.

Chapter Twenty-One

I make my way back to my room when a sudden dizziness overcomes me. Darkness. I have to stop at the next pillar and lean against it. Shadows. Screams. People. I squeeze my eyes shut, the pain is immense. My head feels like it is exploding. The pictures are unclear, blurry. A hut … no not just any hut, *my* hut.

People are running around, being chased. Blood, death.

And it is gone. My head is clear again as if nothing has happened. But they are in danger. Finley!

I have a new goal. I need to go back there. I have to help them. It is still my home and it is in danger.

I suddenly halt. I can never get back to the village alone. I need help. Willow.

I run towards the apprentice chambers and knock on the door I thought is his.

"Aedlin? Wh—"

I storm into his room. "I need your help, Willow. I—I had a vision. I saw my village and the people were in danger. Shadows were chasing them. They were looking for me! I need to go back. What if people were hurt? What if—"

"Hey, Aedlin, focus. Visions?" he asks softly.

"Yes, they've been happening when I'm dreaming. I've never seen something being awake. It was unclear but I am sure. Willow, I am sure!"

He walks around the room. "The Syrivis being outside of this Kingdom is unusual but it is possible. If they have managed to create vessels which can conduct their magic it is possible for them to survive in non-magical territory." He grabs my shoulders. "Are you hundred percent sure?" I nod.

"Okay, let's go. Tell Salem to cover for you, no one is allowed to know that you are gone. Not after what happened."

"Yes."

"It seems like having you around is never boring." He smirks.

-

We decide to vanish under the cover of darkness. Salem will give us a day. If people were asking for me she will tell them I am sick or I was hit harder than we thought in the battle. I trust her. She will figure something out. I have to see for my own eyes what has happened across the border. Everywhere I go, darkness follows. I cannot protect everyone. How can I protect a whole Kingdom if I cannot even take care of my town?

My riding skills are non-existent so I am sharing a horse with Willow. The wind is lashing in my face. The night is as clear as usual and the woods are as scary and mysterious as always. I am thankful for Willow's help, even though he is still recovering from his injury. However, he assured me that he is fine. Something about Elves are healing faster than humans, he has mumbled.

No visions have returned but I am worried to my core.

I just disappeared. They must think I have died. Finley must think I am dead. What will happen if I just appear back there? What if no one is there to welcome me back? What if I come too late? I quickly push the thought aside, we will know once we enter my old home town.

I can feel how Willow tenses under the chilly night wind. I have not returned to the woods from where I first came from. Willow is focused on our surroundings as if he was searching for something.

"What is wrong?" I ask with worry and let my eyes scan the area.

"It is quiet." He says, "Normally this part of is full with Fae."

"Fae?" I repeat.

"Yes, Fae, beings that lure you in and make you promise things you never thought you would give." He says his voice cold. "We are on the edge of crossing the Fate, a area of the death. This is the place where your people as well as our people will go after they have died to ascend into their next life. The Fate is beautiful but it is rather dangerous to cross it unguarded. Creatures of your darkest nightmares are lingering in the fog." He adds. A cold shiver goes down my spine and I squeeze myself closer to Willow.

The Fate, an area where the death are waiting to ascend to their next life. My parents have probably seen this place and went through it. I wonder where they are now.

The woods grew darker and a strange silence establishes among the branches.

"If I say run, you will run , understood?" Willow whispers.

"Why are you saying this now?" I try to find something in the night that would explain his weird behaviour.

"The Fate is no place for an Elf to be. It is even dangerous for us who are trained warriors." He mutters. "Elfhame has agreed to a deal between the Elven and Fae Realm to never set foot in this territory. This is the Fae's hunting region and if they find us there is no way back." I swallow. In my memory this place has been magnificent, filled with light and colour.

"Why has nothing attacked me once I entered?" I ask curious.

"Fae are being of the night, they get their power from the moon and the stars above. You were lucky that is was day time, otherwise, you would have died the moment you stepped into this world." He says numbly. Lovely. Somehow this whole world wants to see me dead. I take a deep breath and continue to look around me but the closer we get to the Fate the harder it becomes to see through the fog. Eventually, I can hear voices. Starting as silent mumbles; becoming cries.

"Try not to listen to the voices," Willow advices, "They are there to lure you in their nest. It is not real." He emphasis the last sentence with great strength. I try to focus on the breathing of the house running through the darkness, but a familiar cry catches my attention.

"Mother?!" My head turns to both sides.

"Aedlin, ignore it!" Willow orders.

"*My sunshine!*" There her voice again.

"This mothers voice!" I try to get through to Willow ignoring the noises around me. "You said yourself, that the fallen once will cross the Fate to go to their next life, what if my mother is here?" I say hysterically. I get pushed against Willow back once he brought the house to stop.

"Aedlin, Listen to me, to my voice to my breathing. Ignore them. You mother is dead, and she is not here. Trust me!" The look in his eyes was pity and sorrow. I swallow but nod. He tightens the reins and the bourse continues its gallop through the mist. The voices grow louder and louder. I can hear my mother screaming my name. Begging me to come back to save her from what awaits her in the night. I burrow my face in Willows back to hide from the memories these voices bring up. I can feel how tears make their way down my cheek.

"It is not real." I hear his voice through my head. I don't question how it is possible for me to hear Aleksander's voice but I let me consciousness take over.

As if someone has poured cold water over my head, I can feel that we made it to the other side of the Fate. I lift my head and look into Willows face which looks a bit anxious. Did he hear voices as well?

I look around and nothing seems to be as it was once I entered. No church no forbidden city.

"When I entered it looked different." I admit.

"Indeed, the fate entrance looks different every time, so no one really knows where it is located." He says. "How did you know then?" A small smile establishes on my face. "Intuition." He smiles. The sizzling in the air is no more, the magic is gone. This is all mortal, vulnerable. Even though it is night time, the landscape looks dull.

From now on I am the leader and Willow will follow my lead. This forest is my home. I also realise, with shock, that his pointy ears are gone.

"Magic, as well. We don't want people to freak out the second they see me, right?"

Right. I don't need that right now. The forest seems like I have left yesterday. It is still cold. The snow is sparkling on the dead branches. Everything is the same, except me. I am not the same as I was when I left. I have changed. And I am trying to accept the new me.

We quietly walk over tree trunks and dirt. Willow is surprisingly quiet as he moves. Considering his height, I cannot hear a sound from him walking on the crunched ice.

Soon, I stop. There it is – the gate to my hometown. The gate to my miserable life. It is quiet. Unusual, as despite the late hour, people would usually be outside. In the market, trading or sitting at a campfire. Nothing.

It smells funny. Rotten. Is my memory of my village so wrong? But this smell wasn't here before. I walk faster towards something laying on the floor. I kick it, nothing. It rolls over and I try to hide my disgust in the sleeve of my coat. A human, dead. It would have been normal for me to see death. So many people have died over the winters due to the cold. But this man didn't freeze to death, he was killed. His face is half *eaten*. As if someone has ripped out a part with their bare teeth. I had to turn around.

"Although animal attacks are not unusual for this place ... this looks like a Syrivis bite." Willow confirmed the worst. So I was right. They have been here.

I am too late. I run towards my old shabby hut and throw the door open. A cold shiver runs down my spine.

We will find you, is written on the wall. I doubt the Syrivis bought red paint to leave the message.

I go outside, I run towards the market. I see more and more faces in the mud. More and more lives have been taken because of me. They died because they are innocent. None of them knew where I was. I cannot help but let out a sob.

"They died because of me!" I said, mumbling into Willow's chest.

"Hey, hey. They died because they were at the wrong place at the wrong time." There is no life left. The last remaining of my humanity is erased.

Finley! I need to find him. I push myself away from Willow and run towards his house. The house which is so familiar to me.

I stop my hand before I can knock on the door. What if he doesn't want to see me? What if he is angry? What if he is dead?

I look over my shoulder at Willow standing here in my home, dressed in casual clothes, prepared for the worst. The first time I met the quiet apprentice boy I could have never thought of what he is capable of doing. He stands there tall giving me space, scanning the village with his grey eyes.

I take a deep breath and knocked.

Silence.

Too long.

There is no one there.

No one will open the door.

I lost him.

But then. Light. I hear voices. A deeper voice lecturing them to be quiet.

Finley.

The door opens and there he is. Alive. He looks tired and exhausted but we all do. I try to take everything in from his brown hair to the freckles on his nose.

I missed him. Did he miss me? The question is answered when he pulls me into a hug. I am thankful for that. Thankful for the acceptance.

"Aedlin, where have you been? I was sick with worry. After our fight ... you left, I thought I'd lost you forever," he says into the curve between my shoulder and neck.

"I am sorry, Finley. I shouldn't have left without a word. But I was so angry and I acted irrationally. I came back because ..." He pulls away to look at me. "What happened, Finley?" His joyful expression has changed into a dark one.

"We were attacked. Attacked by ... by things. I don't know. I have never seen such things before." His voice trembles. I don't want to imagine what they have been through.

"I am so sorry, Finley. That is all my fault." He looks me in the eye. "What do you mean, your fault?"

I swallow the lump in my throat. "They came here looking for ... me," I say.

"For you?" Only now he realises Willow's presence. "Who is that?"

"That's my friend."

"Pleasure meeting you. My name is Willow." He introduces himself, offering his hand. Finley stands still there, not moving, not accepting Willow's hand.

"Finley?" I push.

His eyes meet mine and I know he has figured it out. He is a smart boy. Our fight about the Elves, me leaving unannounced, coming back ready to fight these creatures.

"You are one of them,"He whispers. I don't know what to say next. "How could you? They killed us! The Elves were destroying this village only days ago! How can you be one of them!"

"Finley, you're wrong! Please calm down. Can we please go somewhere private? I promise you, we wish you no harm. I just want to explain everything to you." I sincerely hope he will agree to it.

He pauses, considering my explanation. Then he nods and invites us inside. And I tell him everything. From the moment I entered the forbidden city to now. I don't know for how long we sat there but in the end, he is speechless.

We sit there quietly. No one is talking.

"I know this is a lot, but please try to understand," I say finally.

"So you are part of some sort of sick prophecy. Why are you allowing them to use you?" He asks.

"I—" I realise that I don't know. I do everything they ask me to do even though I could have fled. But then what? Would they kill my people so I would be forced to come and help them?

"They don't use me, well, they don't force. The High King insists I am a tool to them, but I try to ignore that for now as it would not help the situation. I agreed because my gift is their last hope. I want to help. This is my destiny. This is who I am supposed to be," I say honestly.

"So you'd rather help some rich nobles than your own people?" He says, furious.

I am surprised by how angry he sounds.

"You left us here. Do you just have a better life there? How is it to be fed, to be in a warm bed, not to worry about surviving?!"

"Finley, you are irrational, you don't mean what you say

"Oh, and now you tell me what I think? Mind manipulation, can you do that? I don't want to be tricked in some sort of game,"He says while standing up.

"Do you think that little of me?" My voice is filled with rage. How can he say such things? "Yes, I don't have to worry about food or clothes over there but do you think it's enjoyable that so many people want to see me dead? I don't fight for myself, I fight for a nation. People believe in me. People trust me over there. Something you don't."

"I used to trust you, Aedlin. Fuck, I loved you! I loved you all these years but I was just some tool for you, weren't I? You needed the attention. You wanted to be wanted. To be touched."

"Finley! That's enough," I say, furious.

"Oh, and you." He turns himself to Willow. "Do you like to fuck her? Isn't it nice?! Her skin is so soft. Her hair smells divine, doesn't it? Do you at least enjoy it?" He is drunk. How could I have not realised that before. The smell. The whole house stinks of it.

"Finley! STOP IT!" I try to push him away from Willow who sits there uninterested in what Finley has said. He would interfere once I say he can. This is my fight to fight, not his. But it is good to know I have some back up.

"Willow and I are *friends*. No, we didn't sleep together and no I didn't sleep with anyone else there. What is wrong with you?!"

"Leave right now."

"Finley, we should talk once you are sober."

"I am sober enough to tell you that I don't want to see you ever again in my life. You died the day you left. You are dead for me. You are dead to this town, well, more precisely the town is dead because of you. You are a worthless whore used by evil. You should have died in the woods."

I know he doesn't mean it, oh saints, I hope he doesn't. But I cannot control my rage. I hit him in the face.

"Do *not* talk to me like that! We are no longer children. Be a man!" I say dangerously quietly. "I came here to offer my help! To look out for you! But you became an even bigger asshole than you were before." I step towards the door. "Oh, and yea."

"Yes, what?"

"I used you. I never loved you. You were a tool for my pleasure." I shut the door and left. Willow follows me. We pass the town's gate. I am leaving this life behind, for good. I will not cry. There is nothing worth crying for. The Syrivis attacked my village and killed almost everyone in it. There is nothing left that can keep me from accepting my fate.

On our way home, Willow and I are silent. I am ashamed that he had to see this. But I realise I needed this hit in the guts to realise I have nothing left from my old life to mourn.

"That was nothing like I expected it to be."

"I am sorry Willow, I thought he would understand. I thought I could help," I say.

"I know. I don't judge you for having him as a friend. Handsome but no brain, I have to say." Willow has the ability to always make the best out of the worst situations.

"What I said wasn't true. I loved him deeply in the beginning. But I slowly lost feelings for him. I was afraid to tell him, seeing as we had a long friendship. I didn't want to lose the only person in town I could talk to. I am a jerk."

"No, you are not. You are human. Or were. I don't know. Doesn't matter. We love, we fight, we are selfish, we sacrifice. That's life. You should never feel guilty for your actions."

"Thank you for coming with me," I say sincerely.

"That's what real friends are for, supporting each other. And It's been a long time since I have been here. However, I won't miss it." He smiles.

After the ride back to the palace I snuck into my chamber, glad no one saw us. Happy that I am back at home. *Home.* This is now my home and I will fight for it. I will fight for a better kingdom.

CHAPTER TWENTY-TWO

*O*bsidian *eyes are watching me. Intensely. As if they can see right through my eyes into my soul. I feel naked. My thoughts are his and his thoughts are mine. I can feel their pain, frustration and loneliness. I feel connected to these eyes. I feel as if these eyes are everything I would ever need in life. I want to touch these high cheekbones. I want to feel his skin under my hand. I want to touch the tip of his pointy ears.*

"What the—" I shoot up from the bed.

I am looking around the room, looking for those eyes. What is wrong with me? I guess the visit to my hometown influenced me more than expected.

I get ready for the day. Nothing in particular is planned. The days became quiet. Healers are working in silence on the ones hurt from the last attack while Nevan took Aleksander's place in the war councils. He reported to me that the rebels had increased their attacks in the city and had grown in size. Facing the Dark One and the rebels at once is a risky situation.

Yet, the palace halls are never quiet. After Aleksander has announced that some Elves from the town may take shelter in the palace walls, the place got more alive. I can hear children singing and playing around which brings a smile to my lips. I haven't heard any news about the crown prince which is probably a good sign.

I make my way to the library hoping to find Willow or Salem there. I am relieved to find them sitting in a reading corner at the end of the hall.

"Good morning, Aedlin," Willow greets. Since the evening we have gone out to my village, the connection between us seems stronger.

I showed him my past life and I was afraid of his judgment. Yet, he'd accepted me for who I was and me who I am now.

"You seem well rested," Salem observes. And yes, I feel good. I feel alive. As if before I was only half present but now I am fully aware of my body and my senses.

"I am. I believe I needed the visit to my old life. I had to let a part of me go," I say with honesty.

"I am relieved to hear that. Willow has told me some details of your trip but this is your story to tell," Salem says.

"Any news on the Crown Prince?" I ask timidly trying to change the topic.

"You mean the prince who is only alive because of your… whatever." Willow wiggles his eyebrows. I have to laugh. This is idiotic.

"He is alive because of the professional and skilled healers in the castle. But yes."

"He is well. I have heard from others that he attended a council meeting. So apparently he is back to normal." I am relieved to hear this.

I excuse myself and find a corner for myself. I have to do some research. I have to find out more about these Syrivis.

Sadly, there isn't much documented on these creatures. However, I have found several books which describe them.

"Syrivis are Elves who were possessed by shadows. Shadows which belong to the Dark One. Syrivis are Elves who lose control of their bodies and slowly decay over time. They are essentially dead, only kept alive by the evil inside of them."

"There is no way to retransform a Syrivis into Elf form again. Once possessed they are sure to die."

"The object had to die first before being infected with the Shadows. Once possessed the object's body will follow the Shadows' movements."

According to the reading, Syrivis are the undead army of the Dark One. So, after all, there is someone behind this, someone who wants to see me dead. Someone that despises the existence of me. The Dark One. If I'm not on his side, I shall be on none. I am a threat to his plans. It would be horrific if the Dark One has me under his control. I will have to kill him. But how do you kill something that is made out of shadows?

"Aedlin?" I look up. The voice is dark and a bit rusty but recognisably his.

There he stands, alive and well. His air brushed back, dressed in all black as if nothing has happened.

"Alek– my Prince," I correct myself. "I see you are well rested." I speak politely, hiding my shyness.

"Oh well, I heard rumours that your help was a major factor. Is it possible to talk to you in private?" He says while looking around.

"Yes, of course, my prince." I put my book aside, noticing his eyes glancing at the title of it.

I follow him up to his office. If I haven't seen him injured I wouldn't have believed it. He walks as elegantly as he has before. He gently holds the door open for me and I step into his office. It is lovely seeing him again. To see that he is alive and well.

"What a foolish woman you are," he starts, leaving me completely shocked. "You could have died the other night. Use your stupid brain! You are precious to this Kingdom but risking everything just for … what?" He closes the gap between us. I can almost feel his breath on my skin. "You were foolish for risking *everything*. I saw you leaving with Willow. You should have listened to him, listened to his words and ran!" He sighs. "You looked astonishing that night. I was furious with every man who looked at you. Jealous of every man who thought he could ask you for a dance. I was amazed by the power you wielded against those creatures. You were strong, beautiful and I was captured by every bit of you." He raises his elegant fingers to my cheek, hovering over my scar. I have to restrain myself not to shift into his hand.

"You are nothing," he continues. "No one I should care about. You are a tool of the kingdom to help us win the Silver War. And there I was, once the sirens went on and my father forced me to follow him, I ran off looking for *you* instead. I should not care. My life is more important than yours. But I disregarded the orders from my father and searched for you, hoping you were okay. I saw you in the gardens, and I could not turn my back on you! Why is that, Aedlin?"

I am overwhelmed by his words and the meaning behind them. He is as confused as I am. His face is so close to mine. The eyes I have seen in my dreams. The eyes which promise me security.

"You shouldn't make me feel this way. I have to focus. I almost died because I was captured by your being." His hands are wandering down my arms.

I don't know what to say. I want to say something but in my head every word sounds stupid.

We stay like that for what felt like an eternity, I hope the moment would never end. Sadly, my fantasies are interrupted when Aleksander withdraws himself.

"You showed some improvements in your techniques the other night. The healers told me that because of your magic I am able to stand here."

"I heard that too. I am glad it worked." I chuckle. What is wrong with me? He walks towards his desk getting out some papers.

"Would you mind explaining the events of the night to me? I would like to understand how it was possible for you to wield this amount of magic." He looks genuinely curious and I am happy to give him what he wants. We spent hours in his office, which was mostly me explaining to him what has happened. I try to give him as much detail as possible. We have discussions about the elements, the Syrivis and more. The moment earlier doesn't return and I think that is good. Yes, I saved him, but that was because he is the Crown Prince, because he will be the future of this kingdom.

Eventually, the sun makes place for the moon. And I realise I am pretty tired. But there is one thing I have to tell him.

"Aleksander?"

"Yes?" He looks up from his notes.

"There is something concerning me. I thought it was something normal but it has developed. Developed into something that can't be nothing." I don't know how to say the following words and not sound like a psychopath but I carry on.

"I have dreams. Usually they are unimportant, unnecessary but it developed. Firstly it has only been visions. Shadowed places memory glimpse but I believe somehow I may have a connection to your past."

"To my past? Like a vision?" he asks.

"I am not sure. I don't think it's about the future … I saw the past in my dreams."

"Sometimes dreams take memory fragments and turn them into vivid dreams, nothing you should be concerned about. You possess a variety of skills we all have yet to discover. You saw your mother in this very hall talking to me. You should not be worried."

"That's the problem, it wasn't my memories and it wasn't a conversation between my mother and someone from court." Now I have his attention.

"What do you mean it wasn't your memory?" He asks, concerned.

"I believe it was your memory." Silence. He is thinking. He hasn't thought these were my next words. "So you're telling me you saw me in your dream?" He tries to laugh it off. "I believe I made an impression in your head." But this isn't a time to joke.

"No, Aleksander. I saw you. You looked maybe fifteen or sixteen, you killed a man. A soldier. He—"

"Stop right there! Don't say anything more!" I look wide-eyed at him, surprised by his anger.

"You tell me you have access to my memories? You tell me that you could *see* what I was doing? What I did on this afternoon?"

"I am sorry, Aleksander. I didn't mean to—"

"Go!"

"What?" I am confused. " I cannot control it, I wish no to see it but it happened."

"I said, leave this room or you will be dragged outside." I am speechless by his ruthlessness.

"Aleksander!" I cry.

"Aedlin, I am serious. Leave the room!" he hisses.

"Or what, my prince? What are you going to do?" I hiss back.

"You would rather not find out!" This isn't a game. Not a small joke between friends. He is scared. He is serious about his actions and here I am, thinking that the cruel prince act was only a facade.

"With pleasure, my *prince.*" I grin through my teeth, shutting the door with anger behind me.

How can he speak to me like that? The charming and caring prince has vanished in an instant at the mention of me seeing having these visions. I hoped he could help me but instead he made everything worse.

It is too late to go to the library, so I decide to go up to my room taking time for myself.

A knock.

"Yes?" The door opens and a blond Elf looks at me from the doorway. Nevan.

"Oh, my prince! I didn't know you were blessing me with your presence," I say ironically while staring down at my book.

"Always reading, aren't you?" he mocks.

"There can always be knowledge acquired," I answer.

Silence fills the room. I look up and are surprised to see him … nervous?

"I came to say that I am sorry for the way my father spoke to you."

At least one of the brothers has the dignity to apologise.

"Well, it wasn't the nicest conversation I had in my life but I understand your reasons."

"You do?" He asks, surprised.

"Being a prince brings responsibilities and rules to be followed, I am not mad at you." Not at him, rather at someone else.

"I heard of your little trip the other night." Prince Nevan chooses the armchair opposite of me and sits down. I am surprised by the sudden change of topic.

I feign innocence. "I have no idea what you are talking about."

"Don't play with me, Mrs Reckless, I can tell when you're lying." I look up. It is useless to play innocent.

"I had to make something clear," I say.

"Something clear to someone?" I look at him under my eyelashes.

"And if it was so?" I ask closing the book.

"Then I am happy that I see you sitting here." I am confused.

"What do you mean?"

"According to your response to my questions, there was a former lover lurking in your thoughts. Someone from your past life, someone who made it hard for you to accept your new self. I believe that seeing you here confirms that the conversation wasn't easy, it was rather heated, I know you." I am speechless. "And I am pleased to see you here, knowing you have chosen this path over your old one." How can he be so good at reading people? And how can I have never noticed? "He hurt you, didn't he? Not physically, but mentally." I swallow. Every word he said is true.

"How can you know?" I whisper.

"In a world filled with magic, I never got any of it. I am the Prince who has no power. I had to help myself in order to survive in this world. So yes, I am good at reading people. Almost as if I am in their mind." I see Nevan in a different light now. The Prince who has no powers in a world filled with it. The Prince who is more human than Elf has to help himself to survive.

"That is impressive, Prince Nevan," I sa honestly.

"You think?" He looks suddenly shy.

"Yes, that is a skill not many people have acquired. It's impressive. You should be proud of yourself."

"Oh, my dear, I am." I roll my eyes but cannot hide a laugh.

"Now tell me, what did my brother do to upset you?" He is really good.

"Nothing other than being the Crown Prince himself," I say gently, not sure how far Nevan and I are in our "friendship".

"He isn't easy to work with, I can tell you," he says cryptically. "But deep down he is a good man. He is listening to you."

On the way out, he turns around. "I would like you to be at tomorrow's war council. You have the right to be part of it. You are an essential part of the future of this kingdom, you should have your voice heard."

I nod.

-

The next morning, I wake up later than planned and arrive at the council a tiny bit late.

I knock at the door and step into the full room. The last time I was here was with the High King and Prince Nevan but now every seat is occupied, except one.

Aleksander is standing at the head of the table, frozen in motion.

"What—" He begins but Nevan interrupts him.

"Brother and Senate, I thought inviting Aedlin would allow her to analyse the situation better. I hope the rest of the room understand." He looks in every face, none are complaining. I quickly make my way to the empty chair on the right.

"Okay. Aedlin, I hope next time you will be on time. We don't like delays in our meetings," Aleksander says. Of course, he had to throw me under the wolfs. I smile and hope my reaction would please him.

"What happened at the evening of the midsummer festival was a fatal mistake and will not happen. Somehow they bypassed our security system and made it in without anyone in the palace noticing."

"How are you so sure that we do not have a spy among our people? Your Highness?" an elderly man to my left asks.

"This cannot be excluded. We have to consider every possibility," Aleksander says firmly. "Many people could have lost their lives on that day. We were unprepared and this cannot happen again. We are at war. These creatures cannot come close to the folk." People agree with a nod.

"We fought against them and they are as vulnerable as the Elves. They don't own special affinities besides decay," says another Elf sitting opposite me; his beard so long so it reaches the table.

"Nevan, how are the Golden Warriors? How extensive has their training been? Are they soon ready to deploy?"

"The soldiers are ready waiting for orders," Nevan says shortly. "We all have a common enemy and we all want this to be over." I can see how this situation is frustrating him. He doesn't know what to do.

"Any news about the Dark One?" an Elf sitting on my left asks.

"Not any new details, no, but we know that he is still located in the North, in Alastas to be certain. He is using his puppets in the south. If we just knew why? What is his aim?"

"It's me," I say. And immediately, all eyes are focused on me, as if the majority of the room has forgotten I am here too.

"The Dark One is looking for me," I clarify.

"How are you so sure, girl?" an Elf asks.

"Because I talked to him."

"You what?!" This time it is Aleksander who interrupts me.

"I thought nothing of it, sure that it was a hallucination. It happened once I entered this world. It all felt so strange. But there was a darkness waiting for me, offering me everything I could ever want. I declined his offer. I am the only one capable of defeating him. If I am not on his side, I am a major threat to his life."

The room is quiet. Aleksander is the first one to get it together again.

"That would explain the increase in incidences since your arrival."

"They attacked my village. I was there. I had a vision of it but I was too late," I say almost whispering.

"You went back? Into the human world, without telling me?" Aleksander raises his voice.

"I wasn't alone, I was guarded."

He rolls his eyes. "Let this be for another time." He sighs. "You are excused, gentlemen," he said to the others. "Aedlin. Would you stay?" This isn't an order, it is a question.

"Of course, my Prince."

He waits until the room is empty and the door is shut.

"I owe you an apology." This man can always surprise me with his actions. "I was too harsh on you, thank you for sharing your concerns with me. Tell me more about these ... encounters."

"It happened twice. When I entered the forbidden city in my country. There was this shadow. More like a figure hidden in the darkness. It was talking to me but didn't threaten me. I was confused, at first. But I got more and more concerned."

"He wants you by his side. With you on his side he would be superior to all of us," Aleksander mumbles.

"This is frustrating, my prince." Aleksander looks up,

"I thought we had talked about it, Aedlin. Aleksander, in private." He gives me a small smile.

"I read several books which might mention the Dark One and his army, but none of them stated how to end his life," I continue.

"The Shadows are the reincarnation of death. Everything it touches dies. But you ... you are the opposite, you have the ability to wield all four elements. *You* healed me. *You* made it possible for me to live." He stands up. "Where he is the reincarnation of death, you are the reincarnation of life. Perfectly imperfect. If you joined with him, we would have no chance because the Dark One would possess both life and death. With it, he'd be unstoppable."

"And because I didn't agree, the Dark One wants to find me, to eliminate me because without me the Elves don't have a chance." Aleksander nods and runs his hand through his hair.

"If the Dark One can't have you, no one can." The truth is worse than expected.

The thought that I might get killed in the future is something entirely different than having to accept that I could get killed any second.

"Hey, Aedlin." His palm is on my shoulder. I notice too late how my hands are trembling.

"You are under my protection, I won't let anything happen to you. The Kingdom will protect you with everything we have." There it is again, the feeling of hope. The feeling that everything will be fine. I cannot trust this emotion. It has lied to me too many times.

"At the end of this month we will leave. Preparations are ready and my father urges me to proceed. I believe you have had enough training. Henry gave me a detailed report. The march up in the north will be long and hard. You should rest for the next few days."

"This is happening, isn't it?" I whisper.

"I believe so."

CHAPTER TWENTY-THREE

I follow Aleksander quietly to the congress room. Over the past few days the palace was busy preparing for the march. I start to get nervous. To question if I am ready for this. I always come to the same conclusion: I am not sure.

Sure, I have fought against the rebels and the Syrivis but an actual war is on another level. Am I skilled enough? Aleksander and I are sitting, brooding over books and papers, trying to find anything we could use against the Dark One. We barely found anything useful. Our sources are cryptically and lack details when it comes to the Shadow Legion. No one has survived an attack to give a detailed report on their behaviour and actions. Books mention that the Dark One is a benign form the Fade. Something so powerful to rip their presence apart from the fog and manifest into something that can live on its own, which got us thinking that they get their power from the Fade itself. Yet, how can you destroy something which is necessary for all life on this planet. How can you destroy the path to the afterlife? It is impossible without breaking the natural rules. I can scream. This whole situation quickly turns into a suicide mission.

The days pass quicker than I would like to. More and more people from the surrounding cities are joking us to discuss the current situation and hope that we have a solution but we don't.

On our way to the next council, Nevan joins Aleksander and me.

"Good morning, brother, Aedlin." He nods towards me.

"I was eager to write the refusal proposal for the Lord Monnoc from Silicenen."

"Refusal? We need his army by our side," Aleksander says grumpily.

"I know, but I checked the numbers, they are requesting far too much than needed. We are in a crisis but we have to stay firm," Nevan says.

"Okay, understood, I will bring it up in the meeting," Aleksander says.

"Are the lords of the neighbouring country present in today's meeting?" I ask in surprise.

"Yes, all three lords requested an audience before moving any further. Trust has never been something they've had for us, and they want to be sure that you exist. Easier said than done. They suspect the High King of being dishonest, however, would never dare to say so," Aleksander says diplomatically, focused on the path ahead.

He seems more tense lately. And that is something, considering that he is never relaxed. Yet, he feels more distant than usual. In meetings he stays quiet and I often catch him wandering off to another place in his mind.

He opens the door to the conference room once we arrived and the Elves inside become silent. The future High King has entered the room and the current High King is forgotten.

People fear the High King and I am certain that the Realm is afraid of Alexander's reign. Will he be like his father or will he change the world?

In my short time here I have heard of several executions under the High King. He wants people to be afraid of him, to rule over A wicked kingdom. But I can see how it is falling apart. More and more people are siding against the High King and I can see why. I don't want to fight for a man of terror, I don't want to be a tool of horror.

As we walk by the men present in the room, I inspect each and every one. The way they look at Alexander, it is not fear but judgment.

"Gentlemen," he says, his voice is firm.

He and Nevan walk to the High King, make a quick bow and sit to his left and right. I feel like I am in the wrong room. So many eyes bore into me.

I dip into curtsey and say politely, "Gentlemen," and then walk to the empty chair on the left.

"This is her?" one Elf on the right asks mockingly. I haven't had much time to learn the different languages but I can hear the same dialect Salem has.

This is Lord Suhan from Cilest.

"She is a child. Barely capable of the dangers out there." I see Aleksander trying to start a sentence but I don't need someone to defend me.

"Lord Suhan, I am well aware of my age and the circumstances we are under. I understand the danger and the risks by bringing me into this war. However, I am unusual, an answer to a prophecy promised by the God Mother herself. So I will fight to my last breath. I don't ask you to trust me or to like me, but to put faith in me." My palms are sweaty. It is hard to understand the situation. I am sitting here in this room filled with powerful Elves and here I am telling them to trust me? I look at the face of the Westerner. His hair is brown and well styled. His eyebrows are thick. He looks at me appraisingly.

"We will see, *girl*." He spits the words out.

"Her name is Aedlin. Not girl or woman or any other names you find humiliating. She is a valuable asset to this war and you will give her the respect she deserves." The room goes quiet. Did he just tell this lord to treat me better? *Valuable asset.* That's what I am. Nothing more.

"Yes, Your Highness. I will, my sincere apologies, *Aedlin*," Lord Suhan says quietly. It will be a long time until they accept me. But I am not trying to get them to like me, I am just attempting to save their home, no need for formalities.

The High King is unexpectedly quiet during the meeting. He is assessing the situation. Watching. Watching me. I feel like I am in an interview. As if I have to prove myself.

"Lord Monnoc, we have read your proposal for stocking up your equipment, however, we refused it," Aleksander says coldly.

Lord Monnoc has short red hair. He looks younger than Lord Suhan but older than Aleksander.

"Your highness?" the Elf on my left asks. "Without funding we will not be able to perform as expected."

"I suggest running the numbers again or are you calling me unreasonable? Don't you respect my decisions, Lord Monnoc?" There he is, the High King. I can see it. The danger.

"No, my prince. There has to be a number problem, I will talk to my finance man," Lord Monnoc says. Aleksander nods satisfied.

"If everything goes as planned, we should be ready to march by the end of the month leaving us with two weeks. The Dark One has not changed his position. He still controls Alastas and with it, Lord Timothe."

Mumbles across the room.

"The Gold Legion is ready to fight, we are waiting for further orders from the High King." Aleksander looks to his father. He seems uninterested in the conversations which is happening in the room. The conversation about saving his kingdom. How ignorant can a person be?!

"The aim in the coming days and weeks is to protect what the Dark One desires mostly. Aedlin." I am surprised to see the lords and the senate nodding in agreement. "If the march goes as planned, we will have an advantage because we have three armies and her." Aleksander looks at me. "The Dark One knows we are coming or at least assumes it. We have to act fast."

Even though Aleksander has enlightened me about the critical political situation among the kingdoms, he omitted one key thing. All of the Lords shared one thought: saving their home. And for this, they are eager to put aside their disputes and pull their forces together.

During the remainder of the meeting I have to answer several questions about myself asked by the lords of this country. Yet, over course of time they showed me more respect, respect the High King has never showed me. I get the feeling that they see me as one of them, not as a tool.

-

"Aedlin, Aedlin."

I open my eyes and immediately see the change. The room is filled with darkness. The voice belonged to the Dark One, I am sure.

"You believe that these walls will keep you safe? That these walls will protect you from me? What did I ever do to you besides offering you a life you deserve? How are you so sure that the evil doesn't live next to you?" The voice asks.

"I believe the fact that killing innocent people is a sign of evil. Possessing these people to fight for you is evil," I say firmly.

"So the High King doesn't have blood on his hands? Your princeling is innocent? Am I right?" Immediately the pictures from my latest memory pops up in my head. Aleksander killing the warrior.

"You saw the evil in them. The cruelty, but still you judge me for wanting peace?"

"I don't think that peace is what you desire."

"How are you so sure? The world is full of cruelty. Unfairness. I need your help to stop that," The voice continues. "Do you really believe that the High King is trying to stop the power capable of ruling over life and death? Imagine if you win this war, are you certain that the High King will let you live?" It is a speculation *but I find myself doubting the words of the palace. Doubting the High King's real intentions. I will not be free after this war. I would stay a prisoner.*

"What do you believe the High King's aims are?" I whisper in the darkness, feeling stupid at continuing the conversation with the enemy. But who really is the enemy?

"Power. The same power a man once sought. A lord from Alastas ready to give everything up for more power." The Elf who the Dark One took control over.

"And if so, you are no better than him. You kill innocent people. This is what you call peace?" I ask, frustrated.

"I never said my actions are peaceful, my goal is to achieve peace. Us together would be fatal for the High King."

"Even if this all was true, I would not join your army. I would not go from one tyrant to the next one. And now leave me the hell alone!" I cry out.

"I hoped we could have talked like adults, I am sorry, Aedlin."

I open my eyes.

I am dragged violently out of my bed.

I try to shake myself free but the grip around my limps only strengthens.

A smell of decay fills my nose.

Syrivis.

"Hey! Let me go!" Nothing. I squirm, ignoring the pain of their claws in my flesh. I get one of my legs loose and kick one of them in the face. It let go of me. I roll myself on my back, throwing my hands to my chest, making the other Syrivis land in front of me. I can feel the sizzling of my magic in my veins. The feeling is like a drug.

I want more of it.

It fulfils me.

"If you want me, then come and get me!" I say quietly.

The two creatures come running and screaming towards me. A lift of my hand and the two beings are flying against the walls. But sadly this doesn't cause them much pain.

They get up and attack. I dodge one set of claws but cannot dodge the second creature whose claws cut the skin. I groan.

"You little piece of—" I hiss and focus my magic on a fire ball. It is hard to keep two of them away from me at once. Shadows are summoned around them, hovering next to them. Getting hit by them feels like death itself hit you.

A cold shiver goes down my spine.

I try my best to dodge and hit them but it seems my magic isn't listening to me properly. It is not as powerful as it was the other night. And the second I am vulnerable, I can feel the rotten teeth of one of the creatures in my arm.

The pain is immense. I scream and sink to my knees.

I feel heat. Fire.

The creatures are screaming and a burning scent fills my nose. I can feel how the teeth loosen on my arm until it finally let go.

I haven't summoned that fire.

I look up and see Aleksander standing in front of me, casually. His hair messy and dressed in a plain white shirt and black pants. It is weird to see him in something else than black.

"Aedlin," He says breathlessly. Behind him guards come running, followed by Nevan and the High King himself.

Aleksander kneels in front of me, appearing to be the only one who actually cares.

"Send a healer to the hospital wing." When no one moved, he shouts, "Now!"

Three guards are turning around, running down the hall.

More and more people are coming to the room.

"Where were her guards? Why was no one here?" He turns to the remaining Elf Warriors.

"My prince, we … we don't know. Two guards were stationed here for the night," the smaller one of the three answers.

"You better find them and if you do, bring them immediately to me!" Are they flinching? I touch my shoulder and wince. I cannot hide a whimper. My hand is covered in blood. Aleksander turns his face to mine, his expression completely changed.

"Are you okay?" He asks, obviously knowing I am not. His hand touches my hurt shoulder gently.

"Aleksander," I hear his father say. "Know your place." I see the fire in his eyes ignite.

"Know my place? Father? My place is to make sure everyone is alright! My place is to care for my folk." He stands up, going toward the High King.

"What do you suggest I do?" He asks quietly.

"Let the healer do the work, you did more than expected from you." Aleksander snorts and turns his back to his father.

"Can you walk?" He asks gently.

I look around at all the strangers' faces.

I look ridiculous. Sitting on the floor covered in blood after the Crown Prince had to rescue me. How should I survive a minute on the battlefield?

I put my remaining strength together and try to get on my feet. My knees are wiggling and cannot support me well enough due to the shock of almost being killed. I sway. Luckily Aleksander is there helping me. I am embarrassed I cannot look any of the participants in the eyes.

"No," Aleksander says simply. He stops my attempts to walk with positioning his hands around my arms. He places one arm underneath my knee and the other around my back and lifts me in his arms.

"Aleksander!" I can hear his father shouting furiously.

"My prince … This is too much to ask, I can walk by myself. I am just a slightly bit shocked. Besides people might catch sight and will talk." I try to get out of his arms but he only grabs me tighter.

"Let them talk, this would give me another reason to burn this place to the ground," He hisses beside my ear. I am shocked by what he has just shared with me in this tiny moment. The disapproval of the reign? Did he figure something out about his father plans? Yet, I am extremely exhausted all of a sudden so I place my head on his chest. Hearing his heartbeat calmes my thoughts.

The healer has to stitch the wound.

During the whole process Aleksander hasn't left the room. He sits there asking the healers about the next steps. I am surprised by how much knowledge he wields about herbs and medicine.

When the healers finally left, I hear them say to Aleksander from the hallway, "She needs to rest. It was lucky that she was well trained otherwise this could have ended differently."

It really could have.

He knocks on my door gently and steps inside again. This feels weird. It feels private, wrong.

He shouldn't be with me, he should delegate the next steps.

"How are you feeling?" The softness in his voice surprises me every time.

"Besides being high on potions and almost being killed … I am fine." Do I see a faint smile on his face?

"I am relieved you are alive." I do feel a sense of Deja-vu. The last time he talked to me like that was when he pushed me off the palace tower. However, this time was not his fault.

"Tell me what happened," He says sitting on the armchair near the window.

"I was sleeping and then I heard its voice in my head and I knew this wasn't a memory of yours or vision. The Dark One was in my head. It was talking about its plan to bring peace to the folk. That I could trust no one. Evil is everywhere." I swallow. I am not sure if I should tell him about the potential wrong aims of his father.

"The Dark One mentioned as well that the High King might not have the best intentions in the war either. It believes that the High King wants to possess death and life to control this country." I wait for a reply from Aleksander but he stays quiet.

"Once I declined to join his army again, he vanished from my thoughts and I was dragged out of my room by ... by these creatures. I was overwhelmed by the fact that they were in my bedroom in the palace."

"From now on you will sleep in the royal wing. It is closer to me and better protected," He says.

"But if they are after me, wouldn't it be dangerous to place myself close to the royal family?" I ask worriedly.

"I know. But I will sleep better knowing you are close."

Wait what?! Did he just say that? I probably misheard it, I have taken lots of medication in the past hour.

"How did you know what was happening? You couldn't possibly have heard me," I ask curious.

"That's correct. However, I felt it ... I know it is weird and I am unsure about it myself. However, lately, I can feel you." I raise one of my brows.

"I know it sounds crazy but I can feel your presence before seeing you. I can feel your emotions if I let myself go. And yesterday, your fear was enormous. I couldn't focus. I was afraid. But it took me some time to realise that I wasn't the one who was scared." What?

"How is this possible." I whisper in amazement and shock.

"I am unsure, yet, I have a theory but it happens rather rare and if, only between powerful Elves, but there is a possibility that we have created a bond." He says as if that explains it all.

"A bond?" I ask.

"Yes, my dear, a bond." He chuckles, "It basically means that our consciousness are connected. Something so rare that barely any books mention it, but I have heard of it." He swallows. "It is stuck in my hand since the night of the Midsummer festival, the wound was too severe as for me to walk out of the hospital wing unharmed. I thought about the possibility, yet, did not think you could create such things." I look at him wide eyed.

"The next days, my mind was filled by you and your emotions. I wanted to seek you out but did not understand why, but now I believe I do." He says calmly.

"So you say, I am magically bonded to the crown prince..." I say lost in thought.

"Indeed," He chuckles again, "How ironic."

"What is?" I ask curious.

"The only other thing I know about being bonded is that if one dies the other will follow their fate soon." Silence establishes between us. "I guess we are stuck together for life, which means I need you to be save, no risk involved actions, you cannot live without me and I cannot live without you." Under other circumstances, his words would give me butterflies, however, this makes everything more complicated. Now I understand why he has been so caring and worried about my wellbeing. He needs me to be safe.

"Is there a way to break this bond?" I ask shyly.

"I am unsure," He swallows, "But I will keep my promise, I will protect you, you will not have to endure such things ever again." I haven't noticed how much closer he came to me. His hand almost touches mine.

A knock. Aleksander shifts himself back in the chair.

The door opens and Henry steps into the room fully armed. Gone is the caring Elf and back is the Cruel Prince.

"Report, Henry." His voice is as cold as ice.

"We couldn't find any sign of the intruders. However, a crowd has formed in front of the gate in the Royal Sector. They are demanding the High King's presence. I believe I have heard the words 'Revolution'." I can see how Aleksander's eyes turn cold.

"Any information about the missing guards?"

"Yes, your Highness. Found and in chains," Henry adds quickly.

"Good, I will handle them." I am shocked at how arrogant Aleksander's voice has become. *I will handle them.* He is going to kill them because they haven't protected me.

"Aleksander, don't!" I cry out, then press my hands against my mouth. He turns around his gaze.

"Aedlin?" His voice is mocking, cruel. "Do you want to tell me what I shall and shall not do? You clearly need to learn the manners of the court." I flinch back and I can see a spark in his eyes.

"Apologise, my prince," I say, looking at the floor.

"Henry, bring me to the guards."

"As you wish, your Highness."

CHAPTER TWENTY-FOUR

Over the coming days, the crowd didn't grow smaller. The guards send them away every day but they return at night. They only have orders to keep the people away from the palace but this might change quickly if the High King feels terrorised by them.

I haven't seen Aleksander since he left my room to interrogate the guards.

However, Salem has told me that the warriors who left their posts will be executed by midday.

"Executed?" I shout.

"It was an order."

"An order by who, the High King or Aleksander?" She looks at me with pity. "Don't look at me like that," I say furiously. "He cannot kill these people."

"But they didn't do their job. Because of their poor work, you could have died. And further interrogation revealed they belong to the rebels."

"The rebel situation is out of control, the High King has not yet made a statement to his kingdom. The people are suffering. He should be there helping!"

"The Realm doesn't want their help because they are afraid of him and the princes," Salem continues. "They want the bloodline to be erased. They want to see someone new on the throne. I have heard rumours that they believe that it would best for the Sorcerer Supreme to take the throne."

"Me?" I gasp. "I should be on the throne? This is ridiculous. I have no intention of ruling this kingdom." Salem looks away.

"What is it?" I frown at her.

"It is not my responsibility to enlighten you with this but in case of the death of the royal family, Prince Aleksander has requested for you to be the next High Lady of the Elven Realm." I look at her in shock.

"He did what?!" I ask. "Me? The High Lady? If they pass away in war?"

"Aedlin, I shouldn't have told you this, yet it is already written down on paper. I assumed he had asked you about it but I am afraid you cannot change it anymore. Let's just hope they don't die." She tries to lift the mood.

"I wouldn't be so certain of it – I might kill them myself."

"Aedlin, relax, you have to understand him. He chose you because he knew you are a strong woman who can rule this kingdom."

"You don't understand, Salem. When he dies, I die."

She looks at me in confusion.

"We are magically bonded. If he dies in this war, I will die as well," I try to explain to her.

"Bonded. You are bonded to the Crown Prince. To the second most influential man in this Kingdom. This is not good. How many people know?" She asks hastily.

"Only you and him," I answer

"Good, it should stay this way. No one has to know that an attempt on your life would be an attempt on the Crown Prince's life." She speaks quickly. I nod in agreement. "Yet the crown prince has shown interest in the folk, he is a good man, Aedlin," Salem continues.

"A good guy who handles an execution this afternoon." I snort.

"He will not rule like his father does."

"So you believe that what the High King does is not ethically correct?" She nods.

"We have to do something," I whisper.

"What do you want to do? There is no evidence of his wrongdoing. He is the law," She says frustrated. "But I have lived several years in the palace. I heard the rumours and I saw people die under his hand who were innocent. I couldn't interfere, I couldn't help them. This is no kingdom of peace."

"If the folk want to see him dead, maybe we should do as they wish."

"Are you telling me we should kill the King?!" She gasps.

"I know this sounds stupid but once we are off to war, we can say he fell in the battle, no one would suspect anything."

"Aedlin, this is insane. He is still the father of two princes, even if he rules as a cruel King we cannot make the decision." I nod in agreement. My idea is pointless.

"I cannot fight in a war for this man." I simply state the truth.

"But if you don't fight with him with whom are you fighting?" Salem points out. "Which side will you choose? The Dark One or the High King's?"

"This is frustrating, I have to talk to the princes." The words come out faster than I can think.

"Aedlin. Stop. They won't help you. They are part of this mess. The only thing we can do currently is wait. Time will tell." She sighs.

"Time will tell."

-

The morning passed quickly and midday is coming way too fast. I don't want to see the execution. I don't want to go there but I was ordered by the High King himself. I don't know why. Maybe so I can see what he is capable of doing. So he can show me that next time I do something inappropriate, this would be me.

We are in front of the palace. This execution is open to the public which is more grotesque and dangerous. This is entertainment for people.

Guards are located everywhere to defend against possible attacks by the Dark One or the rebels.

Two guards are dragged onto the stage. The crowd is cheering. I have the urge to vomit. I see the High King, Nevan and Aleksander. The two Elves who are dragged onto the stage look horrible. Bruises everywhere. How an they still be conscious?

I try not to remind myself that this could have been done by Aleksander. That he is capable of this much cruelty and violence. The two men are pushed to the floor. No one says a word. I stand next to the High King, front row of this spectacle. Aleksander steps forward, my blood freezes.

"You are found guilty of treason, for being a member of a rebel faction. You have been found guilty of dismissing your posts and leaving the palace, allowing intruders. You are sentenced to death." His voice echoes among the crowd.

I cannot drag my eyes away from Aleksander as he lifts his sword and cut it through the necks of the two Elf. Nothing in his face shows regret. I freeze in place once the heads drop to the floor. Blood flows. I swallow.

Aleksander turns around, takes a towel and wipes the blade of his sword clean.

I can feel a hand around mine. I look into Salem's face. She has seen that often. How can she still stand here and serve this monster? But who is the main monster?

Aleksander's expression is as cold as the High King's himself.

The caring Elf who dragged me out of the hall, who didn't care about what other people thought, is gone. He doesn't linger long at the scene. He vanishes into the dark, guarded by warriors.

I cannot stand here any longer, watching the Gold Legion dragging away the limp bodies ... and their heads.

I turn away and squeeze through the crowd. I hear Salem calling for me but I don't stop. I run into the palace where no one really gives me a second look.

I walk past servants and soldiers, making my way to his chamber, hoping he is there. I don't even bother to knock. I storm in and see him sitting on a desk under a bright window. I have never been in his room before but now isn't the time to appreciate the details.

"How could you?!" I ask.

"You highness, I apologise, she was too—" A guard grabs my arms but I wriggle myself free. Aleksander raises a hand,

"It's okay, you are excused." His voice is still monotone. The guard nods and leaves the room, leaving me with him. A murderer.

"How could you kill them?!" I ask again.

"What would you have had me do otherwise?" His attention is back on the books. His question overwhelms me. Yes, what could have he done otherwise?

"There were so many other possibilities. You didn't have to kill them. Do you think they deserved to die? Like that?" Now I got his attention. He turns towards me, anger filling his eyes.

"Yes Aedlin, I think they deserved this and so much more. I would do it again. Sometimes you have to do things, not because you enjoy them but because it is necessary. And this *was* necessary. I had to make a statement, to say that if someone tries to harm you in any way they will have to face serious consequences." His voice is burning with anger.

"You had to make the statement or your father had to make it using you as his puppet?" I say dangerously quietly. His eyes shoot to mine.

"How dare you!" He growls. "I am the Crown Prince of Eskendria. The heir to the throne, I am allowed to do whatever pleases me." He walks towards me like a predator. I should be scared of the Elf in front of me. He is a killer. He murdered Elves to set a statement.

"Tell me, Aedlin, my dear." His face is so close to mine. "If they had made an attack on my life, what would you have done?" His question is filled with so many unanswered questions but I am terrified by my own thoughts. If someone had tried to kill him, I would have found the guilty ones and I am not sure if I would have acted differently.

"But why in public?" I ask, my voice becoming calm again. Aleksander steps back and moves to the centre of the room.

"So the Realm and the rebels will see what I do with intruders who are threatening my kingdom."

"What happened?" I ask. "You seemed to be exchanged … swapped, somehow. Yesterday you were so nice and now you are back to being cruel?" I realise that I was on thin ice.

"Aedlin, I am a prince. Trained to know the etiquettes and behaviours of the Elves. I know what to do in what situation to get the best out of it. It's called acting." His voice is stone cold. I ignore the pain in my chest from his words. For me, yesterday he was a completely different person, a person I would like, a person I wanted to spend time with.

"Who is the real Aleksander Masquelle? Is it the man who executed the guards in front of everyone? Or is it the man who danced with me at the midsummer festival, who cared for me when I was in pain? Who risked his cold reputation by carrying me to the hospital wing?" Aleksander looks at me with his head tilted.

"Sometimes people are not meant to be what they desire." His voice is monotonous.

"You can be whoever you want," I try.

"Aedlin, please stop the nonsense." He shakes his head.

"This is no nonsense. I want you to understand that you are not forced to do all these things. You are not cruel."

"And how do you know?!" His attention is all on me. "You know me so well? You have no idea what I did and who I am. I've lived for decades. I am an Elf. I've fought in wars and killed people. I killed Elves for my amusement." His voice is icy.

"Don't! That's not true." I hope it isn't.

"Maybe your small visions aren't showing you all of it. I killed your mother and father. I killed Elves because I was bored. Their mercy screams ignited me!"

"I earned the title of Cruel Prince, because that's what I am – cruel. Whatever you thought you saw in me isn't there. I don't care for people, I only care for my own wellbeing because I am selfish!" I flinch back at his words. I don't think about what this conversation would turn into but it was definitely not this. I am stupid to think that he has changed, that he started to care. I thought we had something special but it turns out to be fake.

"Tell me, Aleksander, tell me that you didn't feel anything when we were at the midsummer festival, when we danced, when we fought together on that night. Tell me you didn't feel something when you brought me to the wing. If you tell me that none of this was real to you, I will go and leave you alone." My breathing is getting faster. My heart beats even faster. I ask him indirectly but he is smart.

He probably figures out the intention of my words. But to be honest, I am not sure if I want him to figure it out.

He wets his lips, looking at me. He searches for eye contact and here I am captured by his obsidian eyes.

He moves towards me and I back off until I feel his desk against my knees.

He puts his hands beside me on the table, lowering his head so his eyes meet mine on the same level.

"You pathetic woman. How could I care about you? Me? Did you really think that I actually liked you?" I feel like I have been punched in the guts even though he hasn't touched me. I wish I could tell myself that he doesn't mean it. That he is lying. But he is looking in my eyes and confirming my thoughts.

I swallow. I don't want him to see how much his words have hurt me.

"Good." I push him away from me. I need space between us his presence makes it hard to think. "So it's an equal feeling. Thank you for the conversation, *my prince.*" I turn around and leave his room.

I will not cry. He doesn't deserve my tears.

Yet, I cried in the darkness of the room. This fight made me realise that even though he is the cruel prince, my heart belongs to him.

Chapter Twenty-Five

O ne day to go and I would leave this palace to march into war. The last few days I had an armour fitting and it felt odd to wear such garments. I chose the weapons I wanted to have equipped for the march and the horses were prepared to leave. I am worried about the endless hours I would have to sit on the back of such a creature.

I have talked to Prince Nevan about possible tactics, but I have not seen Aleksander since our fight. I thought it is better this way.

"Do you want to join us this afternoon for lunch, my prince?" I ask Nevan after one of our meetings.

"Is this a date, my lady?" He jokes.

"No it is not. It is only a lunch between colleagues. A last meal together before we go. I thought it would help them to see your face, to strengthen their will," I try to convince him.

"*Their will?* Or is this just an excuse to see me?" He says, stepping in front of me.

"I guess we'll never know." I chuckle and move around him. "See you then, my prince!" I call.

The afternoon arrived and along with Salem and Willow I prepare the plates in the great hall for lunch. Willow came up with the idea of sharing a last meal together, showing unity. I hope Prince Nevan will be there as well; it would motivate the soldiers, showing that we are all one.

In the next few minutes the room becomes more and more crowded with Elves. The kitchen prepared a nicely cooked meal and my stomach answers to my hunger with a growl.

People are chatting and exchanging thoughts. I soak it all in, hoping that this isn't the last time we will all be together like this. I don't know half of the Elves present here, yet I want to get to know each and every one.

Suddenly the room goes quiet and I try to find the cause of it. I look over the crowd and my eyes lock with dark ones.

Everyone is looking at the Crown Prince and his brother entering the hall. Both of them are dressed casually. No luxuriant attires. Both wear a T-shirt and pants.

"Please, do not stop your conversations. We are here to enjoy lunch," Nevan says loudly so everyone can hear him. They step into the hall, walking towards a bench we have prepared. Individuals start to bow in front of the royals.

"Today, we are one," Aleksander starts. "You certainly don't have to bow in front of your own kind." I look at Salem and Willow who are as confused as I am.

"Prince Nevan, you managed to come," I say enthusiastically, and my gaze flies to his brother. "And I see you brought his Royal

Highness as well, delightful." I try to keep up my smile while dark eyes pierce through the mine.

"I thought both of us attending such an event would be for the best." Nevan chuckles. "And I promise you I came hungry."

We all come together as one huge group. It is odd seeing the Crown Prince sitting around his people, joining in conversation. For Nevan, this is his favourite thing to do. Talking about himself and only himself. I have to smile once I realise how many Elves hung on his every word, listening to war stories I am not sure were all true. I even think that Aleksander enjoys his time. We still haven't talked and I have to admit I am avoiding him.

Lunch passes quickly. I am involved in a heated discussion with Salem and Willow about the pros and cons of elements when I realise some of the Elves have excused themselves already. I am glad that they have enjoyed the time spent together. I am just about to get up and start cleaning the table when a loud explosion goes off and fires me against the back wall. I see black. A high pitch noise establishes in my ear. It slowly fates to the screams of people. I try to open my eyes and to move up. A dizziness overcomes me but I attempt to find the Prince and Crown Prince among the Elves but couldn't find them. The room is filled with smoke and my ears are still ringing from the noise.

I look around the room at the faces of the guards who have not moved an inch after the loud explosion happened, as if they are waiting for a signal. In this moment all step forward and tie a yellow cloth around their head.

I don't understand what is happening but it seems so real.

"Aedlin, get down!" I hear Salem scream from the back. But I cannot move an inch. Intruders. The rebels have got into the place under our eyes and we haven't noticed. Are the men and women from the lunch included into this massacre?

We were surprised. We have secured the place as well as possible but forgot to look into our guards. I try to summon my magic but I cannot feel it. It is gone. Not even a sizzle. I look to Salem who is helping Elves to get out of the room but soon it is impossible as the guards block the exits.

"Willow. I don't feel my magic," I say over the loud noises to my right where I see his red curls.

"Me neither!" He looks at me shocked.

"How is that possible?" I ask.

"Mint powder," He says.

"Mint powder?" I raise an eyebrow.

"In the right consumption it can lessen the magic. It's like a pain killer. It kills the magic for several hours," He says, worried.

"So there is no way to get our magic?" I ask and he shakes his head.

"I will try to get weaponry, stay down here!" He says while getting up and running into the crowd. I will definitely not wait here. Screams are echoing from all around the hall. This is a perfect trap, made by the rebels. Throaty sounds of pain are filling the room mixing with the sounds of steps, falling bodies and the clinging of swords.

Willow is back in a second and gives me two daggers to defend myself with. I see Salem fighting in the centre so I decide to help her out. We fought back-to-back. People we have never seen and guards we thought were loyal to the crown. I have to manoeuvre my steps over fallen bodies.

"How is this possible?" I ask her over the screams.

"It can only mean that intruders were lingering among us the whole time and we haven't noticed." She hisses in anger. I growl and toss one of my daggers in the chest of a tall man who gazes at me wide-eyed. I tense up once I heard a scream from my back.

Salem.

I turn around and see a guard sticking a knife from her back until its tip could be seen in the front. I throw my dagger into the guard's face and he falls backwards. I see how Salem's limb body collapses on the floor. I run towards her.

"Hey Salem, hey look at me," I say. At the sound of my voice, her eyes open but the light in them is gone.

"Salem, stay with me," I continue. I look at my hand and have to grasp for air once I see it is covered in blood. "I will bring you to a healer," I assure her.

"Don't be stupid, Aedlin. Don't waste your time trying to fix things that cannot be fixed." Her voice is rusty and she starts spluttering. She coughs up blood.

"Hey, don't say such things. I can help you. I will help you," I whimper.

"It's okay. I died as a soldier and I made my family proud. And now I will see them again. I will be united with them again," she whispers. "Promise me one thing, Aedlin—"

"Anything, Salem," I assure her.

"Turn this kingdom upside down. Make it your own. And once everything is done, think of me. Of me being there with you supporting you in every aspect of your new life." She coughs again. My eyes fill up with tears and I have to try hard not to break in front of her.

"I will promise you that!"

"It has been a pleasure to be your friend, Aedlin," are the last words she says to me before her body goes limp in my arms. I squeeze her body against mine and hugg her tightly.

"Thank you, Salem. Thank you for being my friend," I whisper against her forehead.

Then, someone pulls me aggressively away from the body so I am out of the range of the guards sword.

"You foolish woman." Aleksander's voice is quiet behind me.

"What are you doing here?! You should be safe!" I cry.

"And let all of my people die?! No, because it is true. I care about them. Every single one and I won't let them alone." He looks at me with honesty in his eyes. His gaze goes to Salem who is laying on the floor and I see him swallowing slowly. She has been a great friend, general, and master for everyone.

He pushes me away from him, giving him space to bring one of the guards down who tries to attack us.

"Rebels?" I pant. He nods.

My gaze goes right and I see Willow kneeling on one of his knees shooting arrows in the crowd. He has to be sure of his aim he could easily hit one of ours. But who are our people?

"You were right," He says while scanning the enemies

"I am pleased to hear that, my prince, would you specify?"

"My father. He had plans," He replies.

I look at him hoping he would continue. He does: "One afternoon I went into his office hoping to find him there so we could talk about the current situation. He wasn't present but several papers were flying around the room and I had a quick look into them." A small smirk appears in the corner of his mouth.

"He planned on uniting death and the life to create the ultimate power to ... to bring her back." He doesn't need to say her name. He means the Queen, his mother. "Such wishes have consequences. Bringing a dead back to life cost a life and not just any," He says over the sound of clinking swords. We are lost in thoughts that we haven't notice that a rebel suddenly appeared in front of us, pointing his sword at Aleksander. He shouldn't be here. He should be somewhere safe. This is my fault. I brought them into this situation. I don't know what to do, running isn't an option but I am still too stunned to move. I look at Aleksander and he looks at me. Amusement appeared on the guard's face. He turns his weapon towards me as if he knows Aleksander cares for me, as if it would be more painful to watch me die in front of him. How wrong he is. I grab one of my daggers tighter but I have no chance against a longsword. I can see that Aleksander is stuck as well. I face the guard's dark expression and am motionless. I only see a blurry vision of Aleksander's shirt as he jumps on me. But he misses me. I fall backwards, hitting my head on the stone floor.

"I have him," someone screams. "Look for the King!"

I hear several joyful screams by the rebels. More and more furniture gets destroyed and Elves fall to the floor.

"Are you hurt?" Willow screams over the noise.

I shake my head.

300

"Don't move!" He orders, but I don't listen. I can fight. I have to fight. This is a war only I can win. I get up and look at the rebel holding Aleksander by his throat to secure him in place.

He is bleeding.

He struck him.

They want to hurt me, so he has sacrificed his life for me. He is stupid so very stupid.

I run towards them but once the rebel sees me, he tightens his grip.

"If you move one step closer to your princeling I will cut his throat in two." His voice is cold and steady. I know he would do it. So I stop and raise my hands.

I look back at the crowd. I can see Nevan, thank the saints he is alive.

He is surrounded by his best warriors from the Golden Legion. We have lost too many guards to the rebels. The hall is a massacre but no one has found the High King, lets hope he was able to flee, as much as I despise this Elf I want to kill him myself.

I try to back off but I feel a dagger in my side.

"If I were you, I wouldn't continue moving," a deep voice threatens. I nod and move forward.

"Aleksander. Are you okay?" I ask the most stupid question.

"Aside from the fact that we are under attack and my life is threatened," – He lets out a breath – "I am happy to see you breathing." I give him a small smile. I would have never expected this to be the moment that we finally sort out our problems.

The doors open with a loud noise and rebels are storming in the hall, celebrating, shouting one sentence over and over: "The High King has fallen!"

"The High King has fallen," the rebels in the hall echoes. Men walk into the hall holding the High King's head.

I take a deep breath. He is dead. A small part in me feels relieved. The Elf who had precisely planned to ruin his kingdom is killed by his own people. I see Nevan in the crowd, lowering his sword. My gaze move to Aleksander. He looks like he has been hit in the face. The rebels are cheering for their victory. The High King has been a father, perhaps not the best but he was an important figure in both of the princes life's.

Suddenly, the room goes dark and cold. I swallow. The coldness is nothing new to me. I know who is coming.

Shadows are forming in the middle of the hall and when they disappear, they left behind a man-shaped figure. It is the first time I see him fully as a being, not just shadows. His hair is ink black and messy as if he just woke up. He is wearing a casual black shirt yet his eyes are remarkable. They were purple. If the circumstances are different I would have considered him handsome.

"The Dark One," I his.

"So much blood," He whispers. "This could have been prevented, but you were all so stubbornly empty of knowledge," He hisses into the crowd.

His eyes meet mine. "Such a beautiful face covered in blood. I could have prevented that from happening, my bird." His shadow hand forms around my chin. I am surprised when I feel his touch.

"Do not touch her," Aleksander hisses. The guard tightens his grip around his throat.

"The Cruel Prince does have a heart?" He asks surprisingly. "Or has he given it away already?" The Dark One laughs.

"I never was a fan of killing and blood. I really thought you, Aedlin would listen to me." He turns around. From the corner of my eye I can see how he moves towards Salem. She still lays on the floor where Aleksander has dragged me away from. She is a beauty even in death.

"She died because of you," He whispers.

"Salem ..." I cry.

"So many people died because of your stubbornness to realise which side you should be on."

"Aedlin, *do* not listen to the tyrant. Nothing of this was your fault," Aleksander says.

"Silent!" The shadowed figure moves towards Aleksander. "You were the problem. If it wasn't for you she would have had a clear head. She would have decided correctly." He turns around. "Kill him."

I still have no power over my magic. This is all planned. It had to be prepared for months. And we haven't realise. The Dark One and the rebels are working together. What has the Dark One promised them? The High King is already dead. What more do they want?

The rebel is taking his sword out of his sheath.

"Let me go!" a familiar voice screams out of the crowd. "I demand it!" It is Nevan. The Dark One chuckles. "Bring him here." Nevan is dragged to us, struggling furiously. He is raging.

"You demand it? The Prince? The Heartbreaking Prince?" He laughs.

"No one cares about you. You were only an addition to the royal family, never necessary." He lets out a hiss once a sword gets dragged through his lover back. I gasp for air once seeing him going quiet. "And trying to fill this void with the mask of the heart-breaking prince even though you desire something else." I see how he widens his eyes and looks shocked at the Dark One. I have no idea what he is talking about but my thoughts are dull, all I can focus on is his bleeding. He has to see a healer soon in order to survive this.

I look at Aleksander. His expression is numb – the cruel prince everyone is expecting. But I can see the fire burning inside him, I can feel it as it it my own anger. Salem was his friend as well. Her limp body lays in front of me, her eyes closed as if she is asleep. I cannot handle looking at her any longer.

"Guard, stop. I believe I want to have the honour to kill the Crown Prince himself," The Dark One says, dangerously quietly.

The Guard puts his dagger aside but keeps Aleksander in a strong hold. Without his powers and a weapon, he is weakened. We have a disadvantage.

Black shadows are forming and surrounding the Crown Prince. Wandering on his skin. It is as if the Dark One can hurt him through the skin. Aleksander tries to stay calm but I can see how he has to pretend not to feel the pain. The Dark One presses into him and Aleksander lets out a painful scream. I can feel it in my spine. I have never heard such a cry before. The Dark One is laughing, enjoying this moment.

Now I realise who the real monster here is. Aleksander has never been cruel – he acted as everyone expected him to act. He is forced to keep up this pretence, forced to be a man he never wanted to become. I have to focus on my thoughts since through the bond I can feel his emotions. Anger, frustration and pain. I am surprised when I feel guilt. He should kill him, then I would die as well and this would all stop, but I am selfish, call it foolish. I don't want him to die. I don't want this to be over yet. I open my eyes and look into the ones that I thought would be my world. He is not going to die – at least not today.

"Stop!" I shout with my remaining energy. "Please." The Dark One stops and faces me.

"I see, I see. Someone cares for you, worthless princeling." The Dark One chuckles.

"Stop it! He has nothing to do with what you want!" I say, knowing that Aleksander won't enjoy what I am going to do next.

"Tell me, what is it that I want?" He whispers.

"It's me," I say numbly.

"Aedlin …" Aleksander groans but I ignore him.

"You want me, not them. I will go with you. You can have me, if you let them live." I cannot prevent my voice from shaking.

If I don't accept freely, this will become a massacre. There is already too much blood on the ground, staining it. Let this be the last night I'm here. I see death lurking in the corner of the room. I can smell the fear of each individual in the room.

"But why should I let them live? Isn't it entertaining to see people die?" He turns to Aleksander. "You can tell, right?"

"If you let them go I will be your subject. I will obey." I swallow. "But if not, I will make your life miserable. A living hell!" The Dark One looks at me and then again to Aleksander.

"Let him go." His voice is neutral. "If you ever try to trick me, not only are you dead but your little pathetic friends are as well," He whispers against my ear.

"Aedlin, no!" Aleksander tries to get rid of the guard's arm around his neck.

"Aleksander, let me go. I have to. I promised Salem to make this world good again." I try to sound firm but the wobbling in my voice betrays me. "Let me do this. Let me help this kingdom. They need a good High King. They need a good ruler." I can feel the tears on my cheeks. I don't want to cry but having to say goodbye is hard.

How much I wished to feel his skin one last time, to have him look at me with pure admiration. My feelings have changed for the man kneeling on front of me, fighting to get to me. Once this is all over I will listen to the small voice in my head. But not know. We will see each other again, I am certain.

"Let's go, Aedlin," the Dark One says creating a portal made of shadows. I don't know where it is leading, but I know that I have to enter. "Don't be afraid, just take my hand and follow me," He whispers.

"Aedlin! NO!" Aleksander cries. How much I wish he would not fight. He should be silent. He makes it harder for me to go. I don't look at the remaining Elves. I don't want to see how many have died. I ignore Willow. Salem died due to my actions. And this is how I can fix it all.

I step towards the black shadows. I take a deep breath in and step through the portal, entering my doom.

The last thing I heard before I got dragged in the dark was his voice.

Every moment was real for me!

Acknowledgement

Wow.

I am unsure what to say. This journey has started years ago in the head of a small girl who loves to escape reality. Who maybe wishes to be in one of these Fantasy books a bit too much. In times like these don't we all want to escape somewhere eventually?

This book is a part of me. I am proud of what I have achieved and incredible thankful for all the support I got on my way.

These Characters were all made in my imagination, developing along their way. I felt a bit like the Watcher in Marvel. The one who oversees everything but cannot interfere.

I wanted to create a world with several possible paths, where I decide while writing how a Character will develop. I am surprised by how much I personally have grown with this project. As well as how my characters have grown. Aedlin who used to be the shadow of her village now is the only hope left for the Realm. Aleksander who has been taught to be fearful and cruel finally opened up to the sensation of friendship and possible love. Salem who has sacrificed everything and fought harder than any other warrior in the Realm finally could reunite with her family in the after life. Willow who can always make you smile with silly little words. Prince Nevan, known as the heartbreaking prince might not be all that what Elves mumble about him, even he might have secrets no one knows about.

I have put a lot of thoughts into each of these Characters, hoping the reader will love them as much as I do. It is no secret that I am already working on the second book for this series. I am excited for Aedlin to discover more about the world she is now stuck in. The world she may find to be her home one day or her ruin. I am looking forward to seeing her fight for what she loves and for what she wants. I have to admit that even I don't know where the story will go and how it will end but I cannot wait to share it with you all!

Yet, I have to make another announcement. I am currently working on another project called "The Cruel Prince" A small novella covering Aleksander's past to present and maybe it will reveal some secrets of him no one knew until then.

Now I have talked a lot about the book and its future, I want to take some time to thank the people who have supported me in this process.

I want to thank my boyfriend who has supported me from the start, where I wrote in my math classes while the teacher tried to explain vector to us, to the very end. For motivating me to continue even if I thought I lost the red line. I want to thank my dear friend Katharina for helping me figuring out where the story should be going in the very beginning. By now you probably have noticed I did not do anything we have discussed. Soooorry.

I want to thank my Dad and Rihab for supporting me even though this is not their department to shine. As well as I want to thank my English teacher who supported me through Highschool and without whom I would not have gained so much confidence in my English writing. Last but not least, I want to thank my Publisher Team for supporting me until the publication. It has been a huge step for me to give this book away for people to read and I am so thankful for every single one of you.

I hope I will see you in the next book, until then, try to escape reality from time to time.

The Cruel Prince

Her hair was looking beautiful. The sun made her red curls look like being on fire. Every time she smiled I felt something calming inside me. The pressure was reduced. It was just her and me on this clearing deep in the forest on that afternoon. We were surrounded by trees throning over the place. The wind was light but it started to cool down very soon. The warm days were over and I should not be here. I should be in the palace being on father's side, directing the country, yet, I was here with her.

She closed her eyes to feel the wind around her face, to feel the last sunbeams on her skin. I would do anything for her, to see her happy. I ripped off a blade of grass and twisted it around my fingers. What was I doing here? She looked so peaceful and at ease. How could I have know that she would betray me in just some years? I was innocent, stupid and blind. I would have torn my kingdom apart just for her, yet, she didn't choose me. She chose him. The mortal. I wasn't aware of her adventures at this time. I didn't know that she already had a life back there while we were sitting here and I was imagining my future with her.

For her, I was a friend? The prince? A lover? I don't know.

I just know that the day she turned her back on me, I became who I am now.

The Cruel Prince.

About the Author

Lilian Morgaine is a freshly graduated Student who is passionate about creating worlds to escape to that are filled with magic and mystery. She currently lives in Germany but is a prospective student in Design and Interior Architecture in the Netherlands. When she is not writing she enjoys playing video games, drawing, dancing or watching anime. In addition, she gives love to her cat who barely appreciates her affection.

Visit her on Instagram: @how_to_escape_reality

Printed in Germany
by Amazon Distribution
GmbH, Leipzig

25797225R00179